ON THE LADDER
OF HUMANITY

ON THE LADDER
OF HUMANITY

A JOLENE HARTLEY NOVEL

RYAN JENNINGS PETERSON

FOR
Mom, who thought I'd look good on a book.

7945

ON THE LADDER
OF HUMANITY

PROLOGUE

5 YEARS PAST

The pavement felt cold. Even in his new Ralph Lauren three-button, charcoal suit and overcoat he could feel the cold creep into his limbs and take hold of his lungs, squeezing until his breath felt like it would evaporate into the darkening night. The grittiness of the ground soothed him, letting him know that for the brief last few seconds, his life had some texture, some palpable existence, as his eyes closed and the world around him grew darker.

He had accomplished so many things in his life, personally and professionally, and he thought of himself as a complete, well-rounded human being, a man who had prospered along-side the less fortunate of his neighborhood. They would miss him. They would miss the smiles as he walked with them down the worn, yet promising streets he had made safer. They would miss the light-hearted and determined talks at the soup kitchen as he spooned out creamy chicken noodle or sliced one of many turkeys on Thanksgiving night, all from the kind-ness of his heart and his fifteen dollar Wal-Mart sneakers.

Daniel Vincent was a man of the people. He was one of them and they loved him for it. They would certainly miss him. He had done extreme good for the neighborhoods. Gang activity was the lowest it had been since he took office twelve years ago, giving his oath and promise to take savage shootings and drugs off his streets. He meant it, and he accomplished it. Homeless shelters had been built. Soup kitchens revamped and asbestos removed. Two recreation centers in working order. And all free. The neighborhoods were once again flourishing.

A casino, the brainchild of his personal nemesis, Alderman Harold Johnston, had been put to a stop due to Vincent's constant petitioning of the citizens that would be directly affected and put out on the streets. The building and adjoining hotel, as well as the convention center and fifteen-acre parking lot, would have displaced nearly two thousand tenants and homeowners. Sure, the site for the project was in a faltering neighborhood and would have brought in much-needed money to the city. But that neighborhood was under Vincent's umbrella, his watchful, caring eye, and the people did not want it. Casinos meant constant motion. All night, the in-and-out of tourists. Tourists who did not give a damn about their neighborhood. The homeless would congregate outside the casino, looking for the minute handouts from the occasional winner, thus bringing the shelters into the crosshairs of the higher ups, who in turn would stop financing. No, the casino was not a good idea.

And it was stopped, thanks to Daniel Vincent. The neighborhoods did not need a greed machine running the program, rather an old-fashioned makeover with love and care and a little elbow grease.

His family had been so proud—his wife, Susan, and two daughters, Emily and Elise. They had grown up in the outskirts of the city and moved to the neighborhoods years before Vincent was even considering the exhausting run for Alderman. Even then he wanted to make a change. He wanted things to be better for the people of the city, as well as his family, and the movement he created showed them that he truly cared. He was in it for them.

Now, as he lay on the cold, gritty pavement, feet twitching helplessly in the grass leading into the parking garage, head facing his brand new black 2006 Mercedes-Benz, he could care less about the fresh gang tag spread across the driver side door. He coughed as he heard the footsteps approaching from behind. His chest burned and he could barely catch his breath. His hands reached up to touch his suit coat and he could immediately feel the blood oozing out of his body where he had been stabbed twice. *Funny,* he found himself pondering. *Thought blood was supposed to be warm, but I still feel so cold.*

Vincent turned as the footsteps stopped. Hovering above him, silhouetted against the fluorescent glow of the ceiling lights stood a man, the silver gleam of the knife that had just penetrated the alderman's lungs held firmly in his hand. Vincent raised his head ever so slightly, words trying to form as the figure floating above knelt down next to him.

"P ... please," Vincent whispered, blood trickling down from the corners of his mouth. "My family—"

"Won't be touched." Vincent lowered his head to the pavement, noticing the grittiness and cold fading into the recesses of his mind, the hovering body seeming to diminish into the hazy lights as relief washed over him. The alderman certainly did not wish to die here in this grimy parking garage. He wanted to live. He wanted to watch his daughters marry, have children and witness the great things he was sure they would accomplish. However, the fact that they would have a chance to do just that regardless of his existence soothed him to a point of contentedness, even as the figure lowered the knife to Vincent's throat and cut into his windpipe, severing arteries as he made the incision. He stood as he watched Vincent's life expire, then turned his head towards the black Mercedes, noticing for the first time the shimmering gang tag streaking down the driver's side door and pooling just behind the front tire. He glanced around quickly before moving off into the darkness of the night.

Peering eyes from beneath an evergreen near the black Mercedes watched as the man moved into the darkness. The witness focused in the direction of the killer's exit for several moments before finally shifting back to the interior of the parking garage and the dead man lying half-in, half-out of the structure. The crimson pool accumulating beneath the deceased man's body began to course across the pavement, snaking towards a sewer grate several feet away, the blood red river transfixing the peering eyes, the movement reminding him of an animated, living, breathing gang tag.

A piercing cry echoed through the still night and awoke the witness from his reverie. He lifted his gaze to see a middle-aged couple enter the garage from an entrance to the left. The man, dressed as neatly as the deceased, approached hurriedly, reaching out his arm as he knelt down, mouth agape, eyes wide. "Hurry!" he yelled to the woman who drew nearer, edging along the concrete wall as if it were a safety net. "Call 9-1-1!"

The hiding eyes in the evergreen glanced toward where the killer had gone, waiting for the moment when he would reappear, wielding that glimmering, bloodstained knife once more. He did not come back, however, and the witness approached the scene, the couple looking up in terror and confusion with outstretched hands. "Where did you come from?"

the husband demanded, standing and bracing himself for the unknown.

The witness raised his paint-covered hands. "I didn't do it," he said, "but I saw everything. Call the cops."

* * * * *

PRESENT

The apartment building was located on the north corner of the intersection in the Back-of-the-Yards neighborhood of Chicago, backing up to an empty lot filled with broken concrete on one side and a liquor store on the other. A brown-brick two-flat, the building had been erected in the early 1940s and housed four to six families that employed the stock yards miles up the road. History books of the area showed men in tank-top t-shirts and bowler hats smoking cigars as their children ran freely through fire hydrants opened up for flushing. Mothers hung their family's clothes from lines strung between the buildings, eyeballing their little darlings as they played baseball in the parking lots.

History.

Presently, the building had become dilapidated, broken windows covered with boards and graffiti, bricks from the fallen façade littering the streets and alleys where fights had broken out and stones had been wielded as weapons. Where the children once played baseball, emulating their heroes of ages past, now drug dealers lurked, selling their souls for the right to claim their spot in the present day. The four-to-six family two-flat had been renovated in the late 70s into an apartment complex, housing twice as many families in half the space. The sweet smelling history that had once soared through the dreams of the neighborhood was gone, swallowed whole by the sketchy, dark, abused present.

On the second floor in apartment 204, Benjamin Ochoa returned the phone to its base and fumbled nervously at a desk made from cinder blocks and plywood. He had called 4-1-1 in an attempt to locate a man from long ago, someone distantly connected to him through a foggy past that had a footprint five years ago. Benjamin did not know the man he was seeking out, only his name, and even that he did not know how to spell. Not anymore. He had thought about this man, this ghost, little over the past five years, but now things were different.

Within the last three months, things had changed. Benjamin could feel the cold breath on his neck, the penetrating eyes from each alley he passed boring into his brain. And then he had seen him. A blonde-haired man, alone, in a parked car two blocks away from his apartment. He was back.

Benjamin Ochoa shuffled the papers strewn across the desk and found his blue ballpoint pen, uncapped it, and began writing.

J.

He glanced anxiously out the window to his left, feeling the blonde man would be floating there like the angel of death, his steady gaze penetrating Ochoa's soul.

G-R.

He paused again, the spelling of the name not coming to him. Suddenly, from down the hall, Benjamin heard a commotion. He rose from his seat, staring intently at the apartment door, waiting for someone to burst in. No one did. He turned back to the paper and phonetically put the letters in place, threw down the pen and made his way towards the door. He knew of one more option: Carlos at the local Department of

Motor Vehicles. If anyone knew where this man from his past was, it would be the DMV. And Carlos owed him a favor.

Benjamin slowed as he approached the door, veering to a small, over-stained end table covered in dust and old newspapers. He forced open the sole drawer with effort and retrieved the item within: An aging gun he purchased years ago from his cousin's friend. He had not carried it for a long time, but now was definitely not the moment to be caught without it. He needed to protect himself. He glanced down at the name on the sheet of paper once more. He needed to find this man, this ancient ghost from a time almost forgotten. He folded the paper in half, shoved it in his front pocket and exited, sliding the gun into pants as he closed the door behind him, leaving the apartment to bask in the sound from the neighbors fighting two doors down.

* * * * *

Benjamin sighed with relief after he had made it the mile and a half to the West 51st Street bus stop. He felt safe here, suspended over the Dan Ryan Expressway and a good distance from South Federal Street to his left and Princeton Avenue to his right. If the man were to show up at either of the intersections, Benjamin could easily outrun him to the opposite side and get lost among the buildings. He had done it before when running from the police.

Benjamin glanced at the bank sign to his left. 7:13 a.m. Two minutes until the bus arrived. Two minutes until he could sigh again with relief. He could see the large blue and white bus blocks down the street, pulling up slowly to the South Michigan Avenue stop. He smiled and sat on the bench backrest, leaning into the overpass fencing for support.

15

The pop he heard was only milliseconds before the bullet ripped through his head, sending him sprawling forward in a heap of blood and death. Benjamin smashed into the pavement with such force that two of his teeth flew from his gaping mouth. He crumbled into a pile, wedged between a garbage can and some newspaper dispensers, blood pouring over the curb, mixing with the trash that had settled near the sewer cap.

Seeing no one waiting near the bench, the 7:15 a.m. bus continued past the stop, the driver yawning before taking a long sip from his coffee mug.

ONE

Detective Jolene Hartley slammed into the wall with enough force to knock one of the hanging frames down to the floor. The inside of the apartment pulsated a cherry red as the neon sign from the restaurant across the street flashed from one scene to the next, allowing pedestrians in on the fact that Petzky's was open twenty-four hours a day and had the best Italian wedding soup in town.

Feet away from Jolene Hartley stood a shorthaired, clean-shaven man in his early thirties, handsome by all standards. He wore a gray suit and black tie and seemed out of place amongst the cardboard boxes filled with books and picture frames.

Jolene's breathing was heavy, as if she were entering a late round of a prizefight, yet she stayed put against the wall, her eyes intently fixed on the man now moving towards her. Her arms slid to her sides. The man approached with greater speed and immediately wrapped one arm around Jolene's waist, the other reaching up to grasp the back of her neck. Hartley's breathing became quicker as her partner, Detective Anthony Barailles, placed his mouth on hers in a heated, passionate kiss.

Jolene kissed him back, lust and temptation swirling past her usual sense of control, the consumed alcohol inhibiting her to focus on anything other than the absolute present. She dropped her handbag to the floor and wrapped her arms around Tony's shoulders, her leg sliding around his thigh as she pulled him closer into her body. Barailles gave a slight tug on her hair, forcing her face towards the ceiling, the red glow bouncing off her slender neck. Jolene let out a yearning moan between her panted breaths, a moan that Tony accepted with willing ears. He moved his lips down her neck, kissing and licking down to her shoulders, moving her dress strap out of the way, her shawl falling towards the floor. His hands began to wander and by the sound of it Jolene did not mind in the least. His left reached down to her dress, hiking it up to reveal a long, tanned leg wrapping around him, his fingers meandering up her thigh and to her rear where he gave a good squeeze. His right found her side, a thin, flat stomach and, eventually, her left breast. *Perfect ending to a perfect evening,* Tony thought to himself.

It had been a perfect evening. Barailles and Hartley had shown up separately to an upscale restaurant located on the fourth floor balcony of a lake-side hotel to honor Sergeant Frankie "Potts" Duarson, a thirty-four year veteran of the po-lice force, a man with more friends than enemies and a love for red wine and aged cheese. Barailles had shown up early with detectives Kimberly Banneau and William "Doc" Hester, fore-going the late night at the office for the first time in what felt like years. Jolene, on the other hand, had stayed behind to clean up some paperwork from a recently concluded case. When she finally did make her entrance, conversation had halted and the city seemed to go silent.

Jolene Hartley was, by all means, stunning. Long, brown hair flowed to her shoulders, framing a strikingly delicate, yet fierce face with piercing brown eyes, high cheekbones and lips that made married men look twice while at their anniversary dinner. Her smile could light up a room, but her scowl could set it afire. Jolene was tall and slim, yet toned throughout, having always pulled her weight throughout the academy, as a patrol officer and into the Organized Crime Division's Narcotics Section, where she excelled before landing as a homicide detective within Area One's Detective Division. She could handle her own.

Yet now, as Anthony Barailles moved his hand up her dress and across her back, his lips moving up to meet hers, their tongues flicking one another's ever so gently, for the first time, he felt he had the upper hand with Hartley.

"Jo," Tony whispered between kisses.

"Yeah?" Jolene answered.

"Jo. Let's–" He moved his lips down to her neck, the taste of her sweat on his tongue as his hands moved furiously under her dress, across her back and down her legs.

"What–" Jolene began. Her words failed her as she felt his hand on her inner thigh, moving her underwear to the side. Her head flung back towards the wall, eyes clenching shut in anticipation of what was to come next. His fingers were against her flesh, massaging, his kisses falling on her skin. Her head turned to the side, mouth agape, moans escaping her without her knowledge. "What–" she heard herself ask again, not sure where it had come from or what she was asking.

"Jo. Come to my bedroom," Barailles whispered.

"I … uh … I …" Jolene's mind was flying, thoughts and phrases and situations jamming into every recess of her brain, yet words could not be formed. She opened her eyes and suddenly snapped into reality as her gaze fell on a stack of boxes filled with old sweaters, yellowed paper and pictures by the dozens. Sitting neatly on the top box as if it had been recently looked upon, was an image of a happy family of four: Mr. and Mrs. Anthony Barailles and their two beautiful children, Anthony Jr. and Katherine.

Tony continued to pepper Jolene's skin with kisses and his fingers continued to work underneath her dress. Hartley blinked, almost losing herself in the moment again. His touch did feel sensational. Her eyes opened and again the picture loomed. "I—uh, Tony—" Jolene managed between breathes. "Tony, stop."

"What?" Barailles asked, not hearing her over his lust. "Come to my bedroom."

"Tony," Hartley said again, louder, tapping his shoulder, her eyes never leaving the picture of his family. "Tony, stop. Stop."

"Jo—" Barailles began.

"Barailles! Stop it!" Hartley yelled, pushing him away from her and into a precariously stacked mound of cardboard boxes. He careened off them and stumbled backwards, stopping a few feet away as he caught himself on a floor lamp.

He pulled himself up, his hands going wide. "Jesus Christ, Jo! What the hell?" he yelled, more from surprise than anger.

"I can't," Hartley said, smoothing out the front of her dress. "I can't." She bent down and retrieved her shawl and handbag, staying momentarily hunched while she tried to calm herself and control her breathing.

"Jo—"

"Barailles I can't. We shouldn't be doing this."

"I didn't force you up here, Jo. I didn't start this—"

"I know."

"I wasn't the one who kissed you in the lobby of the hotel—"

"I know, Barailles."

"It's not only me who wants you. You seem to be into me too—"

"I know!" Jolene yelled. "Tony, I know, all right. I know." Barailles remained by the stack of boxes, his tie hanging from his neck in an extremely loose fashion, his shirt missing several of the higher buttons, both remnants of the proceedings that had just been halted. Jolene pulled her dress down across her thighs, shimmying her hips back and forth, the fabric sliding down her legs. She pulled her strap back up and moved towards the couch, taking a seat and running her hands through her hair. Tony moved away from the boxes, situating himself against the wall where his beautiful partner had just been positioned. It was then, as he moved his head to the left, that he saw the picture. He glanced at Jolene and their eyes met, an unspoken understanding crossing between them, floating on the passion that was dissolving into the stuff apartment air. Tony's gaze turned towards the floor.

"It's not wrong, Jo, what we're doing," he stated.

"Yes, Tony, it is," Jolene calmly retorted.

"She's gone, Jo," he said, moving away from the wall and towards the couch, taking a seat next to her. "She's gone. She left me."

Jolene thought of moving yet remained still, the scent of her partner's cologne caught in her nostrils. "Because of us. Because of us being partners." She paused, running her fingers through her hair yet again. "Because of me."

"Not because of you, Jo. Because of—because she can't take you being the main person in my life. This job is our lives. We see each other more than we see our families—" He trailed off at the end of the sentence. He had a family, although a fractured one. Jolene Hartley's family was non-existent. Her's was the job and the people in the precinct. She had no husband or boyfriend, no children to watch grow into adults. There was a brother that she had mentioned from time to time, yet nothing of solid importance that Tony could recall.

It was no secret between them that there was something going on, yet neither one knew what exactly that meant. Barailles was nearing the end of a divorce, which meant, technically, he was still married. He loved his wife and children, and part of him still wanted the chance to make amends, yet he also understood he could not give his wife what she needed: A spouse that would be home every night in time for supper. His life in the force, as a homicide detective, did not allow for that.

Jolene Hartley was a mystery to him, however. She was a mystery to everyone. Besides realizing tonight that his partner was a typical hot-blooded woman with needs, Anthony Barailles knew her only through work. That is not to say they never saw each other outside of the precinct. There were gatherings, get-togethers, parties and the softball league that Hartley attended and enjoyed, but there was no getting close to her, no insight into what made her tick, other than the job.

Tony turned to Hartley. "Jo—"

"I should go, Tony," she said as she stood. He watched her as she gathered her things, wrapping the shawl around her shoulders. As she reached the door she paused and turned, looking into Barailles's eyes. "I'm sorry, Tony. We're partners. You're married. I'm—" She shook her head. "I'm a mess. I'm sorry. I'll see you tomorrow. Goodnight." She left the apartment, looking over her shoulder to him before exiting, Barailles knowing that tonight would most likely be the closest he would ever get to the striking Jolene Hartley.

* * * * *

As the sun climbed higher into the morning sky, Jolene Hartley sat stock still on her apartment couch in her wool pajamas, staring out the window into the city she protected, her knees resting under her chin as she clasped a hot cup of coffee in both hands, letting the aroma flood her senses. Things had definitely gone haywire last night. Not that she had minded for a brief period of time. Had Barailles packed that family portrait away a little deeper she would have been pinned against that wall in nothing but her heels, letting his fingers go anywhere they wished. Sure, she may have had the same thoughts as she had now, but that was a risk she was willing to take. Anthony Barailles was a handsome, good-hearted man, and one that she worked with on a daily basis.

He was right about her being the main person in his life. He was the same for her. He was the man in her life. Her partner, if only by job title. She saw him more than anyone else she knew. She did feel, in a way, responsible for the demise of his marriage. Late nights hunkered down over her desk, digging into the latest case and a box of beef chop suey. Early mornings over coffee, running the suspect list for the hundredth time. Barailles, she could tell, did have intense feelings for her, but nothing that he acted upon beyond subtle hints regarding how she looked or the way she talked. He was an honorable man and had not cheated on his wife.

Jolene's feelings for Tony came more from a longing for a normal life. She loved the job. The job was her life, and with that life came the partner, a reliable, kind, warm-hearted man that knew her ins-and-outs. All things considered, it was inevitable that the previous night had happened. The surprise really should have been that it had not happened sooner.

Her phone's ringer awoke her from her thoughts, chiming loudly in the silent apartment. "Hartley," she answered. A serious look etched across her face and she looked down to the black swirl of her coffee. "Okay, I'm on my way." She hung up the phone and stood, leaving her mug on the end table as she moved to her bedroom. She changed into a pair of bootcut jeans, Sketchers sneakers and a white, form-fitting t-shirt. From a drawer in her armoire she collected her silver star and holster. She placed her finger on the scanner of a locked metal box and opened it, retrieving her Glock 19 semi-automatic pistol and sliding the magazine of .9mm bullets into the handle. A new case had just opened: A young man had been found at the 51st Street bus stop overlooking the Dan Ryan with a bullet hole through the head. Detective Jolene Hartley had been assigned as lead investigator. She threw on a leather jacket and exited.

TWO

Hartley walked to the far corner of the street to her usual coffee shop for her morning latte, the only normal wake-up call before entering into her routine of murder and investigation. Her days were based around death and evidence, research and interrogation, and at times Hartley felt whatever normalcy that had once been part of her existence was rushing from her only to be lost within the concrete jungle of the city. The brief instances where she did graze the average citizen's life—in the morning heading to the precinct and at night as she made her way to one of a dozen restaurants, rented a movie, or watched her favorite television show—were still plagued with bits and pieces of the case she was working on.

She flagged down a taxi and headed to the precinct, the driver glancing back numerous times to stare at the beautiful woman in the back seat. Hartley pulled her long dark hair back into a ponytail and sipped at her latte, staring from the taxi window at a city just waking before her.

Hartley had been drawn to Chicago immediately, living her youth as a daughter to a police chief father in a wealthy suburb where the most that transpired was the occasional DUI of some rich trust-fund baby, a charge that would more than likely be dropped and replaced with a slap on the wrist. Hartley respected her father's position on the force, yet knew his talents had been wasted on such mundane activities. He was an excellent cop, and could have served better in a large, more volatile atmosphere. He had sacrificed being that officer, however, choosing instead to lead a simpler life where his son and daughter could roam the streets without the thought of something awful arising in his mind.

The taxi pulled up to the precinct and Hartley handed the driver the fare, exiting and moving immediately towards the door for the garage. She hopped into her usual unmarked car and headed towards the scene, eager to jump headfirst into the case, knowing that the countdown had already begun on finding the killer.

* * * * *

The scene was that of any other murder in this part of the city. Uniforms had taped off the entire overpass, rerouting traffic down the side streets that ran parallel to the expressway below. Crowds had gathered near the caution tape, bystanders and press intermingling with the officers as everyone tried to get a glimpse at the latest victim. Young men and women grouped together in the same colors congregated at opposite sides of the overpass, wondering if the deceased was one of their own, imagining who was to blame.

Hartley pulled her car under the caution tape as a uniformed officer held it aloft and parked near the evidence team van. As she exited the vehicle she glanced around, checking the immediate area: Vacant buildings with windows shattered; liquor store still gated shut; bank branch with a line of three cars going through a drive-up ATM; members of several different gangs pushing against the fencing of the on-ramps; the remnants of a crumbling building adjacent to an abandoned lot; a stack of broken down, dirty cardboard boxes and an oily, filthy backpack stuffed to the brim.

Hartley was on the job, taking in everything, mentally noting her surroundings, the pros and cons of the area that might help or hinder the investigation. Mainly, she eyed the congregations, knowing the odds were stacked against her. This area of the city straddling the Dan Ryan Expressway was packed full of gang activity from several rival factions. Back-of-the-Yards crews scraped with those from the Englewood neighborhood just to the south on a constant basis and, more frequently than not, someone ended up dead.

As she walked towards the bus stop and the gathering of officers, Hartley began to make out a man lying on the ground. His shoes were against a container holding a garbage can, his torso awkwardly pressed into the space next to the newspaper stands. She could begin to make out a river of blood starting near the victim's head.

"Morning, Detective," a man in his mid-forties said, walking up from behind her with a box. As he passed he handed her a pair of blue latex gloves. "How you feeling this morning?"

"Morning, Mac," Hartley answered. "Better with some coffee. You?"

"Better than our vic," he responded. Dr. Virgil "Mac" McLourey headed up the Mobile Crime Lab within the Forensics Services Section, and Hartley was fond of him. He was a funny man that took life just seriously enough, knowing that at any point, any of his colleagues and himself could end up just like one of the victims they looked upon every day. McLourey was equivalent to the favorite uncle. He scolded if things got out of hand and never pushed a topic unless prodded to do so.

Hartley admired him for the way he looked at his work: It was a job, but not his life.

Hartley looked up and saw Barailles coming towards her, stealing glances at her and the immediate vicinity. They met several yards away from the victim. Barailles made little eye contact, seemingly embarrassed about the previous evening. Hartley continued to stare at the scene, feeling heat rise from her body as the awkwardness settled in.

"Hey, Jo," Barailles said, finally breaking the silence as he turned his head away from her and the victim.

"Barailles," Hartley responded, glancing quickly up at him as he turned towards her. She forced a smile and looked back to the victim.

"I, uh—" Barailles began.

"Tony, let's just—" Hartley interrupted, pointing towards the fresh body lying on the pavement. "I can't talk about this right now." Barailles stared at her in amazement at how cold her comment seemed to him.

"I think we need to—"

"Not right now, though," Hartley interjected again, this time with more force as she glared at him. "We're on the job right now, Detective. I need to know what you've found out so far. I can't relive anything at the—"

"Fine, Jo. Okay," Barailles yielded, raising his arms slightly in defeat. They moved towards the victim, Barailles listing off what he had learned. "I've been here a few minutes longer than you. We've got a young male, early-to-mid twenties with a single gunshot wound to the rear of his head. Fatal, as you can see. Now, I don't have the time of death from Mac yet, but you figure it was within the last two hours. The body was found by the young lady over there, Ms. Angela Reyes, roughly forty minutes ago." Barailles pointed to a woman in her late teens near some uniformed officers. "She was on her way to class. Takes the bus into the city."

Hartley looked to the woman and back to the body. "Okay, we need to get on the phone with Transit Authority. See if we can't get the schedule for all buses that work these streets. Their times and numbers. See if any of the drivers noticed anyone lurking around."

"Jo—" Barailles began, quickly halting when Hartley shot an angered glare his way. "Hartley," he corrected himself. "In this neighborhood, there are dozens of creepy people lurking around." Hartley moved her eyes across the scene, noticing the mass of similarly clad people gathering near the caution tape.

"Have we canvassed the crowd yet?" Hartley asked, staring at a group of rough-looking young men.

"Uniforms got to some of them before I got here. More have shown up."

"Right. Go talk to the group down there. Ask the uniforms what they know." Barailles moved off to one end of the overpass towards a cluster of officers. "Mac," Hartley yelled, stepping back and glancing towards the opposite end of the overpass.

"Yeah, Hartley," McLourey answered from a knee next to the body. "Got a gang tat on his neck. Looks like 51st Street Crew. Come back in a bit."

Hartley left the ME to his business and walked slowly to the west side of the overpass. She eyed the obvious gangbangers lining Princeton Avenue. The odds of getting someone to talk, let alone find a gang-related killer, were slim, but Hartley knew her job. She knew her presence there would send a message—even though a small one—that the police force was involved in their lives. She knew their involvement would not stop the crimes completely, yet it could help.

The group she slowly approached was clad in dark blue jeans and a mixture of red baseball caps, shirts and jackets. They were Mexicans and, judging by their colors and the neighborhood they were in, Hartley concluded they were part of the same gang that the victim seemed to be in, the 51st Street Crew. As she passed a uniformed officer she tapped him on the back and whispered into his ear, "Watch me," knowing that these gang members were violent against anyone and everyone. The uniform nodded his understanding.

Hartley crossed the caution tape, stopping directly in front of the group of males, catching their gaze as they stood their ground, a number of them looking her up from head to toe, noticing the silver star on her hip as well as her tight white shirt.

"*Mamacita*, you fine as hell."

"Damn, *'mano*. I'd fuck that, even with that badge."

"Yeah!" the group agreed in unison.

"Shit, *'mano*. I'd fuck her with that badge on!" one man said, looking from his crew to Hartley. "You can put it right between those perfect *chichis*," he said pointing to her breasts.

Hartley smirked. "You guys are Five-One, right?"

"That's right, *mamacita*. Five-One forever!" This drew a rise from the crowd.

"Any of your crew unaccounted for this morning?" Hartley asked the man.

"Shit, lady, there's a lot unaccounted for. They all probably sleeping it off at some bitch's place." Again, the crowd grew louder. "All of us were at a party last night. So none of us did nothing."

"Anyone see anything here this morning?" The crowd stayed quiet. "Thought not." Hartley turned and went towards the victim.

"*Mamacita,* think about my offer," the gangbanger yelled after her. "That badge would look sexy as hell between those titties!"

Hartley continued across the overpass, coming up behind McLourey as he studied the body. The questions for the Five-One Crew were pointless. No one would talk, and Hartley did not want to start a gang war letting them known one of their own had been gunned down by a possible rival faction. "Got anything for me, Mac?"

"Benjamin Ochoa, 23-years-old," McLourey said, handing a wallet over to her. "Based on body temp and lividity, I'd put time of death at about an hour ago. By the looks of the tattoos and the gun tucked into his belt, I'd also go ahead with the conclusion that he was definitely part of the 51st Street Crew."

"Gun, huh?" Hartley opened the black leather wallet and pulled out the driver's license, her eyes remaining on the ME.

"Didn't have time to even reach for it," Mac replied.

Hartley looked back to the identification and the picture of Benjamin Manuel Ochoa. Born April 6, 1988. His address read to be about two miles northwest from the overpass on the far west side of Back-of-the-Yards, but Hartley knew these gang-bangers tended to lay their head's wherever they were. Perma-nent addresses did not mean much more than a lead to finding the person. "I hate these cases," Hartley said to no one in par-ticular.

"What cases are those, exactly?" McLourey asked, moving towards the bench and fencing.

"These gang-related hits. They're just pointless. One banger killing another banger for selling drugs on the same turf that he sells drugs on. No one talks. Nothing is ever accom-plished."

31

"Except one less drug dealer on the streets," came a reply from her right. Barailles stopped next to her.

"What did you find?" Hartley asked.

"Nothing. Everyone at the far end showed up after the body was discovered and police called. Checked the convenience store and the bank. Both just opened up fifteen minutes ago. Clerk at the 7-Eleven said no one wanders around the neighborhood unless you're at that bus stop or sleeping in an alley."

"Detectives," McLourey called. "Something to brighten your day." Both Hartley and Barailles glanced his way. "If this was a gang hit, it's the weirdest one I've ever seen." Hartley and Barailles moved closer to McLourey, who was examining the bus stop bench.

"Why's that?" Barailles asked.

"Well, first off, Detective Barailles, the blood splatter pattern on the concrete suggests that he wasn't killed by either a drive-by or execution style. Second, take a look at the top of the newspaper stands. What do you see?"

Hartley moved towards the stands. "Blood."

"Precisely," Mac answered, moving his attention to the body once again. "And what do you think, Detective Hartley?"

Hartley examined the blood for a few seconds. "The way the splatter pattern lies, it suggests that he was shot from behind, maybe from someone shorter with the trajectory aimed higher."

"The entry wound," the ME stated from a kneeling position, "is in the lower back of the head, right side. Exit, top forehead. And here's the kicker, guys. You'd have to be no taller than a child to make that trajectory match."

"What are you thinking, Mac?" Hartley asked.

"Well, from the blood splatter and the trajectory, add in the bruising on the head and shoulders, I'm thinking that our vic was sitting on the top of the bench. The shot goes through his head, killing him instantly. He flies off the bench, through the air and lands on the concrete, knocking a couple teeth out in the process."

"If he's on the back of the bench," Hartley began, moving towards the fence, "that means trajectory puts our killer down there." Hartley pointed towards the grass on the side of the expressway. "Barailles, let's head down there and see if we can find anything."

* * * * *

"Hartley, what are you thinking?" Barailles asked, backing up to get a better view of the scene. They had descended to the expressway shoulder behind a wall that hid them from the traffic flying by. The shoulder was at least ten yards wide, with a mound of grass that had recently been placed to give the area a touch of nature. Yards away sat a yellow backhoe, a piece of excavating equipment that had yet to be returned.

"I'm thinking that this is an awfully long way to the bus stop," Hartley answered, backing her way to stand next to Barailles.

"Right."

"Gang hits usually consist of a drive-by or an ambush. Not a fifty or sixty yard shot from the shoulder of a busy expressway." Hartley looked to the on-ramp and back down to the backhoe.

"Could be a stray bullet," Barailles stated. "Maybe someone driving down here let off a shot."

"That would have to be one ridiculously lucky shot. A car traveling fifty-five to, say, seventy miles per hour, gun out the window. The force of the wind would make it impossible to steady that gun. And a random shot that just happens to strike our vic in the head twenty yards up? I find that hard to grasp."

"Hey, stranger things have happened."

Hartley moved off towards the backhoe, staring up at the aged bench above. She pulled her gun from its holster and, with the safety on, held it towards the group of police officers surrounding the scene. She moved forward trying to determine from what area the shot could have been fired. When she neared the backhoe she stopped, gun still aimed high. "Barailles, the trajectory couldn't have come from the roadway. Not unless that bullet had a curve to it."

"You're thinking from around here, huh?"

"Check that backhoe. See if you can find anything."

They searched the equipment, finding various cigarette butts, coffee cups and sandwich wrappers. "Hartley, check this out." Hartley moved towards the front right of the backhoe and knelt down next to Barailles. "I think we have a footprint."

"The ground is covered with them. No counting how many workers have been in and out of this machine."

"Yeah, but this one is above the others, and it's not a boot print. Most concrete and construction employers in the state require these guys to wear steel-toed boots and hard soles. This one looks like a sneaker." They looked closer. Barailles was right. The print was definitely more pronounced than the others and the swirled texture on the sole absolutely did not resemble the square, chiseled bottom of a boot. "I'll have someone from Mac's team come take a look."

The two detectives walked back up the on-ramp towards the scene, noticing Mac had bagged the body of their victim and placed it in the truck for the ride to the lab. "Go tell Mac to give me a call once he gets to the lab. I'd like to come see the body," Hartley told Barailles, rubbing her temples with her index finger and thumb.

"Sure," Barailles responded. "You all right, Jo?"

"Fine. Just a headache. I'm going to grab a coffee over here, see if I can get some more answers." With that Hartley walked off towards a quaint, sketchy restaurant on the corner, across the street from the on-ramp they had just climbed. Barailles watched her go before turning to relay the news to Dr. Virgil McLourey.

THREE

Hartley entered the restaurant and took a seat near the window facing her crime scene. She was surprised when she opened the door to the establishment, feeling as if she walked into another universe. The outside of the building, tattooed and vandalized beyond recognition of its once pristine exterior, gave way to a fresh, tidy inside, free of grime and pollution and the stench of ugliness. It was a haven, it would seem, from the drugs and guns that ruled the world beyond the pain of glass, the world that had in a single instance pulled her from her cozy apartment and into the reality that was her job.

She turned her attention through the pane and to the uniformed officers and technicians still scurrying about the area. She could see Barailles as he caught up to the truck carrying the victim, most likely passing along to Mac her message to contact her once he returned to the lab. She tracked Barailles as he walked slowly towards his vehicle, stopping along the way to glance back towards the restaurant, towards her.

She would have been flattered in any other situation. Hell, she was flattered now, however, her confusion clouded her mind. She knew she would have to confront the consequences of the previous night, yet she was not ready for that. A case had been dropped in her lap, albeit what appeared to be a gang-related crime. She needed to focus. She needed to be clear-headed.

Yet that seemed harder than she anticipated. Flashes of the previous evening, Barailles's hot breath on her neck, his body pressed to hers, his fingers between her—*Stop it,* she thought to herself. *Twenty-three year old victim. Five-One connections.*

"What can I get you, Officer?" the waitress asked, coming from behind her.

"Oh, uh, coffee and a bagel," Hartley responded with not so much as a glance away from the scene.

"Coffee and a bagel it is." The waitress moved off behind the counter leaving the detective to her thoughts. Why kill a kid on an overpass at a bus station? Would it not be easier to hide in an alley and take a shot when he passed? Easier to escape and lose yourself in the surrounding buildings, that was for sure. Unless the killer did not know the buildings? Maybe the killer had a get-away car parked on the expressway shoulder?

The questions began. Hartley knew how her mind worked, knew that the questions that came in an avalanche of thought had produced some crucial leads in the past. It was a blessing to be able to think the way she did, yet the sheer amount of inquiries would sometimes fill her every thought until the breaking point, leaving her with constant headaches, insomnia and the need for vacation.

Things would fade, fortunately, and her team would either solve the case or it would disappear into the past, placed in a box for the future to shape out. Hartley knew her feelings on gang-related crimes, and knew that it was wrong. She tended to have a predispositioned view when it came to homicides on gang turf. Although each and every life that had been taken on her watch meant a great deal, she knew she would much rather find the killer of a noble laureate than a banger. Like Barailles had said, one gangbanger killing another gangbanger meant one less drug dealer or pimp on the streets. In the end, regardless of her thoughts, she was the type of detective that gave it her all, focusing on the facts to try to bring the murderer to justice, regardless if the victim was selling drugs and flesh or not.

"You want cream cheese with that bagel, dear?" the waitress called, rousing Hartley from the scene outside.

"Jam, please. Blackberry? You have that?" The waitress nodded her head and grabbed the carafe of coffee. She placed a toasted bagel in front of Hartley and poured the coffee into a mug. From her apron pocket she pulled several sealed containers of blackberry jam.

"I'm assuming you're part of what's going on out there?" the waitress asked, glancing outside.

"I am. I'm a homicide detective. A man was shot and killed there this morning." Hartley picked up the coffee cup and took a drink. The liquid was bitter, but the taste seemed to wake her slightly. "You wouldn't happen to know what time the buses stop there, do you?"

"Oh, not sure. Quite regularly. I think we've got a schedule around here somewhere. Not sure how old it is."

"That would be great. Thanks."

The waitress moved off to the register and pulled a dilapidated cardboard box from under the countertop. She sifted through items, pulling out raggedy sweaters and holey gloves, tossing aside several books before grabbing a pamphlet and returning the box to its shelf. "Found it," she said as she glanced at the front and walked back towards the table. "Although, it looks to be a couple years old. Don't know if it will help."

"Thank you," Hartley said, glancing at the aged and frayed paper. The cover had the year 2006 written in bold blue typeface, making the book five years old, giving the Transit Authority plenty of time to change routes, times and bus numbers. The book would not help. "Do you mind if I ask you a few questions?" Hartley asked the waitress. She nodded. "What time does the restaurant open in the morning?"

"We are usually up and running at about 6:00 a.m. This morning we didn't get started until about 8. Juan was in a car accident and got here as soon as possible."

"And who's Juan?"

"Sorry. Juan's our cook. He's here everyday from open till about three in the afternoon."

"And what about you? Did you happen to see anything while you waited for Juan?"

"Oh, I wasn't here that early either. Juan gave me a call on my cell to let me know he'd be late. I live in the building right next door. When Juan got here he buzzed me down and we came in together through the back. It wasn't until we were inside that we noticed everything going on out there."

"Did you hear anything? Maybe a gunshot or a vehicle taking off quickly?

The waitress scrunched her face. "No, I'm sorry. I was busy getting showered and blow-drying my hair."

Hartley thought for a moment before proceeding. "Have you noticed anything gang-related going on around the restaurant?"

The waitress laughed. "Detective, there's always gang-related stuff going on around here. Drugs, prostitutes, fights. You name it, we see it. But we try to stay neutral. It's not right, some of the things that happen around here. But if I stay out of sight, no one knows my name and no one is looking for me, you know what I mean?"

"I do. Thanks—"

"Oh, Antonia Herrera."

"Thanks, Antonia."

"Seems like this is turning into a popular police restaurant," Antonia said smiling.

"What?" Hartley asked, looking up at her. Antonia nodded towards the doorway. Hartley looked over and saw Barailles walking in. She shifted in her seat and looked down at her bagel.

Barailles moved past the waitress. "Morning."

"Good morning. Coffee?"

"Please," Barailles said as he took a seat opposite Hartley. Antonia flipped the mug over and poured, then smiled and walked away, disappearing into the kitchen. Barailles put the mug to his lips and sipped. "Holy crap," he exclaimed. "That is awful."

"Yeah," Hartley agreed.

Barailles looked at Hartley who shifted her focus from her bagel to the window and past. He could not determine if it was the early morning sun breaking the building tops or the glow of the fluorescents in the paneled ceiling, but the lighting that reflected from Hartley's skin made her that much more gorgeous to him at that moment. He began to open his mouth to say something but Hartley interjected quickly, sensing where the conversation might go.

"What did Mac say?"

He closed his mouth and looked towards the scene as Hartley turned her attention to him. "He's on his way back. He'll give you a call when he gets there and gets the body on the table." Hartley nodded.

They remained quiet for several minutes, Barailles sipping at his bitter coffee as Hartley picked at the bagel. The tension was palpable. Finally Tony spoke, the words rushing and blending together. "Look, Jo, I'm sorry about last night. Neither one of us meant for that to happen." She continued to look down but did not interrupt. "I can't speak for you, but for me, I'm not regretting it. You're my partner. My friend. I don't want this to be an uncomfortable situation. We need to talk about this."

Jolene looked up at him and shrugged. "I'm just confused with myself, Tony. I don't know what else to say. I don't want this to be a cloud over our heads either, but what do we do? You're married, regardless of what is going on with you guys now. And I—" She paused, looking back out to the orange sun.

"I know you haven't had closure with Ron," Tony added. "But we can't just pretend nothing happened. We can't rewind the last two days. We can't erase it. You and I—" Barailles stopped as Antonia walked back over.

"How you two doing?" she asked with a grin. Both detectives forced a smile at her. Barailles reached for his wallet and pointed to the table, Hartley's gaze returning to the overpass. "Oh, no way. On the house. Let me know if you need anything else." Antonia returned to the register.

Hartley's gaze became fixed as her partner continued. "We can't—"

"Rewind," Hartley interrupted. "I heard you."

Barailles looked at her and realized something was happening in her mind, something that would not be interrupted by his voice. "Jo?" he said. She was staring past the throngs of people, past the technicians cleaning up the scene. Her gaze fell on the opposite side of the overpass, to the bank where cars now parked and pulled up to the drive-thru. "Hartley?" he said again.

"Barailles, that bank. When you went over there before, they were open?"

Barailles followed her stare. "Yeah. Had been open for fifteen minutes. Why?"

"Cameras," she said, turning her attention back to him. He looked back to her and a smile crept over his face. "Cameras, Tony. We can rewind the tapes and see what they picked up." She smiled and a fire lit behind her eyes.

* * * * *

The bank manager was a short, round man in his mid-fifties. His comb-over hid age spots and his large bushy beard hid pockmarks from a youth full of acne. He was a cooperative man, however, and upon learning that his cameras may have picked up something that could be useful to the investigation, he gave the detectives full reign over the security office.

A guard at the bank unlocked the room and took a seat behind the controls, pressing buttons and flipping switches until a screen on the upper right of the wall displayed the video rewinding. "This camera is meant to be pointing straight into our lot next to the street, but that storm a few nights back tore the gutter right off the roof and into this unit," the guard said. "Just might have been enough to point to the bus stop." The guard hit the play button, the right screen blinking to life.

The display was low quality at best, however, the camera pointed directly towards the Dan Ryan Expressway. In the upper left hand corner was the 51st Street bus stop, empty; the upper right displayed the date and time, the latter reading 7:36 a.m. The backhoe was visible in the bottom right. "Yeah," said the guard, "not the best, can't really see anything too clear. Maybe I—"

"No, no," Hartley said, tapping the screen. "This is good. Seven-thirty-six," she said, reading the screen. "Seven-thirty-six. Seven-thirty—Didn't you say the call was made about forty minutes before I arrived?"

"Yeah," Barailles answered. "What time were you there?"

"About eight-fifteen. This is right about the time when—there she is." On the screen, in the upper left hand corner, the blur that was Angela Reyes entered the screen, her grainy, pixilated body approaching the bus stop at a casual pace, the speed of a student heading to class. She suddenly stopped and took a step to the left. "That's Angela. She finds Ochoa and calls the cops. Can you keep rewinding? But show it on the screen."

"Sure," the guard said, fiddling with some of the controls. The blur moved back off the screen, down the overpass and out of the camera's view. "Sorry, it's a little slower rewinding this way," the guard apologized.

"It's good," Barailles said. "Let's see what's going on."

"Seven-twenty-five," Hartley said aloud, eyes not peeling from the screen. "Seven-twenty-two. Seven-twenty-one. We have to be reaching around the point where he's killed."

The video continued to rewind slowly, showing no activity whatsoever save for the tree limbs jumping frantically in the breeze. "Stop it!" Barailles said suddenly. The video timestamp read 7:15 a.m. "Look there, Hartley." He pointed to the lower right to the backhoe. "Play it." The guard hit the play button. From next to the backhoe a figure in black moved from the front of the machine and walked off the screen to the right, an object slung from his shoulder down his back.

"That must be our guy," Hartley said. "Keep rewinding for me." The guard did as told. The screen displayed the figure moving to the front of the backhoe, this time going past the 7:15 a.m. timestamp. The graininess did not help with identifying the man or woman, though the 7:14 a.m. frame did allow the detectives to learn what the person was carrying. The guard paused the video, the mark reading 7:13 a.m. The scene was set. Above, their victim, Benjamin Ochoa, was sitting on the bench, leaning into the overpass fencing, seeming to look to his left for the bus. Below, their suspect hunched next to the excavating machine, rifle resting on the tracks of the backhoe, pointing into the air at Ochoa. "Play," Hartley said quietly. The guard hit the button. There was an immediate flash from the backhoe followed suddenly by Ochoa flying from the bench top.

"Damn," the guard said.

"So," Barailles began, "our vic gets to the stop and is minutes from his ride. The perp positions himself below and takes the shot. I'm betting you he had a car down there to hop right in. Maybe another banger as a get-away driver."

"Right," Hartley agrees, looking up to her partner. "Call it in to see if we can get uniforms to scout the area. See if any other cameras caught anything else. And see if anyone noticed a car parked on the shoulder." Barailles grabbed his phone and began dialing. Hartley turned back to the screen.

"Miss," the guard said. Hartley looked at him. "I realize you guys know what you're doing, but this hardly seems like a gang killing."

"No, it doesn't, does it?" Hartley responded.

The guard nodded. "My cousin's doing time for manslaughter right now. Stupid initiation ritual for the Five-Ones. I've never heard of any bangers planning any killings unless it was a drive-by or street ambush. And I ain't never even seen a banger carrying a rifle. Kind of hard to keep that baby hidden, you know?"

Hartley smiled and nodded. "I was thinking the same thing." Barailles hung up the phone and turned back towards the two. Hartley looked back to the screen. "Can you keep rewinding? I want to see what else we can pick up."

"Sure." The guard began the backward motion of the film, reversing the shooting and giving life back to Benjamin Ochoa. He jumped up to the bench and sat there for several minutes, seconds on the video, then climbed down and walked backwards out of view. Hartley turned her attention to the figure near the expressway, lurking behind the backhoe. An arm would pop up every now and then, seemingly looking at the time on a watch. "Should I stop?" the guard asked.

Hartley paid him no mind. "He knows what time," she said aloud.

"What?" Barailles asked from behind the two.

"He keeps looking at his watch, like he expects our vic to show up any second. He's in place at 7:12am, one minute before Ochoa arrives at the stop. Our killer knew what time he was going to show up." The video continued to play backwards. Hartley, after nearly a minute, reached over and hit the pause button, pointing to the bottom right corner to their killer moving into the screen. "Six-thirty-six. Our killer was on the scene, in place, almost forty minutes before the murder took place."

"That's not your typical gang hit," Barailles said.

"Not a gang hit at all, it seems," Hartley agreed. "Thank you," she said to the guard as she walked past Barailles and out the door. Her partner turned and followed, nodding his thanks to the bank manager as he passed.

Outside, Hartley stopped on the sidewalk. "Gang hits don't work out like this. There's no sitting for forty minutes on the side of an expressway. And there's definitely not just one single, miraculous shot."

"What's the plan?" Barailles said after a few seconds in silence.

"We need more on our vic," Hartley responded. "We need to find out what was going on with Benjamin Ochoa."

"I'll get a copy of that tape and have uniforms pick up the family."

"Let's head back to the station first. Mac may have already called for someone to I.D. the body."

FOUR

The precinct bustled with activity. Uniforms came in at a relatively steady pace, leading handcuffed men and women to the holding cells to wait their turn for interrogation or booking. Detectives roamed in and out of conference rooms the size of closets, shifting papers and writing on chalkboards already filled to the edges with notes on their assigned investigation.

Hartley and Barailles walked through the door, each moving to their respective desks to check awaiting emails and voicemails that had filtered into the system during their absence. This was the normality of the job. Regardless of what case they happened to be assigned to and no matter how many twists and turns it would take, there was still the everyday activities sprinkled throughout, activities that bordered on the mundane and frustrated the officers just as much as a lack of leads.

When Barailles had finished taking stock of his messages, he made his way back to Hartley's desk and waited patiently with hands on hips. He watched as Hartley retrieved a yellow pad and began to write, obviously taking note of importance, her eyes lost between the scribbles and the space between her and the computer monitor. He caught a glance of the paper and read with little difficulty the upsidedown script his partner had etched onto the surface. *Rodolfo & Selena Ochoa.*

Hartley hung up the phone. "Family just IDed the body. Benjamin's parents, Rodolfo & Selena Ochoa. They're on their way up. Let's talk with them and then we'll go see Mac." Barailles nodded.

Hartley stood and walked to the kitchen. From the counter she grabbed a bottle of aspirin and dispensed two pills into the palm of her hand. She filled up a mug with water and swallowed the pills, head lifted towards the ceiling, eyes remaining shut. She was tired. Drinking did not suit her when there was work to be done the following day. She would have to remember that.

A knock aroused her from her thoughts, though she remained still, head cocked upwards, eyes shut, knowing exactly who it was. Barailles entered the kitchen, staring at his partner who seemed to be sleeping in an upright position. "The Ochoas are here, Hartley," he said. "You okay?"

She opened her eyes and looked to the lobby where Mac guided a middle-aged couple to a couch. He made his way towards Hartley's desk and turned as he saw her in the kitchen, nodding his head towards the couple. "Torn up, but not the worst I've seen," the ME said as he entered the room. The three of them stared through the window separating the pit from the kitchen, watching the Ochoa family at the far end of the hall.

Hartley sighed. "Thanks, Mac. We'll be down after we talk to them," she said, her eyes never leaving the couple. "Let's go," she said to her partner. The detectives walked together down the short, open hallway to the grieving couple on the small, black leather couch, the gruff, goateed man consoling his emaciated-looking wife as she leaned into his barrel of a chest, eyes glazed over from crying. He rested his cheek on his wife's head and sat in silence.

"Mr. and Mrs. Ochoa," Hartley said as she and Barailles approached, stopping several feet in front of them to look upon their shattered faces. "I'm Detective Hartley and this is Detective Barailles. I'm truly sorry for your loss this morning. I know this is extremely hard, but I'd like to ask you a few questions if that's all right with you."

"Certainly," Mr. Ochoa said. His wife nodded.

"Thank you," Hartley said softly. "Please, come this way." They led the grieving couple into a snug break room that resembled an apartment dining area. Two couches sat facing one another in the center of the room, a large Venetian rug spilling almost to the surrounding walls. A coffee table separated the couches, as well as four small end tables and several energy efficient floor lamps that produced just enough light to keep the inhabitants of the room from falling fast asleep. Monet and Van Gogh oil reproductions hung on either side of a large, gold-rimmed mirror just above a miniature refrigerator that hummed in intermittent cycles of loud and louder.

These interviews were always tough. Hartley knew that the grief these people felt could affect how smooth the questioning went. She knew she needed to be calm and comforting, yet not overly so. Too much consoling would lead to her becoming another shoulder to cry on, which Hartley absolutely needed to veer away from. Too stiff and the family could begin to see her as insensitive towards their son, thus leading them to throw up a wall, guarding their feelings and the memories of their lost loved one, memories that could break a case wide open.

Hartley knew what she needed to do. She had been through every situation as a homicide detective, seen every sort of reaction imaginable within the confines of the break and interrogation rooms: Thirty straight minutes of sobbing from a burly, Harley-riding man who had lost his only daughter to a random robbery-turned-murder; a scrawny teenager who had admitted to killing his adorable, college-bound girlfriend with his own bare hands before fainting into the metal interrogation table, breaking his jaw; a hundred pound trophy-wife flying across the room in full attack-mode, three-inch dagger-like nails ready to sink in. She had seen it all.

"Mr. and Mrs. Ochoa—"

"Please, call us Rudy and Selena," Mr. Ochoa interrupted.

Hartley smiled. "Rudy, Selena," she repeated looking at each in turn, wishing they would have kept things a little less formal. "Again, I'm truly sorry for the loss of your son. Do you know of anyone who would have wanted to hurt him?"

Selena looked to her husband in thought. "No," she said, bringing a tissue up to her already red nose. "He was a good man. Everyone liked him."

"What about other gang members?"

"Detective," Rudy began, "our son had been in the Five-Ones for years, since he was little. Anyone who gets involved in that is bound to have enemies. But he had straightened up."

"How do you mean?" Barailles asked.

Rudy turned his attention to the male detective. "He was out."

"Out? Out of the Five-Ones?"

"*Si*," Rudy answered. "I mean, he still knew people, and his cousin Miguel is still a high ranking soldier, but he no longer went anywhere with them. Benjamin realized that it wasn't a way to live. It was a way to die. One minute he was out all night, come home stinking of spray paint and alcohol. Who knows what else? Next minute, he doesn't leave the house. He's staying in all night. Barely ever left his room."

"How long ago did this occur?" Hartley asked.

The Ochoas looked at each other. "Oh, had to be at least a couple years, no?" Rudy asked his wife.

"Yes. At least a couple. Maybe a year before he got his own apartment," she agreed. Selena turned back to Hartley. "You think it could have been someone in the Five-One?"

"We have to look at all aspects. The evidence we've collected up to this point doesn't suggest that, but we can't be sure." The Ochoas nodded their heads. "The Five-Ones. We've worked cases that involved their members and have learned that they don't look highly on those who try and leave the ranks. Do you think the higher-ups could have been angry that Benjamin had left?"

Rudy shrugged. "It's possible," he said, shaking his head, "but not likely. Miguel—the cousin I told you about. He's not the best kid in the world. But he knew the life wasn't for Benjamin. He had talks with his superiors, vouching for Benjamin that he'd never tell their secrets."

"And you think they bought that?" Hartley asked.

"No reason not too. Benjamin just wanted out. He didn't seem to care what he knew." Rudy paused, looking to the floor. "As bad as the Five-Ones are, I just can't believe that they would come back years later and kill him."

Selena began to cry and Rudy pulled her closer. Barailles leaned forward. "Ma'am, I'm going to go get some coffee. Would you like anything? Tea? Muffin?"

She nodded her head and answered, "Tea, *gracias,*" between sniffles. Barailles lifted himself from the couch and moved off towards the kitchen.

Hartley continued. "Rudy, you said that Benjamin hadn't been involved with the gang for at least the last couple years?"

"Yes."

"What had he been doing since then?"

"School. Robert Morris on State Street," he said matter-of-factly. Hartley opened her mouth as if she were surprised. Rudy caught the movement and grinned. "See, detective, not everyone thinks a banger can become rehabilitated outside of the system. But our Benjamin—he was different."

Hartley smiled. "What was he doing in school?"

"He was studying general education. Liberal arts. He worked at a restaurant near the college too. He bussed tables."

"Do you know the name of the restaurant?"

"North Corner Pancake House." Barailles stepped in to the room, handing the tea to Selena and taking his place again next to Hartley. Selena forced a smile through her anguished façade.

"What time did Benjamin's classes start? What days?" Hartley asked.

"Every day. Well, every weekday. He would leave his place at seven o'clock in the morning and catch the 7:15 bus into the city. Depending on what day it was and if he had to work, sometimes he wouldn't get back until late. Weekends he had one day off. The other he worked a double at the pancake house."

"Did you notice if Benjamin had been acting differently lately? Nervous or on edge?" Rudy looked at her questioningly. "If he was noticeably different it may help us determine if he knew if something out of the ordinary was going on."

Rudy and Selena glanced at each other. "Well, yes," Selena said. "Now that you mention it, he hadn't really been himself for the last few months. Seemed jumpy. Nervous. We hadn't really seen him as much since then."

"Had anything happened within these last months?"

"No. Nothing other than my sister's death—" Selena said as she held back the tears.

"I'm so sorry, Selena," Hartley said, extending her hand and placing it gently on Selena's. "I know it's hard, but I have to ask. How did your sister pass?"

"She was murdered three months ago," Rudy stated, seeing that the emotions had once again taken his wife. "Miguel came home one night and found her—" he paused, looking up at the detectives. He shook his head. Hartley understood. It was too painful for his wife.

"Did they ever find the killer?"

"They had someone in custody for questioning. A black man. He was a banger too."

"He wasn't the guy?"

"Cleared him. Haven't found anyone since that we've heard of."

"Do you remember his name?"

"Jerome. They never gave us a last name. With the gang affiliation I think they were afraid of action being taken."

Hartley nodded. "Probably nothing there, but we'll take a look into the files to see if there are any connections."

"*Gracias,*" Rudy said. Hartley smiled.

"Do you remember who the lead investigator was on the case?"

"Couple offiers kept in contact with us. Seargent Duarson, I think was our main contact," Rudy said. "Nice guy."

"And newly retired," Hartley added.

"Since when?"

"Yesterday. We'll find out who the lead is now. Again, I'm truly sorry. We'll do our best to find who did this to your son."

Rudy and Selena forced a smile. "*Gracias,*" they said.

Hartley smiled and stood, placing a hand on Rudy's shoulder. "I'll keep you informed if we find anything." He nodded. Hartley turned and with Barailles left the Ochoas in the break room to their thoughts.

The detectives took a seat at Hartley's desk, Barailles staring at his partner as she glanced down to a stack of paper. "What are you thinking?" he asked after a minute of silence.

She looked up at him. "I'm thinking something doesn't make sense just yet." She shifted to an upright position in her chair. "We have an ex-gangbanger who leaves the life years ago. Gets a job. Goes to school. Straightens his life up. If the Five-Ones were looking to silence him, they would have done it soon after he told them he was out. No sense in taking the chance he would open his mouth. But he gets out, untouched it seems. Leads a normal life. Gets an apartment, visits his parents. Then just like that—" she snapped her fingers for effect "—his aunt is murdered and he's looking over his shoulder."

"Do you think what happened then and this investigation have something in common?" Barailles asked.

"I don't know," she answered, closing her eyes again and visualizing the case on the back of her eyelids. "Ochoa gets to the bus stop for his usual morning ride, but he's not going to class."

"How do you figure?"

She opened her eyes. "Because there was no backpack. Kid heading to class for the majority of the day with no quick access to his apartment—he should be carrying his things with him. So where was he going? Meanwhile, our killer knows

Ochoa's schedule. He must have been watching him, learning where he would be at what times."

"Although a man looking over his shoulder doesn't usually keep the same agenda," Barailles added in.

"Right. So the killer's only option is the morning bus ride. Instead of making a scene on the bus or at the school, he takes him out in the morning. He's able to get in his car and disappear into the commuters." They sat in silence again, marinating over the theories they had concocted. "I'd like to take a look at the aunt's murder. Let's pull the files and see if anything pops out at us."

"Okay," Barailles said as he rose from a nearby chair and entered a storage room to the left. Hartley knew they were thin on leads, yet also realized the murder was only several hours old. Being a homicide in a neighborhood controlled by gang activity, the odds were against them from the start. They needed to look at the evidence and question the witnesses, yet the only thing that had turned up thus far was the bank tape, and that only suggested, though strongly, that the murder of Benjamin Ochoa was not a gang hit at all, yet something more planned out.

Barailles returned with a box from the Gomez murder investigation, two months cold. "Who's the investigator on it now?" Hartley asked as he set it down and opened the flaps, sifting through the papers within.

"Doesn't look like it got reassigned," he answered. "Gang hits," he said with a disgusted shake of his head. After a time he halted, sighing and looking up to Hartley as she reclined in her swivel chair. She caught his gaze and tightened her lips together, eyes wide. Barailles, slumped and cocked his head to the side. "You're not going to help with this, are you?" he said in defeat. Hartley shook her head. "It was your idea."

"I think you can manage," she replied. "I'm going to head down to Mac, see what he has for us."

"Probably a cold table and a warm cup of coffee," Barailles answered, diving into the box and pulling out dozens of forms and photographs.

Hartley stood and moved towards the elevator. "Hopefully a pillow and blanket," she said as she pressed the down button. "Let me know if you find something interesting." Barailles waved a finger in acknowledgment as the elevator doors opened.

FIVE

The box containing the Maria Gomez murder investigation was a hard thing for Detective Anthony Barailles to look through. Photographs of the murder scene painted a picture of a brutally painful and excruciatingly slow death. Bruising. Broken nails. Swollen eye. Puncture wounds from a large blade. All before Maria Gomez was put out of her misery.

Barailles knew the gangs in the area where Benjamin Ochoa was found murdered, knew the hostility and violence they brought to the table. Maria Gomez, regardless of her gang affiliation—if she had one—had undergone a horrific night. No one, gangbanger or otherwise, deserved what she had received. He turned his attention from a crime scene photo to the statement made by the first officer on the scene.

* * * * *

Hartley rode the elevator down to basement level, her headache once again spreading its painful tendrils along her skull and curling behind her ears. She closed her eyes and waited for the sensation to pass. The city morgue and forensics labs were located in the building on the opposite side of the next block, a long walk especially when the dead of winter came around. Fortunately, the city council had years ago approved the construction of an underground walkway system connecting the morgue, lab, police station and the St. Francis Hospital, a renovation of the sublevels of half a dozen buildings that cost upwards of fifteen million dollars.

The hall Hartley walked down after exiting the elevator was half the length of a city block, lit by blue halogen bulbs that reflected off the six-inch white ceramic tiles covering the floor and walls, creating a hazy dream-like effect for whomever used the walkway. Hartley did not mind the dreary, lazy effect the corridor had on her. It soothed her, pulled the ache from her temples ever so slowly.

She continued past a locked door on the right with the word *HOLDING* written in red block letters and entered an alcove that held a water fountain and a single elevator. She pressed the sole button on the panel and it lit red.

* * * * *

Date: April 21, 2011.
Time: 21:54.

Barailles made a note mentally, jotting down the statement's date in his mind.

> *Desc.: OFC PETTIMAN received call about African-American man walking quickly down road in BACK-OF-THE-YARDS neighborhood known for 51st Street Crew affiliations. OFC PETTIMAN apprehended one JEROME GRAZER on WEST 54TH STREET between*

ABERDEEN and MAY. GRAZER appeared inhibited. Admitted to alcohol and marijuana consumption. GRAZER visibly shaken. Was cooperative to get into cruiser.

Barailles looked up from the statement and glanced at a crime scene photo displaying the front yard of Maria Gomez's property. Chaotic footprints littered the front lawn from the detectives and Evidence Team as they made their way from the vehicles on the street to the interior of the home. In the photo, Officer Pettiman's cruiser was parked near the corner and Barailles could make out the face of a black male in the back, staring out into the mayhem.

Barailles moved to his computer and entered the name Jerome Grazer into the database, immediately pulling up the man's rap sheet—aggravated assault; public intoxication; breaking and entering; resisting; destruction of property; possession. Grazer was a lifetime member of the Four Star Rings, a gang that, like others in the area, thrived on violence and narcotics. They were into running prostitution rings as well, and had big name clients that were willing to overlook some of their more routine criminal acts.

Barailles pulled up his most recent mug shot. Jerome Grazer was an intimidating man. Just clearing six-foot-five-inches and two-hundred-forty pounds, Grazer was a beast of a human being. According to his record, he was a survivor also, having been shot three times in the stomach, twice in the thigh and once in the left foot, an injury that resulted in him losing one of his toes. He had been stabbed numerous times as well, though these incidents seemed to be domestic occurrences from his youth with a father that was now serving time for second-degree murder.

Barailles shook his head and returned to Officer Pettiman's statement.

* * * * *

"Detective Hartley," Mac sang from the kitchen as Hartley exited the elevator and proceeded towards the lab. "Looking radiant as ever."

Hartley smirked and leaned against the doorframe, arms crossed. "Mac, you cease to amaze me with your upbeat attitude."

"What can I say, my dear? When you're staring at heads with bullet holes and men with their dicks chopped off, there's just a lot to be grateful for." Mac grabbed a banana and muffin from the refrigerator and walked towards the door, Hartley stepping back into the hall and allowing him the exit.

"Funny. You talk about bullet holes and dickless men, and the first thing you grab is a banana," Hartley said with a little laugh as they began down the hallway with the ME in tow.

"Why, Jolene Hartley!" Mac said with mock surprise. "What a terribly crude analogy! Linking my banana to a penis!" He looked out of the corner of his eye towards her. "Is that humor I detect?" he asked as she smiled and looked towards the floor.

"Hey," she replied, "I'm not all work." Mac stopped in his tracks and stared at her, his jaw hanging open in disbelief. "Come on!" she said, tilting her head to the side. They continued walking, Mac's smile filling his entire face.

"I'm just kidding, Hartley," he said. "Brains, beauty and a sense of humor. You're going to make some man extremely happy one day." Hartley rolled her eyes. They continued for several steps in silence before Mac turned all business. "The shoeprint you guys found by the backhoe is useless. The size was that of an average man and the brand is sold in hundreds of stores across the city. It's a dead end." Hartley nodded her head, not surprised. They turned into an intersecting hallway and continued up a stairwell to their left, ascending one flight and exiting into an impeccably clean hallway, the smell of bleach and other cleaning agents resting in the air. The ME led Hartley to a door thirty feet down the corridor, pushing the entrance open for the detective. The bold, white letters *FORENSICS* stared at her as she passed into the adjoining room.

* * * * *

OFC. PETTIMAN learned from GRAZER that he had been in the neighborhood to find one MIGUEL GOMEZ. GRAZER to assault GOMEZ for recent gang activity on 4 STAR RING territory. According to GRAZER, GOMEZ had been seen trafficking narcotics to African-American subjects on 4 STAR RING turf. GRAZER appeared clean of blood or grass stains, signs typical of an altercation.

Barailles continued reading as the statement turned towards the Gomez murder.

Approx. 22:30, OFC. PETTIMAN receives radio transmission. Possible 187 at 4152 JOINER AVE, home of one MARIA GOMEZ. OFC. PETTIMAN first respondent.

Officer Pettiman had pulled up to the home of Maria Gomez with Jerome Grazer in the rear of his cruiser, cautiously taking in the neighborhood around him. A throng of people had begun to congregate near the Gomez home, all staring wide-eyed and open-mouthed as the cruiser pulled up. Pettiman exited the car, glancing at the faces before him, listening to the faint *thump thump* of a bass line rolling down the pavement from a distance away, an obvious sign the Five-Ones were up to no good somewhere in the neighborhood. Lights were shining bright within almost every home in the near vicinity, most likely in response to the scene the officer now came upon.

Barailles flipped to the next page, reading the report like he would a favorite novel, unable to put the papers down, yet fearing the descriptions that pulled his attention like a magnet.

Pettiman proceeded slowly up the driveway, assessing the situation before him: Neighbors forming in mobs; the low, subtle sobs of an individual within the confines of the home; a trail of blood leading to the front door. He had made the wise decision to call in for backup, reporting to the dispatch operator that he had arrived on the scene after picking up Grazer, and that Jerome was now secured in the rear of the cruiser, a person of interest in this possible homicide due to his own confession of hunting down Miguel.

The officer had made it to within a dozen feet of the entrance before Miguel Gomez came through the door, blood coating his arms and chest, red streaks smeared down his face as if he were crying crimson. Pettiman had tried to console Gomez, yet the young man was beyond devastated, his eyes lost to a world of pain and rage. Another cruiser pulled up to the scene moments later, Pettiman handing off the bloodied man to his counterpart before turning back towards the residence.

It was not until Officer Pettiman stepped into the house that the weight of the situation fell fully upon him.

* * * * *

The body of Benjamin Manuel Ochoa lay on the cold, metallic laboratory table, eyes shut as if in slumber, face and clothes stained red from the blood that had poured uncontrollably out of the perforating wound on the right side of his forehead. The bullet had made a relatively clean exit, leaving behind minimal extruding tissue and brain matter, though the loss of blood had been extreme.

Mac walked over to a wall-length counter packed full of medical equipment of all sorts, items Hartley was used to seeing but never quite comfortable around. She could imagine what they were used for and the damage they could inflict if in the wrong hands. The ME pulled two paper towels from the hanging wall dispenser and moved back towards the detective and her victim, placing the banana and muffin neatly on the napkins next to Ochoa's body.

Hartley moved closer to her victim to get a better look. Besides the hole in his forehead, Benjamin was a decent looking young man. Hartley thought to herself that his murder was more pointless than other gang related killings, mainly because this kid had begun to turn his life around. He had not needed the barrel of a gun jammed into his face or a stint behind bars to learn that he was worth more than the Five-Ones. He needed only to flip the figurative switch in his mind, to wake up one crisp morning and decide that this life was not for him. He was going to change.

"As you can see," Mac began, "I haven't really been able to dive into anything just yet. The Ochoas showed up shortly after we got here, so I just had time to lay him on the board and examine the wound briefly."

"Excuses, excuses," Hartley chided.

"Yeah, yeah." Mac turned on an overhead light and pulled it towards the victim, illuminating the wound with such intensity that the brain matter and dried blood could be seen clearly from a dozen feet away. "Now, as you can see—" he lifted the head and turned it to the left, Hartley squatting down so her eyes were level with the table "—the bullet entered in the bottom right of the head and traveled upwards—" he returned the head to the table and pointed at the exit wound "—exiting the left forehead."

"Caliber?" Hartley asked.

"By the looks of it I'd say a .22. But that's not what gets me. This shot was extremely precise." Hartley looked up towards Mac and he crossed his arms. "A distance shot is by all means more difficult."

"Right," Hartley interjected. "You're playing the wind, breathing, vibrations from heartbeats."

"Correct. The easiest area to place a shot on a human from a distance is the torso. You may not kill the target straight out, but initializing a wound slows said target down."

"But this option allows a potential victim to raise an alarm or perhaps get away."

"Military sharp shooters, however," Mac continued, "are trained to, if possible, minimize the time a target has to react. A shot to the brain will disrupt and instantly incapacitate the central nervous system, in essence turning everything within the body off."

"You think our perp is ex-military?"

"Ex-military. Military. All I know is that whoever it is, they know how to use a rifle." Mac unfolded his arms and moved along the table, pulling the sheet covering Ochoa's body down to his feet. He ran his hands up Ochoa's leg and into his pocket, pulling out some change, a Transit Authority ticket and a crumpled yellow piece of paper. He unfolded the sheet and sighed. "It's like I've won the lottery today," he said. "First I get to work with you, and second—" He let the phrase hang as he handed the note to Hartley.

She glanced at it and looked up. "I wonder who this is."

"I don't know, but after years of doing this, I've learned whatever is in the pocket is most likely important."

Hartley nodded. "Where's a phone I can use? Get no reception in here."

"Out the door to the left. Use my office. First door on the right."

* * * * *

The house was in tatters. Chairs were knocked to the ground. Plants had emptied their soiled contents onto the cream-colored carpet, which was stained crimson with blood-splatter from an assault that was wholly one-sided. Red footprints littered the walkway to the door.

In the center of the living room, tied to a chair was the lifeless body of Maria Gomez, a pool of blood formed beneath her seat as she slumped forward as if in prayer. Officer Pettiman walked delicately up to the body and checked for vitals, being careful not to taint any evidence that may have been left behind. Maria Gomez was indeed dead. Pettiman could see the incision on her throat, determining that the cut had most likely severed her carotid artery and killed her in a matter of seconds.

As Barailles read the statement and viewed the gruesome crime scene photos he began to feel that he and Hartley were wasting their time. Grazer was indeed a criminal, however, nowhere on his record did murder or manslaughter show its ugly face. And the killing of Maria Gomez, although horrible as it was, did not seem in any way connected to their current investigation other than pure coincidence. The odds of multiple family members with gang ties being threatened, assaulted or even murdered within months of each other was, unfortunately, not an isolated event, especially on Five-One turf. Revenge for a fallen brother or cousin ran high in the streets. It was just part of gang life.

Barailles looked up and rubbed his eyes. He needed coffee. Hours spent pouring over paperwork, especially that of a cold case, needed fuel beyond the urge to bring about justice. From inside his breast pocket Barailles's cell phone sprang to life, causing him to jump and laugh at himself.

"Barailles," he answered.

"Hey, it's me," Hartley replied. "Mac just handed me a piece of paper found in our vic's front pocket. Want to run a J. Grazer. G-R-A—"

"Grazer? You've got to be kidding me," Barailles interrupted, sitting up and sifting through the box.

"Why? You know who this is?" Hartley asked in surprise.

"Yeah, I'm looking at him right now," Barailles answered, lifting the picture of their suspect into his line of sight. "Jerome Grazer."

"How are you looking at him now? I'm confused."

"Brace yourself. Jerome Grazer was at the scene of our vic's aunt's murder. He was the initial person of interest before he was released."

The line remained silent as Hartley took in the news. "Well," she finally replied, "that must be a role he likes to play. Find an address on him. He's our focus for Benjamin Ochoa's murder right now. Let's bring him in."

SIX

All was quiet at the run-down bungalow listed as Jerome Grazer's last known address in Englewood. Hartley and Barailles had pulled up to the opposite corner and parked, binoculars set to their eyes as they peered into the lower windows. There was movement inside, yet the detectives could not make out if it was their suspect through the pulled drapes. There was only one way to find out.

They exited the vehicle and moved to the trunk to fetch two Kevlar vests. Though a confrontation was not expected— nor wanted—the two officers knew they could take no chances in this neighborhood. Gangs avoided tangles with officers, yet when backed into a corner, shootouts did occur and both sides had experienced casualties.

They crossed the street at the corner and walked up the sidewalk, pausing just outside the front gate of the home. Bushes and trees hung low and sporadic within the yard, the grass long enough to begin reseeding, though the odds the new blades would penetrate the jungle of dandelions was a stretch. "Let's get in and get out," Hartley said. "I want to get him into the station as quickly as possible. If there's a fight, we need to go in fast and quick. There's nothing to fall back to besides the car, and I don't want to be exposed for that long."

Barailles nodded and followed Hartley through the gate and up the porch steps, the wood bending and groaning as they ascended. Just as they reached the landing, the handle on the front door began to turn slowly and the door creaked open. The officers stopped, hands immediately darting to their respective sides and unlatching their firearms. "Police!" Hartley yelled out. There was no response. Hartley looked to Barailles. Their Glocks were immediately in their hands and raised towards the door. "Chicago PD!" Hartley yelled again. "Open the door slowly and show your hands!"

"Oh, come on now," came the sweet, melodic reply from inside as the door swung open. In the threshold stood a squat, elderly woman in a purple sweat-soaked t-shirt and skirt, her large frame supported by a wooden cane. "I raise my hands up and you gonna be picking my fat, sweaty ass off the porch. I don't think you want that," she said with a smile.

Hartley and Barailles lowered their weapons, but did not holster them. "We're looking for Jerome Grazer, ma'am," Hartley said. "Do you happen to know where he is?"

"Well, you at the right place, but he ain't here. Hasn't been back since yesterday afternoon. Don't know when he gonna be back neither." Her voice carried with it the sound of her origins, a southern drawl that sung of better days. She leaned against the doorframe, cane positioned directly in front of her with her hands folded on top. She had an amused smile on her face as she glanced back and forth at the visitors on her porch through squinted eyes. "Now, y'all wanna come in you have to put those away," she said turning into the dark of the house. "I seen enough of those things around here."

Barailles glanced at Hartley who shrugged and holstered her weapon, keeping it unlatched and hand at the ready as she walked towards the front door. She slowed and peered inside, letting her eyes adjust fully to the interior before stepping in. The woman had moved off into the living room and stood waiting for the officers, sweat beading on her forehead. "Y'all want something to drink? I just made some tea."

"Ma'am," Hartley said as she entered the living room, "we're looking for Jerome Grazer—"

"I know. I heard you the first time," the woman interrupted with a smile. "And, as I said, y'all have the right spot. Jerome's my grandson, but he ain't here. Now, would y'all like something to drink? It sure is hot out there."

Hartley looked quizzically at Barailles who tried to hide a smirk. "Ma'am," he said to the woman, though his eyes did not leave his partner, "I'd love some tea. Thank you." The woman nodded her approval and turned to Hartley.

Hartley looked back to her and realized she was still waiting for an answer. "Uh—No. Thank you. No," she stammered.

"All right," the woman said as she moved into the kitchen. "Make yourself comfy. I'll be back directly." Barailles moved along the left-hand side of the room, eyeing an ancient upright piano resting against the stained, dingy wall, an antique from another world that definitely seemed out of place in a dangerous neighborhood filled with theft and murder. He took a seat on the piano bench and looked up to his partner who still stood in the middle of the room, hand resting on her firearm as she stared after the woman. Barailles laughed loudly and shook his head. Obviously this elderly woman had overtaken Hartley's no-nonsense attitude with little more than a lighthearted, carefree sense of humor.

Hartley heard Barailles chuckle and removed her hand from her weapon, stealing a glance out of the corner of her eye at her partner as she took a seat in a plush chair covered in plastic. "Shut up," she said to him as the woman returned to the room carrying a small tray with three small glasses of iced tea, which she set down on the coffee table.

"Now, I know you said you didn't want nothing," the woman began as she fell onto the couch, "but my tea just too good to pass up. You really must try it."

Barailles leaned forward and grabbed a cup and put it to his lips, letting the liquid cool his throat and chest. "Thank you, ma'am," he said, raising his glass to her. She nodded and turned to Hartley, looking at her with a slight grin, as if she were willing the detective to pick up the third glass and taste her creation.

Hartley looked down to the drinks quickly and clasped her hands in front of her. "Ma'am," she began. "I'm Detective Hartley and this is Detective Barailles."

"Good to meet y'all. I'm Norma Jean Whickerson." She smiled at both detectives in turn.

"You said Jerome isn't here. Do you happen to know where we can find him?"

"Oh," she said, waving her hand in the air. "Who knows with that boy? Never tells no one where he's going. Or when he's coming back."

"You said he hasn't been back since—"

"Since yesterday," Norma interrupted. She turned her head towards Barailles and without missing a beat asked, "She repeat like this?" Barailles smiled and let out a laugh, silencing it immediately when Hartley tensed her mouth.

"Mrs. Whickerson," she said, "I need to ask you some questions and I'd really appreciate—"

"You sure are a pretty thing, you know that?" Norma interrupted again.

Hartley smiled nervously. "Uh—thank you, but I—"

"You notice how pretty she is, don't you?" Norma asked Barailles.

He continued to grin as he answered, "Everyday, ma'am. Makes it hard to do the job." The old woman laughed with Barailles as Hartley looked from the table to her hands and back to her partner, her cheeks flushing red.

"Well, I been around for quite some years," Norma continued. "And I hardly seen anything quite as pretty as you. Which makes me wonder why in the world you gone and made yourself a cop. Putting that pretty face out in the line of danger." She shook her head and sipped her tea. "You don't mind me asking, what y'all doing out here? What you want with that boy? What you investigatin' now?"

Hartley took that moment to assert herself as the alpha female in the room. "A homicide," she answered, face calm as she stared at Norma. The old woman held her cup of tea aloft and stared back at Hartley, the humor of the conversation seeming to be released from her in one breath, leaving an air of shock and panic. The realization that these two members of the police force had shown up on her doorstep asking about her grandson as part of a homicide investigation hit her like a ton of bricks.

"Jerome," she said in a whisper. "Is it Jerome? Dead?"

"No," Hartley answered. "We need to know where he is though. We believe he has some part in this investigation."

Norma set her cup down on the tray and shifted her weight on the couch. "Yes, well, he was here around noon yesterday and then left. Hasn't been back since."

"Do you know where he is?"

"No. Probably out with those fools he hangs out with."

"Norma," Barailles jumped in, "do you know of Jerome's ties with the Four Stars?"

Norma straightened and grew more serious, her lips tensing together. She nodded. "I knew those no-good fools would get him in trouble. Jerome's been in and out of jail for things. Nothing like a killing though. I knew this would happen some day."

"Norma," Hartley said sternly, "we don't know if Jerome is involved directly or not. But we need to talk to him—"

"Leave me a number," she interjected. "I'll call you when I see him."

Hartley looked towards Barailles, wondering why Jerome's own grandmother was so willing to give up her grandson. Norma caught the look and stood. "Detective, I love that boy. But he's gonna end up dead on the street. I'd rather see him behind bars than lifeless in an alley. I'll call." The detectives stood and Barailles handed Norma a card with his and Hartley's phone numbers on it. She took the card and nodded her understanding. "I'll call."

* * * * *

"You think she'll really call?" Barailles asked as he drove their cruiser back to the precinct, weaving in and out of the evening rush hour.

Hartley nodded. "Yeah, I'm sure she will. She may not know exactly what Jerome is involved in with the Four Stars, but you heard her: She'd rather see him in jail and alive. She'll call."

After a few minutes Barailles let out a chuckle, causing Hartley to jump and turn towards him. "What the hell was that?"

He contained himself just long enough to let out a squeaky, "'You sure are a pretty thing.'" His attempt at the southern drawl failed miserably, yet the jab hit home fully. Hartley rolled her eyes and looked out the window. "She really had you flustered. It was hilarious!" he said.

"Shut up," Hartley answered.

They rode in silence for several minutes, both thinking of the day's events and what they needed to accomplish going forward. Hartley had called in an APB on Jerome as soon as they left the home, yet the odds of a patrol locating him in a Four Star Ring neighborhood was highly unlikely. They would need to wait until Norma Jean Whickerson called back.

Barailles looked over to his partner, her head thrown back against the rest, eyes closed. *You are beautiful,* he thought to himself. "Hartley," he said, rousing her slightly. "You want me to drop you at home?"

Hartley remained still. Finally, she opened her eyes and turned to the passenger side window. "No," she responded. "I'll catch a cab." They remained silent for the rest of the ride to the precinct.

SEVEN

Jolene Hartley entered her Lakeview apartment and closed the door behind her, resting her weary body on the frame and breathing deeply. It was good to be home. The majority of her cases saw her parked in front of a chalkboard of evidence until the early hours of the morning, sometimes longer. On numerous occasions she had decided to make a couch in the break room her bed, and on others, sleep was not an option.

She knew how her mind worked, knew that sometimes sleep would only erase a thought that had been floating in the recesses of her brain, one that very well could break a case wide open. Tonight was not the night for a sleepover at the station, however. Tonight was about one thing and one thing only: Recovery.

Jolene removed her shoes and placed them neatly in her front closet. She moved slowly across her living area, sliding her leather jacket down her arms and setting it over the back of the red microfiber couch. She pulled out a chair from her kitchen table and sat, leaning forward as she pulled her hair tie out, letting her locks fall to her shoulders and around her face. She closed her eyes and took several deep breaths, settling her body into the state of relaxation she had needed all day. Her fingers moved to her face and massaged, working their way up her cheekbones, across her forehead and streaking through her brown hair as she tilted her head back and opened her eyes, a word forming in her mind: Bath.

She stood and made her way up the steps to a loft over-looking the kitchen and stepped into her bedroom. Her apartment was spacious, yet contained only one bedroom and one full bath, both located on the upper floor. Jolene loved it. It was her place, her sanctuary and getaway from the cruelty that surrounded her life at the precinct.

She entered the bathroom and turned the handle on the tub, the pipes making a creaking sound before the water came rushing out. She flipped the lever to close the drain and grabbed a bottle of soap, turning it upside down and squeez-ing a good amount of liquid into the path of the water, bubbles forming immediately as steam wafted up from the growing puddle, carrying with it the scent of soothing lavender.

Jolene moved out of the bathroom and down the hall, making her way to her bedroom and the large, fluffy king-size bed situated against the wall, framed by two mahogany end tables cradling a pair of silver lamps. She opened her armoire and pulled out the drawer that held her firearm lockbox, scan-ning her finger and hearing the click as the box disengaged. She placed the gun in the container and closed it, removing her star and holster and setting them next to the receptacle.

Jolene moved to her closet and undressed, trading her work clothes for a short cotton robe to cover up while she walked back to the bathroom. *No need to give the neighbors a free show,* she thought to herself, glancing out the windows that lined the opposite wall.

In the glow of the bathroom lights she let the robe slide from her shoulders, leaving her standing naked in the cool apartment air. She reached over to the iPod docking station near the sink and pressed play, setting off her own personal concert starring Jefferson Airplane as they started into *White Rabbit.* Jolene stepped into the hot, steaming water and sunk in, letting the suds flow over her skin and rejuvenate her senses. She turned the faucet off with her toes and leaned back, breathing in the fragrance rising from the suds and letting the heated water soak into her body and soul as she began to finally relax.

She lay there for nearly half an hour before moving, her joints feeling as if a new spring had been set, tendons shaking off the years and becoming new once more. With her foot she released the drain, letting the cool water shoot down the pipe as she turned the faucet on once again, warming her cauldron to a more desirable temperature before completely immersing herself and running her hands through her hair, releasing bubbles of air from her nose and mouth and watching them as they danced sporadically towards the surface.

When she emerged, Jolene wiped the suds from her face and positioned herself once again against the slanted backrest, her eyes locking onto the metal faucet. The case continued to sit poised in the recesses of her mind, though her partner, Detective Anthony Barailles had now jumped to the forefront. They had been assigned together for four years, Barailles starting over after his previous partner took a bullet to the temple, killing him instantly. Barailles had taken an extended leave of absence, yet forced himself back into the job, leaving his precinct in the Morgan Park neighborhood and moving into hers, a desperate attempt to run from the past and start anew.

Hartley had become somewhat of a celebrity in the police force the moment she took her first assignment, a case that saw her track down and apprehend a serial killer linked to at least a dozen murders. She had been the driving force of the case, testifying and bringing the murderer to justice, though missing the death sentence she and the victims' families had sought due to a verdict of insanity. The outcome was disappointing to Hartley, however, she knew the man would never again roam the streets of Chicago. She had done her job.

The assignment that found both she and Barailles working together was initially Barailles's alone. He had been following a lead that linked an owner of a grungy gentlemen's club in Chicago Lawn to his victim's murder, yet had stalled due to the fact he could not get anyone to spill the beans. What he needed was someone to infiltrate the staff, to gain knowledge of the owner's whereabouts, and to do it without jeopardizing the investigation.

What he needed, Captain Nolan assigned to him in an incredibly attractive, long-limbed beauty with sleek, dark hair and fierce brown eyes that drew attention like a black hole. Detective Jolene Hartley was brought in to play the role of a waitress, passing the interview process with flying colors after toying with the idea to management about possibly taking the stage. She was incredible to look at, and the management did not think twice about bringing her aboard as she sat before them in a small skirt, legs crossed, fingering her hair, her perky breasts trying to make an escape from the extra small white t-shirt that had cropped up just above her belly button.

The whole operation took less than a week and to the disappointment of the club's management—as well as the officers working the operation—Hartley was able to keep her clothes on. She had formed a connection with a newly-hired dancer who, unknowingly, handed over the information that indeed their suspect had been on the premises that night, rushing into the private restroom to wash from his hands and face what looked undeniably like blood. An apartment search warrant hours later found the victim's phone and wallet buried within a kitchen cabinet, and a purse jammed into an overflowing dumpster just down the block. All items were coated in the victim's blood.

They had worked so well together on the operation that Captain Nolan assigned them to the same cases from there on out, with Hartley taking the position as lead investigator on most cases. Barailles was one of the few detectives in the precinct that was willing to let Hartley, a woman, take the lead. He was a good detective as well, yet realized quickly that his new partner had something special, something that led her to think differently than any other officer he had ever seen. They had gotten along well from the start, working cases to their conclusions like they had been partners from day one, sifting through evidence and determining between them the best course of action. They were good for each other.

Two years into their partnership Jolene had met Ronny Debarsi, a detective heading a team assigned to city bank robberies. Ronny was tall and handsome with wavy black hair and a chiseled jaw line. Sparks flew immediately and Jolene and Ronny became enamored with one another. Due to strenuous cases, however, free time away from the precinct was limited. Ronny would visit Jolene when possible, and she, in turn, would bring lunch to him as they bounced ideas off of one another, shaking through the evidence with an outside perspective on each of their investigations.

Months into their relationship Barailles began to show signs of jealousy, signs that did not go unnoticed by Hartley. She was confused as to why these feeling were arising in her partner, seeing as he was a married man with two children. Tensions mounted while Debarsi was around and flooded into their cases, causing Hartley to take a stand as lead investigator. She had done nothing wrong with her actions and needed not to justify them to her partner.

It was nearing this point that Hartley learned of Barailles's marital issues. Obviously with the late nights a connection more than partners had been made, and Mrs. Barailles was not pleased in the least to have such an attractive woman by her husband's side day in and day out. Hartley had tried to talk to Barailles about his situation but he was unresponsive, wanting—or needing—to deal with his personal matter on his own. She needed to focus on the case, he would tell her. And she would.

For an additional two years this became the norm as Barailles and his wife moved into divorce court, Hartley feeling more and more like the nucleus of their problems. There was nothing she could do, however. This was her life. Her partner was the one who needed to make the decision. She could tell that he did not want to proceed with the divorce, yet he also had an air of relief about him at times.

Ronny and Jolene grew closer, as relationships tend to do, yet neither one ever seriously considered moving into each other's lives on a more permanent basis. Each kept their own apartment, although nights were spent at the other's on numerous occasions when time permitted. Debarsi eventually broke the news that he had been offered a position at the FBI offices in Philadelphia to head a team tracking a well-known thief that had terrorized banks in the city for years. He had accepted. Jolene was hurt, knowing that she was going to lose the most constant thing in her life, yet also understood the job was more than a nine-to-five deal for Debarsi too.

He left the following weekend, Jolene seeing him off and immediately returning to the precinct to bury herself in her work. Barailles was there as well, doing the same.

* * * * *

Six months ago, Jolene thought to herself as she shifted the bubbles of her bath. *Six months and I still don't know what to do.* The previous night with Tony had obviously happened to fill a void in her, yet she felt whole-heartedly that it meant something entirely different to her partner. It could not happen again. At least not until she got her head on straight.

Jolene exited the bathtub and toweled off, draping her robe over her shoulders as she walked back to her bedroom, changing into a pair of gray, cotton shorts and an old t-shirt that belonged to her ex. She left the room and walked down the stairs and into the kitchen, pulling from the freezer a carton of chocolate fudge chunk ice cream. *Recovery,* she thought. *This definitely falls in the recovery category.*

She took a seat on the couch and flipped on the television, surfing through the channels for something worth watching and stopping on *Animal Planet*, her eyes focusing on the dry, barren desert and the tiny, armored lizard scooting across the sand. Her mind, however, was elsewhere. The case had stolen the spotlight from her reveries of Ronny Debarsi.

Hartley envisioned the face Norma Jean Whickerson had made when the word *homicide* was released into the air, recalled how every movement had ceased as she realized the gravity of the situation was well beyond that of the usual interrogation regarding destruction of property or where her grandson was on a given night. Hartley knew the old woman would call if she saw or heard from him, yet Jerome, himself, was the question.

She had learned from the past that gangbangers were hardly reliable. Jerome could return in a matter of minutes or not for years. Gangs were like fraternities, spread across the country in dozens of cities, and if he was responsible for Ochoa's murder or knew something about it he could easily disappear within those factions, leaving her case with a non-existent person of interest, which could wreak havoc on the investigation.

Hartley felt in her gut that Jerome Grazer was not the man she was looking for. He did not fit into the knowledgeable military marksman category they were after. He was a typical drug-pushing street thug. Yet there was something there, obviously. Why else would Ochoa have Grazer's name written down on a piece of paper stuffed into his pocket?

She yawned and realized she was exhausted. Her ice cream was only partially eaten, yet she could not will herself to take another bite. She moved back to the freezer and threw the carton in its place, turning off the light located on the end table as she slumped back onto the couch. She covered herself with a blanket and gazed into the picture dancing across the television, letting herself become transfixed with the changing images until they blended into one and she fell into a deep, relaxing sleep.

EIGHT

At some point in the night Jolene must have been up and moving. She awoke to the sound of her phone chiming, signaling she had received a voicemail. She rose from her bed, realizing she had somehow made it up the steps and into her room, though she had shifted her pillows to the foot of the bed and lay crooked with her feet hanging into space, her gray shorts missing in action and her t-shirt now inside out.

What the hell did I do last night? she thought to herself as she stood and stretched the sleep from her limbs. Her phone showed two missed calls and collected just as many messages. She called her voicemail and punched in her password to listen to the first, the quiet, southern drawl creeping through the earpiece.

Detective Hartley, this is Norma Jean Whickerson, Jerome's grandmother. I'm sorry to call you so early, but you did say to call. Jerome showed up here sometime in the night and when I woke he was asleep in the den. Please, when you have a chance, give me a call back. I don't want no trouble in my house. She left her number.

Jolene saved the message and moved onto the second voicemail. *Hey, Hartley.* It was Barailles. *Surprised you're not*

83

up yet. Hey, listen, I just got a call from Mrs. Whickerson from yesterday. Seems her grandson is at home. I told her to stay put and we'll be in contact with her. Said it doesn't look like he's going anywhere, but she'd call back if he left. All right, I'm on my way to pick up coffee. I'll swing by your place and pick you up in about thirty. See you then. The timestamp on Barailles's call read 7:35, twenty minutes ago.

"Oh shit," Jolene said, deleting the message and rushing to the bathroom, her lethargic limbs feeling as if they weighed more than they actually did. Her bath the night before had worked well to rejuvenate her mind, yet seemed to set her body in a state of slow motion. "I need to wake up," she said to herself as she turned the nozzle for the shower, water shooting out and immediately beginning to steam as she removed her shirt and underwear and climbed in, tiptoeing around the out-skirts of the tub towards the handle and turning the heat down. When the temperature was right she stepped into the middle, letting the water soak her hair and run down her body. She had no intentions of actually using shampoo or soap. Just a good old-fashioned soak.

* * * * *

Hartley opened her door to Barailles five minutes after stepping from the shower. She had her damp hair pulled into a tight ponytail on the back of her head and a toothbrush stick-ing from her mouth, toothpaste dripping from her lips.

"Morning, sunshine," Barailles said, smiling as Hartley jumped back to avoid a dribble of toothpaste dropping like a bomb from the corner of her mouth. They both looked down at the spot on her floor for a moment then refocused on each other. Hartley nodded her good morning to her partner and turned, rushing to the kitchen sink and relieving herself of the frothy mess.

"Yeah, um, sorry about that," she said as she returned with a towel, bending down to wipe up the puddle.

"No worries," Barailles said, stepping around her and to the table. "Got you some coffee."

"Thanks," she said as she returned to the kitchen, throwing the towel towards the sink. "Any more from Norma?"

He shook his head. "Figured I'd come and get you before calling her back. I assume he's still there since I haven't heard from her." Hartley nodded and grabbed her coffee. "Rough night?" he asked.

Hartley shrugged as she took a long sip from her cup. "Don't remember much of it," she said as she lowered her mug. "Seems I either sleepwalk or the aliens were nice enough to turn off my TV and put me upstairs." Barailles chuckled. "Hang out for a sec. I need to get my things."

"Take your time," Barailles responded as she moved up the steps and out of sight, his focus on her bottom as she ascended towards the bedroom. He took a swig of coffee as she disappeared into a doorway, his eyes lazily searching the vicinity and coming to rest on a pair of cotton shorts hanging from the end table near the couch.

"All set," she said, dropping from the last step and onto the main floor, silver star and gun set on her hip. She had changed from the raggedy t-shirt into a light blue button up blouse with short sleeves, her toned arms reaching out for the leather jacket draped across the couch. How he ever kept a level head to focus on the job was beyond him, he thought to himself as he stood and handed his partner her coffee. She nodded her thanks and they turned towards the door, Hartley locking the apartment as they exited.

The street below was bustling with people leaving for their morning commutes. Cars pulled from the curbs at frantic paces, their spots immediately filled by men and women desperately looking to flag down a taxi to make it on time to their business meetings or interviews. It was mostly sunny with clouds moving quickly through the sky, a slight breeze blowing through the trees and weaving in and out of the activity currently driving the city streets. Hartley knew it was not supposed to stay this nice for long, as a storm front was forecasted to cover the area in a matter of hours. The brief period of sunshine, however, was all she needed to feel as if her day was starting off on the right foot.

They walked to the corner and hopped into Barailles's cruiser, Hartley pulling her knees to her chest and resting her feet on the dashboard, a maneuver that her partner found adorable, like she was a carefree teenager just out for a ride.

The detectives decided to head to the precinct first, opting to call Norma from one of their desks, a plan that allowed them to determine if they would need more officers to apprehend Jerome. "You want me to call?" Barailles yelled over to her after they each checked their messages and emails.

Hartley shook her head and picked up her phone, punching in Norma's numbers. "Take a quick look into the system at Jerome. I want to know what we're dealing with before we get there. I don't want any surprises—Hi, hello, I'm looking for a Mrs. Norma Jean Whickerson," she said, turning her attention away from Barailles. "Yes, thank you." She covered the mouthpiece and mouthed to her partner, "I think that was just him." Barailles nodded and rolled his chair towards her.

"Hello?" came the voice on the other end.

Hartley set her phone to speaker and placed it on the desk. "Hi, Norma? This is Jolene. We spoke the other day." She kept the conversation cryptic to start, letting Norma decide if it was prudent to speak.

"Jolene, yes, yes. How are you today?" Norma responded cheerfully.

"I'm doing well. Is this a good time to talk?"

"Well—" Norma let her sentence hang.

"Is it a good time to listen?"

"Absolutely! It's like you read my thoughts."

"Okay. Was that Jerome?"

"Yes, ma'am."

"Is he leaving?"

"I believe so. Uh, hold on a sec, baby." She moved the mouthpiece away from her face but continued talking loud enough so the detectives could hear. "Jerome, where you off to?" There was silence. "Jerome, I'm talking to you, boy! Don't you go ignoring me." There was a muffled response in the background, followed by Norma answering, "Well, you wanna pick me up some Earl Grey on your way back? All right, baby. Be careful." Hartley and Barailles could hear a door slam in the background.

"Norma, where's he going to?" Hartley asked quickly, Barailles picking up the desk phone next to him.

"Not sure. But he's heading west on 63rd, past the grocery store."

"Are you sure?"

"Yes, dear. I can see him through the blinds. He's moving down the street. And Detective, he has a gun." Barailles immediately made a call, putting out an updated APB on Jerome Grazer. Patrol units in the area were notified of his whereabouts and the direction in which he was moving, yet given the order not to apprehend him without either Barailles or Hartley on the scene. He was to be considered armed and dangerous.

"Thank you Norma," Hartley said.

"Just don't hurt my baby," she responded.

"It's the last thing we want." Barailles approached as Hartley hung up her desk phone, the latter standing and pulling on her jacket, zipping it up to her neck, the holster carrying her firearm jutting from her hip. She looked to her partner. "We get the Kevlar on now. No messing with them there and giving our guy time to react." Barailles nodded as he and his partner moved towards the elevator and readied their gear, their minds racing as they planned their next moves.

* * * * *

They pulled into a grocery store parking lot near the corner of West 64th Street and South Racine Avenue nearly thirty minutes after leaving the precinct, parking next to a marked squad car with a pair of uniformed officers wearing their Kevlar vests inside. They had located Jerome Grazer on West 63rd Street walking into a convenience store and followed him at a distance to their current location, reporting it to Hartley and Barailles who were en route to Whickerson's residence.

The officer rolled down the passenger window as Barailles pulled in next to them. "Morning guys," Barailles said. "We still got him?"

"He's moved across the street to the auto shop," the officer in the passenger seat responded. "What's the plan?"

Barailles looked to Hartley, her eyes fixed on the shop, the gears obviously running at full speed. "Why don't you guys pull around and park on the Racine next to the shop. Cover the alley and any exit to the west. We'll take the sidewalk and come from the front." The uniformed officers nodded and pulled away, taking a right out of the grocer's parking lot and coasting slowly past the auto shop. Hartley and Barailles exited the car, pulling their jackets over the bulletproof vests and crossing the street as they made their way slowly towards their suspect. "Keep your gun ready, but don't do anything unless I do," Hartley said to Barailles, knowing the directive had been embedded in her partner's mind since his days in the academy. "I don't want to spook whoever's in here. We'll make ourselves known and grab him."

They crossed the street hurriedly and began down the sidewalk, stepping over broken glass bottles and litter plastered to the cracked concrete pavement. The neighborhood had seen better days, and worse. Hartley knew, regardless of the gang activity and murders that occurred at a stunningly grotesque rate, there were still good-hearted people in the area, people that had no means to create their own exodus and enough sense about them to keep their lives to themselves and their mouths shut.

At that moment several men in a blue minivan pulled up to the front of the shop, parking in the entrance lane but not exiting the vehicle, one of the men gesturing towards the open garage doors. The detectives slowed, but continued on. A tall black male appeared from the garage and walked up to the van, leaning into the window. An exchange was made, Hartley distinguishing a small plastic bag that held at least a gram of cocaine. The man laughed as a joke was made amongst them and turned his head, the smile fading as his gaze fell upon the white couple walking towards him, very much out of place in a predominately black neighborhood. He took a step away from the van, turning towards the two and reaching his hand into the front of his jacket. It was Jerome Grazer.

Hartley and Barailles paused, each of their hands darting to their weapons and unholstering them. "Jerome Grazer!"

Hartley yelled out, leveling her service piece on him. "CPD! Stay where you are and put your hands on your head!" There was a moment of complete silence as the detectives stared at their suspect from thirty feet away, each waiting for some response, each more aware that the clouds had become dark and rain began to fall. The standoff resonated like a scene from a movie with Hartley, the long, drawn-out affair between the Earps and the Cowboys in *Tombstone*, eyes wide, noses twitching, tongues flicking the air waiting for the initial scent of fear.

The driver of the van made the first move, peeling away from the store with squealing tires as they hooked a u-turn across the median and away from the approaching altercation.

It was then that Grazer reacted, bolting from his current spot and into the shop. Hartley and Barailles gave chase, breaking into a full sprint with guns in hands toward their suspect. "Grazer! Stop!" Hartley shouted after him, knowing the words were lost in the wind. They slowed as they neared the opened garage, guns raised and fingers near the triggers. Three men sat inside the shop, staring at the officers as they moved after Grazer, each seemingly oblivious there was a manhunt taking place a dozen feet from them. From somewhere inside came a crash and immediately Hartley bolted into the work area, sprinting through a door leading into the shop's kitchen and past a garbage can lying on its side, contents strewn about the floor. She leapt over it with Barailles in her wake, charging through another side door that led into an alley.

The uniformed officers stood with guns drawn near the street, making their way cautiously into the lane in the direction of the detectives. "Where?" Hartley asked as she saw them, breathing rapidly from the sprint.

"That way," one of the officers said.

"He poked out into the street but came back when he saw us," his partner added. Hartley turned back to the scene and eyed several connecting alleyways leading into hers. She sprinted towards the second as a loud commotion broke the silence.

"Chicago PD! Grazer! Stop!" she yelled, jumping over a crate leaning against an overflowing dumpster, her suspect ahead taking a quick left and making his way south down Racine. She followed, her streamlined figure cutting through the air and making ground on the much larger man.

Barailles and the uniformed officers followed close behind Hartley, though at a slightly slower pace. Grazer continued down the sidewalk, knocking into several kids as they played near a fire hydrant, sending them flying onto the pavement, the collision slowing him down slightly as he darted into the wide two-lane road, cars screeching to a halt to avoid the crazed lunatic moving into their paths. Grazer flew across the sidewalk and up an embankment that led to a vacant dirt baseball field, now covered in a soupy, brown mud from the steady rain that had begun to fall.

Hartley jumped onto the hood of a stopped vehicle, descended on the other side into a forming puddle and sprinted up the embankment close behind Grazer. Ahead a fence loomed ten feet tall, a single gate on the left the only way through to the filthy creek on the other side. Grazer, looking over his shoulder at the officer gaining ground, set his sights on the opening.

Hartley holstered her weapon as she ran and latched it shut, knowing that she needed to bring Grazer down without an errant shot being fired. As he passed through the threshold he slowed, reaching back to grab onto the fencing to close the gate in hopes to impede the detective's progress. The pause was all Hartley needed. She moved slightly to the right and at the last moment jumped left, crashing her shoulder into the closing door and bouncing through the opening, grabbing around Grazer's shoulders as she twisted him into the air with her, the momentum from the gate sending them both head-long into the creek.

Hartley leapt to her feet, arming herself once again and aiming at her suspect, mud and water dripping from her entire body. Grazer resurfaced and crawled slowly towards the opposite embankment, holding a broken wrist to his chest and groaning. He turned and laid on his back, gasping for breath, the wind having been knocked from him.

"Jerome Grazer," Hartley said between breathes, "what part of the word *stop* do you not understand?"

"My hand, you bitch! Fuck you!" he responded.

Hartley reached down and grabbed his wrist, pulling him back towards the gate. Grazer shouted in pain as she moved him with no compassion for his mangled limb. She pushed him face-first into the fencing and kicked his legs apart. "Put your hands on your head." He did as directed, wincing as he raised his injured arm.

Barailles and the uniformed officers appeared on the scene with guns raised, Hartley nodding to her partner and holstering her weapon as she moved in to frisk Grazer. From deep in his back pocket she pulled a .38 Snubnosed Special and handed it to one of the uniformed officers. "I'm going to bet that's not registered to you."

"I ain't saying nothing," he responded.

She reached into his jacket and pulled from an interior pocket a large, sealed plastic bag containing at least a dozen smaller bags of cocaine. "Look at that," she said to Barailles.

"That looks like enough for a possession with intent to distribute."

"Oh yeah," Barailles added, gun still pointed at Grazer. "You won't be taking anymore swims for a long, long time, I'm guessing." Grazer clenched his teeth.

Hartley finished searching the wannabe track star and cuffed him, passing him off to one of the uniforms. "Take him back to the precinct for me, will you?" The officer nodded, turning to begin the long hike back to the squad car. Hartley turned towards Barailles and ran her hand over her muddy hair, the rain continuing to fall as they followed the officers step-for-step through the field once again.

"Nice tackle," Barailles said to her as they walked.

She looked to him and smiled. "Yeah," she agreed. "I think I have a shot as a cornerback if this detective thing doesn't work out."

NINE

"That's quite a bag of coke you had in your possession," Hartley said as she entered the interrogation room where Jerome Grazer sat, her face and hair cleaned from the dive in the creek. "Either you have a real problem or you have some friends that do. And I'm guessing by the way you don't seem to be itching for any right now it's your friends." Hartley took a seat across the table from Grazer, who sat caked in mud, his wrist displaying the only clean fabric, having been wrapped in a medical bandage to prevent the joint from moving. "And the gun—" She paused and let the phrase hang. "Screw the gun," she continued. "The bag of coke will be enough to put you away for a long time."

"Fuck you," Grazer said from his reclined position in the metal chair.

"No," Hartley said as she leaned forward, smirking at her suspect, "not me or any female for years. But who knows? I hear in prison you're able to find a willing partner relatively easy." Grazer stared at her but said nothing, his eyes displaying the hatred he contained for her. Hartley let the moment sink in then leaned back in her chair, opening one of the case files she had brought in with her. "The way I see it, the little marathon you pulled was possibly the dumbest thing you could have done. My partner and I only wanted to ask you some questions. But no, you had to make your move." Grazer laughed and rolled his eyes towards the ceiling. "What's funny, Jerome?" Hartley asked, closing the file and folding her hands, her eyes intently focused on him.

He leveled his gaze on her and his face turned serious once again. "You think I'm that dumb? Like you weren't going to pull me in here after what went down with the van? Shit. I saw you! You seen it go down!"

"No, Jerome, I don't think you're dumb. But tell me this then: When have you ever seen drug busts in your neighborhood run by anyone other than uniforms or guys with DEA spelled across their chests?" The question hung in the air, Grazer not removing his eyes from Hartley. "See, Jerome, I didn't give a shit about the drugs. I didn't give a shit about the gun. But then you had to run into that filthy creek and get my new shirt and jacket all dirty." She leaned back in her chair again, an agitated look spreading across her face. "And I loved that jacket, Jerome!" she said. "Now, I'm going to ask some questions, and I'm hoping you'll just choose to answer them, because the thing I love most—next to my now ruined jacket— is my questions answered."

Jerome leaned forward and said slowly, enunciating every word, "Fuck—you—ass—hole."

Hartley sat up slowly and looked at Grazer as she weighed her next move. She smiled and looked down to the files stacked neatly in front of her before pushing her chair out and walking to the door. "Make yourself comfortable, Jerome. With what we're looking at, we may just throw out those cocaine charges altogether." He turned his head to her, making eye contact with the detective, hatred and a tinge of curiosity escaping from his gaze. "What's an additional twenty years tacked on to life in prison? Doesn't really matter anyway, right?"

"Life?" Jerome asked sitting straight up. "What the fuck you talking about?"

"Yeah. See, I told you I don't care about the coke or the gun. I'm a homicide detective, Jerome, and you are my new star. Running from me a day after you're linked to a murder? It doesn't look good."

"Wait a minute!" he said, his tone incensed and pleading in the same instant. "I didn't have nothing to do with no murder. I—"

"I highly doubt that, Jerome," Hartley interrupted. "Like I said, get comfy." With that she walked out of the interrogation room, leaving her suspect stewing.

* * * * *

"What else did you find?" Hartley asked Barailles as she passed his desk and headed into the kitchen.

Barailles stood and followed. "Well, nothing really. I don't see a connection."

"Besides the fact that he was found near Maria Gomez's murder scene and his name was on a piece of paper in our vic's pocket? Which also happens to be Maria's nephew, don't forget." Hartley looked at Barailles quizzically. He returned the look and sighed. "Yeah," she said, "I don't feel it either." They moved from the kitchen to her desk where she grabbed a muffin and took a bite.

"What's going on with our guy?" Barailles questioned, gesturing towards the interrogation room.

"He's thinking things over right now. I'm guessing we won't get anything from him that's useful. Probably just send him with the uniforms for charges of cocaine possession with intent. What else do we know about the Gomez murder?"

Barailles opened a file. "Regarding Jerome? In the statement he said he showed up to confront Miguel, maybe throw a tag on his house. Looked in through the window and saw the mother dead."

"And how was he cleared?"

"Arresting officer found him a few blocks down several minutes later. He had no traces of blood on him at the time. Techs found no evidence of him being at the scene either. There were definitely prints from someone other than Maria Gomez, but they don't lead anywhere."

"Change of clothes?"

"Officers didn't find any items when they made a sweep of the area. Besides, Jerome couldn't have cleaned up that fast. There wasn't enough time between Officer Pettiman picking up him and Miguel getting home and finding his mother."

Hartley stood. "All right. When we go back in there, let's play stupid with this. I want to get the story out of him again. Maybe there's something they missed or held back when he was questioned before."

"Okay. But he'll know we would have already researched this once we bring up Ochoa," Barailles said, standing up next to her.

"He will," she agreed, "but right now he's thinking he'll never see the light of day again. Maybe he'll just be willing to play ball."

They headed off towards the interrogation room again, opening the door and finding Grazer leaning over with his head in his palms, foot tapping rapidly on the linoleum floor.

"Look, I had nothing to do with no murder. I swear to God!" he stammered as they entered.

"Good to know," Hartley answered as she moved into the room and pulled out the chair opposite her suspect. "Jerome Grazer, this is Detective Barailles. I'm sure you recognize him from earlier."

"Morning," Barailles said. "Have a nice jog earlier?" Grazer's face flashed anger but was quickly replaced by concern.

"I didn't do nothing," Grazer said.

"See," Hartley said, "that's just hard to believe."

"I swear!" he yelled. "Look, I ain't no killer."

"You're a banger, Jerome," Hartley responded again.

"That don't make me no killer! I sling rocks and bags. I didn't kill no one."

"Rocks and bags. I've seen bangers kill for a lot less."

"Fuck you!"

"Jerome, you're mouth isn't helping you right now."

"Like I give a shit?"

"You will if it comes to the DA asking my opinion on whether you cooperated or not." Jerome stiffened, yet closed his mouth and stared to the observation mirror. Hartley looked to Barailles, both of them remembering the record sheet on Jerome Grazer and the lack of manslaughter or murder charges. "Do you know a Benjamin Ochoa?" Hartley asked.

Grazer looked at her questioningly. "I know that punk. Why?"

"How do you know him?"

Grazer stared silently for a few seconds. "I scraped with him from time to time."

"What about?" Barailles asked.

"Anything and everything."

"Want to clarify a little?"

"Those fools used to come on my turf and sling drugs. Tag our shit. You don't do that to Four Ring territory."

"What happens if you catch someone doing those things in your area?" Hartley asked.

"They going to catch themselves a beat down."

"That's it? You're going to sit there and tell me a Five-One tags your turf or sells rocks to your girl, and you're just going to give him a beat down? Jerome, you're going to have to do better than that. Like I said, I've seen killings for a lot less."

"Yeah, but not me. I ain't an enforcer, you hear? I do my shit. Other's do their own. Just how it goes."

The room was silent for a minute as the detectives glanced into their files, Grazer's gaze moving back and forth between the two. Finally Hartley spoke. "Jerome, how well did you know Benjamin Ochoa?"

Grazer lifted an eyebrow to her. "Not well. He was a fucking Five-One. We didn't much get along. Why you keep asking me about him?"

"Because Benjamin Ochoa was found dead yesterday morning with a bullet hole to the head—"

"Good. Fuck him," Grazer interrupted.

"—And your name written on a piece of paper in his pocket," Hartley concluded. Grazer became agitated as Hartley continued. "So, you see, Jerome, things aren't really looking up for you right now. A murder conviction may hinder your freedom just a little bit," she stated.

"I didn't kill no one! I told you!" he yelled.

Hartley leaned forward quickly, causing her suspect as well as her partner to jump. "Stop dicking around, Jerome," she replied. "Coincidences don't just happen like this. Benjamin Ochoa is Miguel Gomez's cousin. You remember Miguel

Gomez?" Grazer remained reclined, his eyebrows furrowing closer as his anxiety rose. "I'm sure you do, seeing you were smart enough to outwit the detectives that interrogated you about his mother's murder. But guess what? I'm a lot smarter than those detectives, Jerome. I find things that no one else can. I'm like a fucking hound dog on the trail." She stood and leaned into the table, bending towards Grazer as his gaze fell onto the floor. "I'm not sure how it happened, but I'm sure you were involved. First you kill Maria Gomez, a brutal murder to show her son and nephew that you mean business. Next time it's them. Then you stalk Ochoa, learning his moves, figuring out where he's going to be until you get him right where you want him and—" She slammed her palm against the table, creating a loud *bang* that once again sent Barailles into the air.

"Fuck no!" Grazer yelled. "I didn't kill that bitch! And I didn't kill that Five-One motherfucker neither! What the fuck do you want from me?"

"Tell me what I want to know!" Hartley yelled back. "Tell me why you killed them!"

"I'm telling you! I didn't kill them! There was a guy there! A white guy with a tattoo on his neck! He killed them! I didn't have shit to do with it!"

Hartley turned quickly to Barailles who looked from Grazer to her, a shocked expression crossing his excited face. He shook his head slightly. Hartley understood completely: There had been no mention of a guy at the scene in the original statement. The officers knew someone had been there, what with the bloody footprints and corpse of Maria Gomez. Yet Grazer had not told the officers about seeing the murderer within the home. There had been nothing regarding the tattoo on his neck nor had Jerome relayed the crucial information that he had potentially witnessed the killing of Maria Gomez by the hands of another man.

Hartley looked back to the frantic Grazer and smiled. "All right, Jerome," she said in a soothing voice, stepping back from the table and smoothing out her shirt. "I want you to tell everything to me again. Let's start from the top. Pretend I don't know anything about you or the night of the Gomez murder. Tell me about when you showed up at Miguel's house. What happened?"

TEN

Jerome Grazer sat stock still in the interrogation room, looking from Hartley to Barailles and back again, conjuring images of that night three months ago. He could tell by the look between the detectives moments before that the man with the tattoo was new information that could potentially benefit his current situation. He knew he needed to tread lightly.

At the same time, Hartley knew exactly where Grazer was, knew what was going through his mind. She did not want to play hardball by getting into a shoving match with this man. She did not care about the gun or the drugs nor did her thoughts linger on about the morning's events. All she cared about now was a new lead in a cold murder that, at present, had fallen into her lap, all thanks to Jerome Grazer.

"Look," she said as she sat down in her chair, Barailles next to her with a pen in hand. "You're not a stupid guy, Jerome. Let's say we completely start over here. Forget the gun. I saw no gun."

"And the bags?" he said.

"If you're willing to tell us what happened that night and what you know about Benjamin Ochoa, I'll put in a good word for you with the DA. The intent to distribute charge will go away."

"I want it all to go away."

"Something's got to stick. I'm good, Jerome, but I'm not that good." She stared at Grazer as he processed the options. "It's either a couple years due to your existing record, or the rest of your adult life. You don't want to be in there until your sixty, Jerome."

Grazer pulled himself to the table. "I'm game," he said. "But how do I know after what I tell you, y'all ain't gonna go and forget?"

"I'll have my partner go right now and make the call to the DA. You tell us information that helps out the Gomez or Ochoa investigations, we cut a deal. But, Jerome, if you dick us around any, I'm calling them back and requesting the max. Deal?" Hartley stuck out her hand, elbow resting on the table, Grazer looking at her for a moment before reaching out and shaking an agreement with the detective.

Hartley looked to her partner as he exited the room and headed into the captain's office. The call was made to the DA requesting that Jerome Grazer be taken into custody with a plea of guilty for possession of a controlled substance in exchange for his knowledge of the night of Maria Gomez's murder, as well as information regarding their current investigation. After a brief conversation, Barailles returned to the room and shut the door, nodding his head to both Hartley and Grazer as he sat. "DA says it's a go. You tell us what you know and the gun and distribution charges go away. You have to plead guilty to a possession charge. You'd be back out in no time." Grazer nodded. "The paperwork is being faxed over now," Barailles added.

"Jerome, what happened the night of Maria Gomez's murder? Why were you in a Five-One neighborhood to begin with?"

Grazer cleared his throat and thought momentarily before diving headlong into his memories of that evening. "Earlier in the day me and my homie was cruising through the strip and saw this Mexican dude slinging rocks to some of our people. I realized it was either that Gomez dude or Ochoa. By the time we made it around the block to bust him, he was gone."

"You say it was either Gomez or Ochoa. You couldn't tell the difference? Seems odd seeing all the confrontations you had with them."

"You'd think, right? You ever seen those two? They like fucking identical twins. Could be brothers." Barailles began jotting down on his pad of paper, Grazer pausing to take note of the detective before continuing. "Well, this wasn't the first time he was in our area. Couple other of my crew saw the same thing a few days earlier. So me and my guy decide to go see Gomez later that night."

"Who's your guy?" Hartley asked.

"Come on," Jerome replied, palms wide.

"Spill it, Jerome," she pushed.

"Shit. Lamarcus Millan. Goes by Caesar."

"Caesar? Really? Caesar Millan?" Barailles had to keep from smiling.

"On account of him being real good with dogs," Jerome said, an edge in his voice.

"Yeah, word is you guys are making money off of those dogs too."

"Barailles," Hartley interrupted, giving him a glare. She turned back to Jerome, confident her eyes had quieted her partner and set the interview back on track. "Continue."

"Anyway, my guy drops me off a couple blocks away and takes off."

"Why would he do that? Why would he leave you?" Hartley asked.

Jerome shrugged. "Keep an eye out around the hood. Come back if there was any fools comin' up on me. Just how we do."

"All right. How'd you know where Gomez lived?"

"Got his address through a connection."

"Who's the connection?"

"Shit, I don't remember. Some broad that hangs with Caesar's girl." Hartley stared at him, trying to grade his level of honesty. "I swear to fucking God!"

"Okay," Hartley said. "So you get his address and your guy drops you off. What happened then?"

"You know, I figure I'd come up on him near his house, give him a beat down for slinging in on my streets and then I'd bounce."

"What time did you get over there at?" Barailles asked.

"Shit, I don't remember. It was months ago."

"Try," Hartley said sternly.

Jerome titled his head back in thought. "Must've been around ten. Ten-thirty maybe. It was dark. That's all I know. So I get up to the corner right across from the house. I got my hood up so no one can see me, plus the place was dead. No one walking around. No bangers neither."

"Anyone awake in the houses around Gomez's place?"

"Yeah. There was lights on, if that's what you mean."

"What about the Gomez residence itself? Any movement or anything?"

"Not that I could see," he responded. "I remember the house being pretty dark. There was a light coming from inside someplace. Turned out to be the kitchen. Saw it on when I got closer."

"Step me through what you did when you got up to the house."

"I remember rushing across the street and going straight to the front. The porch light wasn't on, so I figured no one would see me. I was gonna tag right there on the door, but I heard some movement inside and didn't want no one walking out on me."

"Did you see anyone inside?"

"I tried to look into the front window, but couldn't see nothin'."

"What did you do next?" Barailles asked.

Jerome thought for a minute and continued. "I remember going around the side of the house. There were taller bushes that would give me some cover if anyone came out. When I got there I got out my cannon and—"

"Cannon?" Barailles interrupted.

"Can of spray paint," Hartley answered without taking her eyes off Jerome. "Continue, please."

"So I got my cannon out and gave it a good shake and was about to start tagging when I saw some somthing. I stepped back into the bushes and saw some dude pulling something into the room."

"Were there lights on in the room, Jerome?" Hartley asked.

"Like I said, they was on in the kitchen. I could make out the silhouette. I remember staring in and thinking, *'What the fuck is going on?'*, you know? Like something ain't right. Then the guy turned and I knew shit was definitely fucked."

"Why's that?"

"The guy had a mask on. Covered his face and head but not his neck. He was a white dude. Had a tattoo on his neck of a circle. Fucked up. Never seen a white motherfucker in that neighborhood or mine. If you're lost or getting your rocks, sure. But never like that. And the chick, she was all messed up. Her face was swollen and she was bleeding everywhere. Looked real bad."

"Jerome, Maria Gomez was stabbed multiple times in the chest. Was she already stabbed by this point?"

"Had to be. I didn't look away at all. Didn't see the dude do nothing with that knife except put it to her throat." Jerome paused and looked to the table. The memory obviously was painful to him. Such brutality, regardless of your background of violence, had an effect on people. "Anyway," he continued, clearing his throat, "the woman bled out right there. And you know what that motherfucker did?" Hartley shook her head. "He stood there. Stood right in front of her and watched her bleed. Like he got enjoyment from it."

"What did you do? Why didn't you run?"

"I couldn't. If I would have moved, that asshole would have seen me and come after me. There was something about him. No adrenaline pushing his hand. No emotion. It was just cold."

"Jerome," Barailles chimed in, "how'd you see the tattoo on this guy's neck if it was dark in the room? Seems to me you'd just see silhouettes."

"The light from the kitchen was bouncing off this shitty old lamp or something in the corner. Thing was like a giant fucking mirror. When the dude was moving the chick he stopped and the light reflected was right across it."

The room was silent for a minute, Grazer pulling himself out of the moment when the man slit Maria Gomez's throat, the detectives taking every little detail in. "What happened next?" Hartley asked.

"That was it. Dude waited until she slumped forward then turned around and walked out. He closed the door behind him and everything and just walked off down the street. I stayed put for about ten minutes. Didn't want that dude to come back and catch me walking around the house."

"Where was Caesar this whole time?"

"Shit if I know. Probably across the park, couple blocks down. He was gonna wait for me and then we'd take off after he seen me cutting through the park. I didn't make it that far. Walked away from the house and got picked up by some pig. First time in my life I was grateful to see a cop, man." Jerome laughed at himself and shook his head. Hartley smiled and looked down to her papers.

"Jerome," she said in a serious tone. "Why didn't you tell this to the officer before? None of this is in the report from three months ago. Why not tell all of this?"

"What was the use?"

"To clear your name."

"My name was already cleared. The amount of blood and the bruising on that woman's body, there was no way it was me. I ain't no fool, Detective. I knew it was only a matter of minutes before those cops realized that I wasn't part of that."

"But why not help the officers out?"

Grazer sat silent, staring at Hartley with cold eyes. "Because, shit like that happens, it's bound to find you out sooner or later. Plus, those Five-Ones thinking my crew had our hands dirty, puts the fear of God into a man. They think twice about fucking with us."

"Jerome, a woman is dead and you could have helped with bringing her killer to justice. Instead you blew it off as Four Star publicity?"

"I do what I can to survive. Those Five-Ones, they would put a bullet in my head in a second. No questions asked. Sometimes it's a game. It's strategy to survive out on those streets. I'm sorry that chick got killed, but her death may have let me live longer."

Hartley glared at Grazer for a moment and shook her head, rising from her seat. "You play a sick game, Jerome," she said as she exited the room, Barailles following behind.

* * * * *

The detectives ordered a meal for their detainee from a Chinese restaurant a block away, wanting to avoid moving to Grazer's bad side after a day in the interrogation room. Hartley knew that Grazer's remarks were true, regardless of how callous they seemed. Life on the streets was a harsh game of survival. A reputation not only put a bulls-eye on your back, but also increased how dangerous you were. A killing like Maria Gomez's could send a message that Jerome and his crew meant business, that they no longer would tolerate such indecencies as drug dealing on their turf.

Yet Hartley also gathered from the interview that Grazer, like many gangbangers, was a lot of bark. He had reacted to the retelling of Maria Gomez's death. There was a definite understanding within him of how incredibly awful the acts that befell her were that night. It was beyond her that he had not come forward with this information beforehand, letting the system work its way through the investigation before releasing him as an innocent man. Yet the proof to clear his name was right there: The amount of blood that Maria Gomez lost would have been present everywhere on the killer's body. Jerome Grazer was clean. In cases as brutal as this, the detectives learned to look for visible signs on their suspects, especially so soon after a murder happened.

Jerome Grazer was definitely not the killer of Maria Gomez, and in her gut she did not believe he had killed Benjamin Ochoa either. The figure they had seen in the bank security video was unrecognizable, so they could not rule out that it had not been Grazer, yet the sheer will to sit on the shoulder of an expressway for three quarters of an hour displayed a patience and cunning that her suspect seemed to lack. It was the cunning and patience that Maria Gomez's killer seemed to embrace.

Hartley knew she was jumping to conclusions and that they were no closer to finding Ochoa's killer than before, but these were how homicide cases panned out sometimes. One murder led to another, like a vicious game of connect-the-dots. Hartley could only hope she would eventually end up at her initial mark. The Ochoa investigation seemed to have taken a back seat to the events that had unfolded within the last few hours and Hartley knew they needed to get back on track. Yet she felt there was something more here, a possible connection from three months ago that needed to be thoroughly scrutinized. The only way to find out was to learn more about Grazer's relationship with Benjamin Ochoa.

They entered the room as Grazer finished his carton of orange chicken and washed it down with a can of soda. He looked up to them as they took their seats and nodded his thanks.

"Jerome, I need to ask you a few more questions," Hartley said. "Benjamin Ochoa, how did you know him?"

Jerome stared at the detective. "Man, are you serious? Didn't I answer this fucking question like three times already?"

"And you'll answer it again if you don't want me to make another call to the DA."

"Man, I told you, I didn't really know him. I knew of him. You have enough scrapes with the Five-Ones you start to pick up on who's who, you know?"

"And were there a lot of scrapes with Ochoa?"

"I guess. He used to show up on our turf to tag our shit. We'd catch him and give him a beating before he ran off."

"You ever find him selling dope or anything of that nature around your turf?" Barailles asked.

"He was a Five-One. What do you think?"

"How many times? Couple? Dozen?"

"Shit, I don't know. Maybe a half dozen times. Lot of the time it was Gomez."

"Where were you yesterday morning around seven-fifteen?" Hartley asked.

Grazer titled his head back in thought. "I was at my girl's house."

"Name?"

"Latonia Watson."

"Can anyone support that?"

"Her family had a breakfast for her uncle who just passed. There was a whole mess of people there."

"When's the last time you saw Ochoa?" Hartley questioned.

"Shit, I don't know. A while. He used to be tagging all the time. Sometimes we'd catch him, sometimes we didn't. But then, *poof!* He was gone. The tagging happened, but definitely not at the same pace. Like he just quit or something."

"Do you remember how long ago that was?"

"Had to be a few years. I'd seen him after that, you know, but mainly when we was cruising. Seemed to be minding his own business. Stayed on his own turf. Wasn't worth the effort anymore, you know?"

"If you hadn't seen him in a few years, why'd you think it was him in your neighborhood the day of Gomez's murder?"

"I don't know. You hear of guys from time to time getting out of the life. They always come back though. People gotta make money somehow."

Hartley looked to Barailles. "Let's go make a few calls and verify his whereabouts. Jerome, I need Latonia's phone number so we can talk to some family members."

He nodded. "Where's the agreement I need to sign?"

"We'll bring it in once we verify that you aren't Ochoa's murderer. Until then, sit tight."

They exited the room and closed the door behind them. "Go check with the Watson family and see if that pans out," Hartley directed Barailles. "I'll get someone to book him for the possession charge and get that agreement signed."

"Great," Barailles said as he idled near his desk. "Hey, listen, it's been a long day. What do you think about grabbing a bite to eat when we take off?"

Hartley turned slowly towards him and sighed, her thumbs resting in her front pockets. "I can't, Barailles."

"Can't? Or won't?"

"Both," she replied. "I'm going to eat with Kim. And I need to go get cleaned up. Just fill me in tomorrow if anything comes up, okay?"

Barailles nodded and took a seat at his desk, Hartley watching him for a second before turning and making her way to the stairs. It *had* been a long day and she could smell the filthy creek on her, the mildewy, rancid scent of rotting vegetation seeping into her skin and sickening her senses. What she needed was a hot shower and a large, warm meal with some good company.

And, by all means, Detective Kimberly Banneau was just the company she needed.

ELEVEN

Jolene cleaned and dressed, throwing on a pair of form-fitting jeans and a black, sleeveless shirt that plunged down her back to just between her shoulder blades, revealing a sophisticated yet playful taste of her chiseled muscles from years in the gym. She exited the precinct in a hurry, not wanting to run into her partner for a last ditch effort at tagging along to whatever eatery she was headed to. From behind she heard the sound of heels tapping on the pavement and turned to see Detective Kimberly Banneau hustling over, a smile spread across her face.

"Hey, Jo-Jo!" Kim shouted. "How's my favorite home wrecker?" Jolene stood and gave her a look that would have stopped most people in their tracks. "Oh, I'm just messing with you. You know that."

"Yeah, yeah," Jolene said, wrapping her arms around her friend. Kim Banneau was an attractive woman, yet paled in comparison to Jolene. She was stylish and kept up with the latest trends from all the major fashion designers, considering herself quite the guru when it came to the most recent summer dresses or winter boots. Kim was shorter than Jolene by a good six inches, a noticeable difference that was pronounced only next to the taller homicide detective. She was jovial and flirtatious, her layered, bouncey blonde hair and rambunctious attitude adding to the party girl persona she so easily portrayed. She was a good cop, but an even better friend. "And 'Jo-Jo'? Really?" Hartley asked with a furrowed brow and a masked grin.

Kim shrugged and put her arm around Jo's waist. "Eh, I was just trying it out."

"And?"

"Don't think it's working for me."

"That's a relief."

"Not unless we were back in college and you were my sorority roommate with benefits." Jolene laughed as Kim looked up to her. "Hey! It could have happened. I happen to know women find me irresistible. I don't think the giggling is called for."

"Oh, okay. I'm sorry," Hartley responded as they began down the street, the two falling into conversation like they had not seen each other in years and desperately needed to catch up.

Kimberly Banneau was a free spirit and one of Hartley's closest friends. The two had met after Kim completed a year-long stint as a homicide detective, choosing to forgo the unwanted relationship with murder and death in exchange for a union that, for the most part, came with a positive outcome and warm body at the end of the day. She and her partner, Doc Hester, worked kidnappings within the city, the majority ending on a positive note, making the duo a prized possession for Chicago.

The two of them walked arm in arm to the corner, chatting and smiling as they flagged down a taxi, the driver eyeing the women as they slid into the back. It was not every day he gave a lift to a couple of seemingly beautiful lesbian—

"Hey, buddy," Banneau said to the driver. "Not what it seems, so maybe you can wipe that grin off your face and stop eyeballing my friend here."

"My apologies, miss," the driver said, still smiling. "Where to?"

"Lakeview. Belmont and North Orchard."

Jolene turned quickly to her friend. "Belmont and Orchard? Isn't that Propellini?"

Kim smiled and nodded, her tongue moving back and forth across her pearly whites. "Yep. Figured it's been a while since we went out. Let's do it up!"

"But how'd you get a spot? I heard this place is impossible to get in to."

"Oh, no worries there," Kim said, waving her hand in the air. "When you suck dick as well as I do you can get anything you want." Jolene covered her face with her hand as she chuckled, catching the toothy grin from the taxi driver staring back in the rearview. Kim caught his eye as well. "I'm just kidding, guy," she said. "None of that here. I'm into the ladies and my friend here—" She paused and looked to Jolene, who had stopped laughing and stared back with a wide grin. "Eh, she's a dude." Hartley shook her head in disbelief and turned towards the window.

The sun shone brightly from between the buildings in the crisp Chicago skyline, its rays creating a strobelight effect within the cab as they sailed north on Lake Shore Drive towards the Lakeview neighborhood. It had been a while since Jolene had been out with Kim Banneau on what the latter liked to describe as "an adventure." The word could not be more perfectly placed within Hartley's mind when associated with her blonde friend.

Banneau was a spitfire, a force to be reckoned with, armed with a witty mind and an appetite for brunette punk rockers. Jolene had known Kim to be involved in several relationships in the past, each flaring up and fizzling out within several months. Banneau always said it was because her fling had become self-conscious about a relationship with a woman of the law. Hartley almost always chalked it up to an over-abundance of attitude. "What are you going to do?" Banneau had said after the most recent breakup. "I'm looking for something more serious, but how are you going to find it if you don't try? And really, who actually completely hates a few months of off the wall sex?" Kimberly Banneau had no shame.

The two rode on amidst an avalanche of good-humored chiding and exhalations of needing to see each other more frequently until at last they pulled up to Propellini. They exited the taxi, handing the driver a decent tip and walking onto the sidewalk, each feeling the eyes within the cab following their bottoms as they moved.

Propellini was packed. The line stretched around the building and down the block, each customer waiting patiently to walk through the doorway and into the hottest new spot in Lakeview. Kim grabbed Jo's hand and walked towards the front doors, her heels clicking on the pavement as she moved. The maître d' stopped them as they approached, pointing to the back of the line. "Is that how you treat your best customers, Johnny?" Banneau asked as they stopped.

The man looked up from his reservation book and his mouth went wide in a grin. "Kim! Hey, wow! I didn't even recognize you. Look at you!" he said, moving in for a hug. "You look great!"

"Don't I always?" Kim said as she struck a pose.

"Every time I see you. Must be the hair down. And who's your friend?" he asked, looking behind Banneau to Jolene.

"Johnny, this is Jo Hartley." Hartley stepped forward and reached for his hand.

"Holy shit, aren't you gorgeous!" Johnny said as he pulled her in for a kiss on the cheek. "Good job, Kimmy! Who knew you had it in you?"

"Not like that, Johnny. This is a friend from the force. Jo, this is my cousin Johnny. Maître d' and partner in Propellini Italian Steakhouse," Kim said, doing her best impression of a *The Price Is Right* model.

"Nice to meet you," Jolene said.

"Likewise," Johnny replied. "Careful of this one," he said pointing to his cousin. "She'll buy you dinner, get you drunk and in the morning you'll be wondering why you're walking around like you just got off a horse."

"Johnny!" Banneau yelled as Hartley laughed hysterically. "Just give us our table."

The interior of the establishment was exquisite. Dark wooden tables accented the rustic, plaster walls. Chandeliers of crystal hung from strategically placed locations, the light reflecting off the glazed floor creating a hazy effect that set the mood for each patron. The aroma of freshly baked breads, oils and vinegars, and herbs and peppers floated throughout the restaurant, pulled along by waiters carrying prime cuts of steaks still sizzling as they made their way through the packed aisles separating each table.

Kim and Jolene were situated in a somewhat secluded area in the back left of the restaurant, overlooking the street where patrons were not lined up to get a taste at the happening establishment. The kitchen was through a pair of swinging doors just to the right of Jolene and every so often Johnny would set a plate full of appetizers in front of them as he dashed through the mayhem. "Bruschetta eggrolls!" he said on his most recent flyby.

"Oh my God!" Kim exclaimed as she eyed the plate. "He's going to have to grease up my ass to get me through those doors after eating all this."

"Get out of here," Jolene responded.

"If I wasn't in that gym every morning working out, I'd have the fattest ass you've ever seen."

Jolene laughed and took a sip of her wine, letting the liquid splash around her mouth before swallowing. "So how's everything else going?" she asked her friend.

"It's good. Can't complain. When was the last time we were out together?"

"To dinner or—"

"Well, I know we were just out for Potts's thing the other night. To dinner. Few months ago, maybe?"

"Yeah, that sounds about right," Jolene responded, thinking that the last time they were out for dinner was right around the time Maria Gomez was murdered. The smile on her face faded as she began to think about the case.

"Hey," Kim said, "not yet you don't. I know that look. Whatever's going on with the case you're on, it'll have to wait."

Jolene nodded her head. "Got it. Sorry."

"Unless it's not the case you're thinking about. Maybe it's that partner of yours." Jolene looked up from her wine glass at Kim who was smiling mischievously as she bit into a sautéed shrimp.

"What are you—" Hartley tried.

"Really? I was drunk, but not that drunk. You two were flirting all night long. And you really ought to be more careful.

Making out in the lobby of a hotel isn't the most discreet thing in the world."

"Oh God!" Jolene said, lowering her head and rubbing her eyes. "You know about that too?"

"Yep. I also noticed that you two left right around the same time. Please don't tell me what I think I already know?"

"What?"

"Did you go home with him?" Jolene remained quite, her eyes fixed on Kim. "Jo! Jesus! He's your partner. And married!"

"I know. I know," Hartley said, bringing her wine glass to her lips. She could feel her cheeks turning red, though did not know if it was because of the wine or the conversation.

Kim leaned in closer. "Did you sleep with him?"

"No!" Jolene said a bit louder than intended. Several tables turned towards her. She held up a hand in apology. "No, we kissed and … I didn't sleep with him."

"Good," Kim said, leaning back and grabbing her glass of wine. She took a long sip and set it back on the table, turning to Jolene. "Look, I like Tony and all, and I think he's a good looking, charming guy, but it's not right."

"I know. That's what I told him. He's still married. I can't do that. He's married and I—" She paused, staring into the distance at nothing in particular. "I have Ronny still on my mind. And this case. I just can't deal with that. It was a mistake."

Kim sat in silence for a moment and let Jolene wander with her thoughts. Finally she said, "It's not a mistake. Well, it *was*, but he's a good guy. Just the wrong time, you know? He's got to be all messed up from the divorce anyway." Hartley nodded and Banneau could tell the excitement of the night was vanishing. "I'll tell you what you need. You need a tall, dark and handsome guy, mid-twenties, rock-hard abs and a dick the size of your forearm!"

"Kim!" she said, looking around at several tables that had overheard Banneau's dialogue. Jolene laughed and swung her hand at her friend.

"Oh, come on now," Kim said quieter, stifling her laughter. "You of all people are in need of a good lay. How long has it been? Since Ron left town? Six months ago?"

"About that, yeah," Jolene replied.

"Hey, if you don't care how it comes, I'm willing to pull out the machines I have hidden in my—"

"Kim Banneau!" Jolene said. They both laughed heartily, enjoying their wine and appetizers. "Let's just eat."

"Fine," Kim replied, "but if in another six months we're having this same conversation, I'm picking out the man you are taking home for that night."

"Fine," Jolene agreed.

The two ordered and ate mainly in silence, each devouring the food set before them, allowing the aroma of their meals to encompass them and take over their senses entirely. The atmosphere of Propellini was very casual, yet had an elegance about it that made the restaurant an instant success. The food was exquisite and the staff extremely on the ball when it came to removing plates and bringing refills, Jolene's wine glass never getting anywhere close to being empty.

After the meal they sat back in their seats and relaxed, sipping their wine and watching the crowds continue to pour in. "So how's it been the last couple of days working with Tony?" Kim asked.

Jolene shrugged. "It's been fine. He's tried to bring it up a couple times. But, you know. He thinks it's more than it really is."

"I mean, you knew he had something going for you, right?"

"Yeah, I knew. And I think part of me was willing to let it happen. Obviously. As we've already stated, it's been awhile." She took another sip from her glass. "But we've been doing our jobs. I can't afford not to. Not with this case I'm on."

"What's it involve? And don't say 'a homicide.'"

Hartley laughed. "Well, yeah, one of those. Kid was killed. Shot in the head. Looked like a gang hit, but a bank tape shows otherwise. Too planned out."

"Got a suspect?"

"No."

"Any leads?"

"Nothing of significance, no," Hartley answered.

Banneau leaned back with a grin. "Sounds like a bust. Where's this get interesting?"

"This kid. He's a former Five-One. Got out of the life a few years back. Hitting up school and a legal job. Seems to have turned his life around."

"Well, that's good," Banneau chimed in.

"Right. We interviewed his parents and the mother's sister—this kid's aunt—was brutally beaten and murdered just three months ago."

"Any connection?"

"A person of interest in the aunt's case. His name was found on a piece of paper in our vic's pocket. We bring him in and question him on both murders. There's this whole other story that wasn't in the aunt's file."

"Something he didn't tell before?" Hartley nodded. "Why would he keep something out?"

"We wondered the same thing. Turns out that our guy is smarter than we figured. He watched the aunt's murder from a bush. He'd been there to tag the house and just happened upon everything. The way it read in the statement was that the inside of the house was a mess. Blood everywhere. There was no way the killer could've been free of the aunt's blood. He would've been filthy."

"Let me guess: Your guy was spotless?"

"Yeah."

"Why'd he keep the part about witnessing the killing to himself?"

"To increase their reputation on the street."

"That's disgusting," Banneau said, shaking her head.

"Disgusting, but smart. He's obviously innocent. There's no way to connect him or his crew to the murder. But speculation and heresy on the streets go a long way."

"So where are you guys at now?"

"That's it. We're nowhere. We're running a check to see if our guy was around at the time of our vic's murder, but I highly doubt he's our killer."

They sat in silence for a time, each running through the case in their minds. "So what are you thinking is the next step for you? Seeing that your guy will most likely come back clean?"

"I'm not thinking anything just yet. My brain hurts," Hartley replied.

"Well, you want to know what I would do?"

"Please, anything will help."

"When did your vic get out of the gang life?"

"They had said a few years back at least. Barailles looked into our vic's financials and he had been paying on an apartment for about four years. So right around that time then."

"I'd look into his past. See if anything right around that time triggered something. Moving into an apartment takes a while. Shopping, saving up for utilities. I'd see if there was anything going on within the last five or six years. Most of the kidnappings we deal with, they are within the family. An uncle or a cousin end up taking the kids because of an altercation in the past. Things happen and make people change. Make them react a way that isn't necessarily the way they are, you know what I mean?"

Hartley nodded her head. "I do. Thanks, Kim. I knew I could count on you to help me think outside the box."

"You're welcome. And if you ever want to get in the box—"

"Stop it!" Jolene interrupted with a laugh. "You're so gross."

"Fine, if you're not willing to switch teams yet, how about we get that tall, handsome guy's number for you? You know, just for a long night of fun." Kim laughed as she pointed towards the bar at the man ordering a drink.

"Kim, would you stop it!" Jolene stated, reaching up and pulling her hand down to the table. "Six months." Kim looked towards her. "Six months, and if it hasn't happened by then, I give you full permission. But not yet."

"Deal?"

"Deal," Jolene agreed, shaking her friend's hand and sipping her wine.

"Oh, I can't wait. I really hope you don't get laid. I have got the cutest, freakiest guy already lined up for you. Holy shit, it'll be the best night of your life!"

"Oh great," Jolene said rolling her eyes. "I can't wait."

TWELVE

The night with Kimberly Banneau turned out to be exactly what Jolene needed, an evening filled with an abundance of laughter, superb food and delectable wine. They left the restaurant around nine o'clock in the evening and shared a cab back to the corner near Jolene's apartment in Lakeview where they hugged goodbye and promised to make their excursions out more frequent.

The cab pulled away with Kim waving through the back window and Jolene crossing the street, the tall, slim detective making her way down the sidewalk with a smile spread across her face as parts of the evening danced through her memory, fueled on by the two bottles of wine the friends had split throughout the night.

She made her way to the gate of her apartment and unlocked it, walking up the stone steps and through the door into the foyer where she checked her mailbox and began the long hike up the stairs. Even through the pleasant, drunken haze she was now cozily enveloped in Jolene chose her usual mode of transportation to her apartment: Her legs.

Once on her floor, she began flipping through the mail. It was amazing how many pre-approved credit card applications she received via the postal service. Her financial history had been pristine ever since college. Jolene had grown up listening to her father preach upon the necessities of paying off one's debt. She had immediately followed in his footsteps, shelling out the full balance upon her credit cards each and every month, her college friends and roommates in awe of the responsibility young Jolene seemed to posses while they struggled with minimum payments. Years built up on such a routine allowed her an absurd amount of credit with a multitude of agencies, all of which she turned down.

It was not until after rounding the corner into her hallway and raising her eyes from the envelopes that she caught her breath and stopped dead in her tracks. Before her, leaning against her apartment door was a short-haired man that appeared to be asleep, his legs stretched before him and nearly crossing the entire width of the corridor. Hartley's heart pounded as she began to breath, dropping the mail to the carpeted floor and reaching for her firearm that sat holstered within her purse. She was off-duty, yet had not had time to make it home before her evening with Kim. The alteration in her daily routine seemed to benefit her at this exact moment.

"Chicago PD," she said, the words coming out in a raspy whisper as the firearm in her grasp lifted to aim at the man. Hartley inched closer, bracing herself against the wall to her right for some much needed stability. "Police!" she said louder, rousing the man. His head lifted slowly, his face turned away from her as he seemed to gauge his bearings. "Sir, stay still. I'm a Chicago police officer. I need you to stand up and put your hands—" She stopped as he finally turned towards her, blinking the sleep from his eyes while Hartley lowered her weapon and stared back in disbelief. "Ronny," she said, more of a statement falling from her lips than a question.

"Jo?" he asked, shielding his eyes from the hallway light shining brightly above her head. "Is that you?" Jolene leaned fully into the wall, her shoulder holding her entire weight as she stared into the face of her relatively-recent past. Ronny stood, reaching down and hoisting his small duffel bag and motorcycle helmet up with him before smiling at Jolene, his eyes noticing the gun she still held firmly in her grasp.

"How'd—" Hartley began but trailed off.

"I, uh—Mrs. Gerard saw me downstairs and let me in the gate."

"She remembered you? She's almost ninety-five."

He shrugged and chuckled, his laughter sending shivers down her spine. She had always loved his laugh. It was one of the wonders of their relationship that she found exceptionally sexy. He looked towards the gun in her hand again and pointed. It registered to Jolene that the weapon was still at the ready, yet the shock of the situation at hand did not allow her to place it back in her purse. "Mind if I come in?" Ronny asked with a grin.

Jolene glanced at him and then to the door, nodding her head. She moved to the entrance and unlocked it, pushing it open and flipping on a light switch. She stood in the threshold for a moment, peering at him out of the corner of her eye. He smiled and said, "After you." Jolene moved into her apartment, Debarsi following behind and shutting the door.

Jolene's mind was reeling. She had not seen Ronny for six months, and had not spoken to him in just shy of that time. The split had been amicable, yet the pain of losing such a major part of her life had been something she had dealt with every day. She had not gotten over him, yet had, within the past half year, learned to deal with the gaping hole he had left.

Jolene moved into the kitchen and flipped on another light, Ronny placing his duffel bag on the floor and turning towards her as she set her purse and firearm on the counter. She stared up at him and their eyes connected, Debarsi smiling at her as she looked him over. He was an attractive man with jet-black hair atop an olive skinned, muscular frame. He had chopped off his longer waves and now sported a messy look, though Jolene did not know if the hairdo was done on purpose or from his nap against her front door. Either way, he looked good to her. "What are you doing here, Ronny?" she finally asked.

He continued to smile and looked down to his hands. "I—I had some time off and came back to see my mother," he answered, his smile fading slightly.

Jolene nodded slowly. "I heard. How is she doing?"

"Hanging in there," he responded. "Cancer seems to have stopped spreading. She's doing treatment, but—who knows?"

"Well, she's tough, Ronny."

"Yeah. Yeah she is." They remained quiet for a moment until he looked up at her again. "You look great, Jo."

Jolene smiled and glanced away, her cheeks flushing a slight red. "Thank you," she responded, looking back to him again, a fire growing in her stomach. "You do too. I like the short hair."

"Oh yeah?" he said as he brushed a hand over his head, stepping forward into the kitchen. "Thought you always liked the shaggy look?"

"Anything looks good on you," she replied, blushing once again. She felt heated all over, her senses rushing from the wine she had consumed early that night. Seeing him again brought back the realization that she was alone, though it also churned up a feeling that she had not confronted other than in her mind in a long time. She was fully aware that she was biting her bottom lip while looking him over, and he smiled as he walked closer, stopping feet from her and placing his hands on the counter. "When did you get to town?" she asked.

"Earlier today. Went straight to the hospital. Left there and just rode. Found myself outside your place." He paused as their eyes locked. "I—I just needed to see you, Jo."

She smiled wide and stepped away from the counter directly in front of him. "Would you like a drink?" she asked.

"Absolutely," he responded. Jolene moved away from Ronny and towards the pantry, opening the doors and retrieving two wine glasses and a bottle. She poured the wine and handed the glass to him, taking a long sip from hers, her eyes still locked on the man standing before her.

"Where are you staying?" she asked, her hands shaking slightly from the urges that were taking over.

"Well, I hadn't gotten that far," he answered. "I was going to see if there were any vacancies at the Hyatt or something. If not, maybe ride out to my mother's."

"That's a long way."

"Yeah."

They stood in silence near the counter for a time, each sipping their wine and trying to overcome the awkwardness that draped over the room. Jolene could not control the feelings she had repressed over the last several months, although she knew what she wanted was going to possibly lead to more heartache. She so badly wanted to feel his mouth on hers, experience his hands sliding across her body like they used to.

Ronny could feel the tension between them. He knew when he came to her door things would be strange, yet they had spent so much of their lives intertwined together that eventually they would break through the barrier. He did not, however, realize that he would be dealing with a woman fueled by lust and alcohol, a stunning being that obviously still thought of him as much as he thought of her.

As he stood there, looking upon the beauty of his former lover, Jolene decided that the heartache she may feel in the future was not going to determine her actions of the night. With her hands shaking, she placed her glass on the counter, reaching for his and setting it next to hers. Ronny stared at her as she moved gracefully towards him, positioning herself directly next to him, her body grazing his. She reached her hands up and clasped the back of his neck, pulling herself up to him and placing her lips on his, kissing him passionately. He did not hesitate, immediately wrapping his arms around her and returning the kiss.

They remained in this heated exchange for nearly a minute, their mouths pressed together, hands groping each other's bodies. Ronny reached down with both hands and lifted her up, her legs wrapping around his waist. They moved together away from the kitchen towards the couch, knocking into tables and chairs, sending a container of incense flying to the floor, the contents rocketing out in all directions. Jolene leaned back into the couch as Ronny lowered her, pulling him to her body in the process.

He pulled away from their kiss enough to say, "Jo, maybe—"

"Shut up," she responded. "Please. Shut up." He obeyed, locking his lips with hers again as she pulled his jacket from his shoulders, his hands unbuttoning her jeans and sliding them down her legs. She sat up suddenly and pulled her shirt over her head, throwing it on the floor in a heap before lying back again on the couch. Ronny, one knee on the sofa, gazed down upon Jolene who looked ravishing, clothed only in her underwear. He pulled his shirt off and undid his pants, Hartley leaning forward to pull them down, taking his boxers with them. Debarsi unlatched her bra strap and slid it down her arms, smiling as she leaned into the couch, arching her back as she removed the last bit of fabric.

They remained still for a moment, each looking over the other's body, taking in pieces of the other's anatomy that had faded over the last six months. Ronny had a muscular build, athletically cut and in shape with a scar crossing his right shoulder, a souvenir from a battle that ended with the attacker being shot and killed. Jolene was flawless; her dark, brown hair falling around exquisitely defined facial features, the lights of the kitchen shimmering off her smooth tanned skin.

Finally, able to take the waiting no more, Hartley reached down and grabbed between Debarsi's legs, pulling him to her. He bent down to her, his lips resting on her neck, kissing to her shoulder as she pulled him into her. She moaned loudly as she tilted her head back, enjoying her former lover for the first time in half a year.

*****

"You understand those weren't my intentions," Ronny said, lying next to Jolene, their bodies glistening with sweat. He stroked her side, running his fingers gently from her ribcage to her thigh and back, his chin resting on her shoulder.

"You didn't seem to mind much," Hartley responded, a smirk growing on her face.

"Well, no," he replied. "I didn't mind at all. In fact, since you broke the ice, I'm sure I have another round in me—"

"Okay," she interrupted, tilting her head back towards him. "Take it easy. Let me get my second wind here first."

"I'm just saying." They both laughed and replayed the last hour in their minds, their bodies moving together as one, their moans and breathing battling in the air. The intensity of the event could not be matched by anything in their past.

"Why'd you leave?" Jolene asked aloud.

Ronny lifted onto his elbow, staring down at her. "Jo, you know—"

"I know," she interjected. "I know why you left. That was more of a rhetorical question. You know, like—I don't know—"

"I get it. I've missed these past months too." He paused for a moment and then stated, "I've missed you."

Jolene turned on her back, her naked body facing the ceiling, his hand making circles on her stomach. "Then why didn't you come back?"

"You know how it is," he began. "You know the job. It's too much. There's no time. Believe me, if I knew how to do anything else, I would have quit the force and stayed with you. But—" He let the statement hang in the air, yet Jolene understood where he was going with it.

"I know," she said. "You're the same as me." They smiled at each other, relishing in the fact that they were once again together, although for an unknown amount of time. "That's why I fell in love with you." Debarsi looked into her eyes and leaned in to kiss her, placing his hand on her cheek. He pulled away suddenly and lifted off the couch, stepping over the back and into the kitchen. "What are you doing?" Jolene yelled after him.

He came around the end table with the two glasses of wine and a smile on his face. "No reason to not drink these." He sat on the couch near her feet and handed her a glass, pulling a blanket from under the coffee table and covering himself, leaving her naked. She smiled at him and sat up, bringing the glass to her lips, though not moving towards the blanket.

"So what now?" Jolene asked, placing her glass on the coffee table and pulling a pillow to her, her knees against her chest.

"Well, I'm thinking I'm going to be in town for at least a couple days. I've got to meet with the doctors again about my mom, but other than that, I'll just be around. What about you?"

"Nothing planned besides work."

"Maybe dinner? A night on the town for old time's sake?"

"Perhaps," Jolene said coyly, bringing her glass once again to her lips. "I'm assuming you're just going to stay here for the night then?"

"Well," Ronny said, "I was going to head to the hotel. Like I said, I didn't plan on coming here and, you know, doing what we did."

Jolene smiled and set her glass down again. She stood up still clutching the pillow to her, Debarsi gazing at her long legs as she moved backwards and around the couch. "You may want to get used to it," Hartley said as she made her way towards the stairs, "because I think I've caught my second wind." She stopped midway up the steps and threw the pillow down, Ronny catching it as he sipped his wine. "I'm going to take a quick shower," she said as she turned. "There's only one towel in there, so you may want to get one for yourself." Debarsi flipped over the back of the couch and followed her upstairs and into the bathroom, watching as she slid into the falling water.

THIRTEEN

Hartley called into the precinct early the next morning to let her superior know she would be in around midday. The night had given Ronny and her very little sleep, having moved from the warmth of the shower to the cool hallway floor and ending up in her cozy bedroom, each spot devouring a good deal of time in the early hours of the morning. She woke around 11:30 and rolled over, realizing to her extreme pleasure that the previous hours were not a dream. Ronny was next to her, the covers pushed down to his waist as he slept facing her. She reached over and slid her fingers down his back gently, smiling as she did so.

Jolene moved from the covers and grabbed her robe, closing the bedroom door as she left and descended the staircase. In the kitchen she made a pot of coffee and poured herself a mug, sitting at the table and staring through the window into the city. She was surprised that she had no signs of a hangover from the previous night with Kim Banneau, and was even more grateful that she felt no remorse for her actions with Ronny. She felt good. She felt a connection again with her ex, one that had been missing for a long while. She knew things would not turn out the way she exactly wanted, yet there was a definite comfort in knowing that after all this time he still had obvious feelings for her, as she did for him. It made life a little easier to deal with.

Her phone rang from the countertop and she moved across the kitchen to answer. The caller ID read *BARAILLES.* "Hartley," she answered.

"Hey," Barailles replied from the other end. "Everything okay with you?"

"Yeah," she answered. "Everything's great. Why? What's up?"

"Good. Just making sure. I don't think I can ever remember you taking the morning off."

"Oh, well, just catching up on some sleep. What's going on?"

"Well, two things. We checked in on Grazer's alibi. Seems he was at the family brunch from about six o'clock in the morning until about one. Don't know where he went to before or after, but he's accounted for during the time of the killing."

"Thought so. What else?"

"We've got a guest in here this morning."

"Who?"

"Miguel Gomez."

"Ochoa's cousin? What's he doing there? Did he get picked up for something?"

"No," Barailles said, speaking quietly into the phone. "Just came in about five minutes ago. Was asking if we knew anything about his cousin's murderer. I'm pretty sure he's looking for a name."

"You haven't told him anything yet, have you?"

"You kidding me? Yeah, I want to start a gang war. No, I haven't said a word. He's hanging out in the break room enjoying some donuts and coffee."

135

"Can you keep him there?"

"Yep. He's not going anywhere. Said he'd wait for the lead detective to get in."

"Great. I'll be in soon."

"Oh, and Jo—" Barailles said.

"Yeah, I'm still here."

"You aren't going to believe this, but when Miguel walked in, it was like seeing a ghost. He and his cousin look like twins."

Hartley remained silent for a moment and then replied, "Keep him there. I'll be right in."

* * * * *

Jolene dressed quickly and caught a cab into the station, making a quick stop at her corner coffee shop for a to-go cup. She had felt bad not waking Ronny before she left, but knew he would understand. Before she left she had written a note and taped it to his motorcycle helmet: *Help yourself to anything you want. Dinner tonight? Case calls.*

She walked into the precinct and to her desk, her eyes searching the pit for signs of her partner. He snuck up behind her and took the first seat he could find. "He still here?" she asked.

"Yep," he replied. "I set him up in the break room still. He's getting a little anxious. Don't think he's ever been set up in anything but Interrogation."

"Probably because he's never been in a station this long without being charged for something." Barailles laughed. "Okay, why don't we go talk to him?"

"Sounds good. Hey, I'm thinking about staying a little later tonight. You want to hit up the Thai restaurant down the street with me?"

Hartley scratched her head and rose. "Uh—I can't. I have plans tonight."

"Yeah. Okay. Well, maybe tomorrow or something." Hartley nodded and forced a quick grin before moving past him towards the break room. The pit of her stomach wrenched as she passed on the sudden urge to tell her partner of Ronny's return to town. She knew fully that it was none of Barailles's business what she did on her own time, whether that was getting a bite to eat at a local pizzeria or sleeping with her ex. Regardless, she felt as if she were hiding something from him. Their mistake from the other night had put Hartley on eggshells, and she felt in certain situations she was treading lightly.

They walked into the break room and closed the door behind them. Miguel Gomez sat sprawled out on the sofa with one of his legs extended to the coffee table. The resemblance to Benjamin Ochoa was uncanny. They were absolutely cut from the same mold, a likeness Hartley had never seen before between cousins. Their builds, facial features and even identical haircuts caused her to pause as her gaze fell upon him. Miguel looked up as they entered. "You the detective I've been waiting for?"

"Mr. Gomez, I'm Detective Hartley," she said, taking a seat on the opposite couch with Barailles next to her. "You've already met Detective Barailles."

"Yeah. I want to know what's going on with my cousin's case," he stated matter-of-factly.

"Mr. Gomez—"

"Miguel."

"Miguel, the investigation is ongoing and we're not able to share anything right now."

"That's bullshit!" he said fiercely. "You pigs got to have something. Those motherfuckers got to pay for what they did to Ben!"

"And they will, but not by you and the Five-Ones. We'll find the person who did this and they'll stand trial for it." Miguel put his foot on the floor and shook his head, wringing his hands together. "Did you really think you'd come in here and get names from us?" Hartley asked, her eyes level on the gangbanger.

"I don't know. I don't know what I wanted." He shook his head more and rose. "Fuck this."

Hartley stood as he passed in front of her and began his exit. "Miguel," she said, causing the man to slow. "If you want to find your cousin's killer, maybe answering a few of our questions will help."

"What's it going to help?" he asked as he turned around. "I don't know shit. And if I did, I wouldn't be in here talking to you. I'd be out there finding whoever did this, like you assholes should be doing."

"Miguel, we're investigating this as we speak. I realize you don't think you know anything, but answering some questions may set us up with a new lead. We want to get this guy just as bad as you do." Hartley paused as Miguel seemed to think about it. "We need your help to find Benjamin's killer."

Hartley's pleading and her use of Ochoa's first name made it seem to Miguel that the detective was taking this case personally. He nodded his head and walked back to the couch. "I'll answer your questions, but I don't know if I can help any."

"It's worth a shot, Miguel. Thank you," Hartley said as she returned to her seat as well. "You want anything to eat or drink? Coffee?"

"No."

"Okay." Barailles pulled out a pen and pad of paper and scribbled a few preliminary notes. "Now, I need to know about your cousin. We talked with your aunt and uncle on the day of Ben's murder."

"I know that. I talked with them too," Miguel replied.

"What did they tell you?" Barailles asked.

"They told me to talk to you."

"What do you want to know from us?" Hartley questioned, causing Barailles to look up to her. She was smart, he thought. Allowing Miguel to ask them for information would put him more at ease and establish a trust between.

"Do you have anyone? Any suspects?"

"No," Hartley responded. "We have a piece of material showing the killer from a distance, but it doesn't do us any good. We can't make out anything. What else?" Miguel thought for a moment and shrugged his shoulders. "Okay, can I ask you some questions then?"

"Whatever," he replied.

"How long ago did you help your cousin get out of the Five-Ones?"

"Got to be at least four years. He just wasn't right for it."

"How so?"

"He was into tagging. Did some dealing once in a while, but not much. He wasn't big enough and didn't have what it takes to enforce things either, you know?"

"Is that why you got him out?"

Miguel shrugged. "He was family. That means something. Five-Ones mean something, too. He wasn't ever pulled into doing anything that was really that dangerous, so it was easier to get him out."

"You think tagging the neighborhoods of rival gangs isn't dangerous?"

"You know what I mean. Shit goes on between us and other crews all the time. Violent shit. He didn't want any part of it. And I didn't want him to be involved either."

"Did you still see your cousin?" Barailles chimed in.

Miguel looked to him. "Yeah, he was my fucking cousin. What do you think?"

"How often?"

"I don't know. After I got him out, he wasn't around all that much. Not even at our family parties. Just didn't show his face. Then he started coming around more. We'd go to eat, play some pool. Shit like that."

"You're uncle said that Benjamin had been acting a little anxious the past couple months. Do you know why?"

Miguel tensed up slightly, the realization that they were referring to the timeframe of his mother's death grabbing him instantly. "I noticed it too. I know you know about *mi madre*. Everything happened right around then. My mother was killed. Everyone acted differently."

Hartley looked to her hands and then back up. "I'm sorry about your mother, Miguel. We took a look through the files. It was a horrible thing that was done to her. She didn't deserve it." Miguel's eyes glazed over as he held back the tears. Hartley glanced at Barailles who nodded. "Miguel, I have to tell you, but I don't want you to get overly optimistic. Some new information came our way through your cousin's investigation that deals with your mother's death."

Miguel perked up. "What? What is it? Do you know who it is?"

"No, we don't. We don't have much to go on, but we have something that could help us identify the killer. I need to know a few more things first."

"Sure," he agreed quickly.

"Benjamin began acting nervous around the time of your mother's murder, you said," Hartley stated.

"Yeah."

"And before that it had been roughly four years or so?"

"Right. Around there."

"What happened back then? Was there something that triggered his behavior?"

Miguel thought for a moment and stuck his finger in the air. "Yeah. He saw some dude get killed. I remember him showing up that night and he was wigging out. Said the guy— the killer—was a mean motherfucker. Showed no emotion. Just killed this guy and walked off. Ben was tagging this car and when these guys showed up he hid. Said he didn't want to move and just watched it all."

"Where was this murder at? Do you remember who was killed?"

"No. Never really looked into it. It was a big deal, though, to my cousin and in the papers. After that, Ben wanted out. Took a little while to do, but eventually the higher ups let him go."

"Do you remember anything from the papers? Anything at all?"

Miguel thought for a moment, shaking his head in the process. He shrugged and said, "No. Only that the dude killed was some low level politician or something like that. An alderman, maybe? Shit, I don't know. He just wasn't your regular Joe, you know?"

Barailles scribbled down the information quickly on the pad of paper before him. The killing of a city official was a huge deal in the force, especially if you were a homicide detective. The pressure to find the killer and bring them to justice was a weight unlike any normal murder.

"All right, Miguel," Hartley continued. "Thank you. We're going to look into the things you've told us and see if we can't find something to go on." She reached into her folder and pulled out her card. "If you think of anything else, will you give me a call?"

Miguel took the card and nodded. "If it helps to catch my cousin's murderer, sure." Hartley extended her hand and shook Miguel's. "Hey," he said. "I took the bus all the way here. You wouldn't mind having someone drop me off, would you?"

Hartley smiled. "We'll take you back. Come on."

FOURTEEN

Hartley left the precinct shortly after returning with Barailles from dropping Miguel off in the Back-of-the-Yards
neighborhood. She caught a taxi home to her Lakeview apartment and entered with hopes Ronny would still be there
awaiting her return. Her wish disappeared into the darkness of
the empty room before her as she made her way inside. Her
disappointment was only apparent for a split second. Jolene
reached the kitchen and flipped on the track lighting to see a
note resting on the counter in his pen. *Dinner sounds perfect.
Call me when you get in. –R.*

She dialed his number immediately. "Hey," he answered.
"Home early? Did the precinct blow up or something?"

"Funny," she answered, smiling. "I decided it's not every
day you're in town, so I left a little early. Besides, I've got plenty
of vacation left."

"How many days have you used so far?"

"Counting today? Almost one." They both laughed into
the phone, Jolene rolling her eyes at her juvenile, schoolgirl
attitude. "So, you still up for dinner?"

"Absolutely. Where are you thinking?"

Hartley bit her lip, thinking back to their past. "How about
our old spot?"

"Carlisle's?" Debarsi exclaimed. "Oh, I haven't been there in so long! That sounds great. Want to meet there at about six?"

She thought about it for a moment and responded, "You know what? Why don't you come and pick me up."

"I've only got the bike."

"You know how I like the Harley."

Ronny chuckled. "Okay, I'll be there in about twenty."

"See you then." Jolene hung up the phone and ascended the stairs with a skip in her step and a grin crossing her face. She removed her blouse and pulled on a white tank top she had retrieved from a basket of clean clothes near the door, pulling her hair into a tight ponytail as she stepped in front of the mirror and determined with a quick glance she indeed had the stuff to pull off the chosen attire. Hartley moved downstairs and snatched her spare leather jacket from the closet hallway, thinking the choice to remove the coat from her donation pile was absolutely the right decision.

Outside, the streets were buzzing with life as people seemed to be taking advantage of the incredibly beautiful weather that had descended upon the city. Pedestrians moved at a snail's pace along the sidewalks, stopping at every other store to glance through the windows at items they had no intention of purchasing. Bicyclists moved quickly through the streets, the breeze blowing through their hair or over their helmets as they zipped next to motorists making their way home early from their day in the office.

From her left she heard the grumble of what could only be Ronny on his Harley Fat Bob, a beauty of a machine growling its way through traffic and pulling up to the curb in front of her. Ronny kicked it into neutral and turned towards her, smiling from underneath his black helmet and riding glasses. He retrieved a second helmet from his saddlebag and handed it to

Hartley who eagerly placed it atop her head before sliding her left leg over the leather seat directly behind him. She wrapped her arms around his waist. "All set?" he asked over the purr of the engine.

"Let's do it," Hartley responded. They pulled away from the curb with a roar, carefully making their way into the midst of other city travelers and towards their favorite restaurant of six months ago.

* * * * *

"So how come you just stopped calling?" Ronny asked her as they sat at an outdoor table at Carlisle's. The restaurant was a quaint hole-in-the-wall eatery nestled in a garden type of atmosphere on a side street in a quiet neighborhood. The owner of the establishment was the father of Joe Paligulia, a longtime friend of Debarsi's parents and one-time patrolman for the force. Jolene and Ronny frequented the establishment several times a month since the moment they started dating up until his departure to Philadelphia, falling in love with their toasted sub sandwiches on homemade rolls and handcrafted wines they fermented in the downstairs basement. Trees lined the outdoor patio and the scent of lilac filled the air.

"It turned out to be easier that way," she replied, biting into a ring of calamari, the red marinara sauce dripping onto the napkin she held aloft under her chin. "I was busy. You were busy. If I kept moving, it was just easier."

"Like you weren't busy when I was still here. Both of us were swamped in the job." He grabbed a fried zucchini from the tray and plopped it in his mouth, chewing and blowing as the temperature of the breaded appetizer burnt his tongue.

"Oh shit!" he exclaimed as he washed it down with some cool water.

Jolene laughed loudly. "That's true. But I figured you weren't heading back anytime soon and I obviously wasn't going to leave here. With the way we both work, a long distance thing wouldn't have panned out."

Debarsi shrugged, nodding his head. "Yeah, I guess so," he agreed. "Doesn't mean I didn't think about you all the time and want you to call."

"I know. I realize that. But at the time I needed you either here or not. I couldn't drag myself along like that. It's not how I work."

"Understandable," he said, grabbing his beer from the table and taking a sip. He pulled the bottle away and set it next to the appetizers. "Speaking of how you work, how are things going for you? Still partnering with Anthony?"

Jolene glanced up at him and saw the smirk cross his face. "Yes, Tony is still my partner. Why do you say it like that?" she asked, a smile forming on her lips.

"No, nothing. No reason. He's a good partner."

"Yes. Yes he is."

"Right." They each drank and ate for several moments before the conversation resumed. "I bet you he was glad I took the job in Philly."

"He didn't seem to mind, no."

"Yeah, I'll bet." Silence followed again as they took in their surroundings, each relishing in the fact that they were once again together and sitting in chairs that had so grown accustomed to their forms. "So what's on the agenda nowadays for you? What are you guys working on?"

"Weird one. Homicide on an overpass."

"How's it weird?"

"The investigation isn't going anywhere, but it's shedding light on another homicide three months ago, and there's also been talk of one from years back. It's—" she shivered. "I'd rather not think about dead people while I'm eating."

"Okay," he said, putting his hands up in defense.

"What about you? How's Philly?"

"It's, uh, good."

"Really? That sounds convincing."

"Yeah, well, the job is good. Still settling in, you know? Missing a few things," he said as he looked up to her, Jolene catching the gaze and smiling, saying nothing. "Been following things with the same case."

"The Phantom Robber? Is that the one?"

"The one and only. It's been slow, but we're catching pieces here and there. Lot of robberies going on in Philly right now."

"Yeah?"

"Yeah. Must be the weather or something. Brings out the crazies and the thieves, I guess."

"What, are they banks?" Jolene asked.

"Banks, restaurants. Couple of ransom cases a few guys are working on. Just a whole mess of things. But yes, several banks within the last couple months in Philly."

"Have you been getting your guys?"

"Yeah, some of them are popping up. Got one group inside the bank. Real amateurs. Had one gun with three bullets and the other two guys had knives. The moment we got on the phone two of the guys bolted out the front door and turned themselves in."

"What about the third guy?"

"Stayed for a couple more hours. The guard inside finally got enough courage to hit him upside the head with a desk lamp. Knocked him out cold."

"Well that seems like a nice, tidy case," Hartley said.

"Yeah, but then you have the Phantom Robber where it seems everyone seems to just disappear. See, the one with the three guys, all of these kids were friends. Grew up in the same town. Two of them shared the same apartment. This other one seems like no one knows anyone else. How they come together, I'm not sure. But as soon as they are out of the bank, it's like they never existed. It's frustrating." He shook his head and took a drink from his beer.

From the restaurant doorway appeared a short, elderly man in his mid-eighties, approaching the two with a crooked brown cane and a limp. "You two," he said, stopping and raising his hands to the sky, "I tell you, you show up week after week and then—*pow!* Nothing!" He stopped next to their table, reaching out to pull Ronny to him, kissing him on each cheek.

"Mr. Paligulia," Ronny said, kissing him back. "How are you doing? Been a long time."

"Oh, don't ask me that," he said as he made his way towards Jolene. "Bladder's keeping me pissing all night long, feet hurt, and my wife just won't leave me the hell alone. How do you think I'm doing?" They all laughed. "But then you bring this wonderful young lady back into my restaurant and I'm walking on daisies. How are you, my dear? You look as beautiful as ever."

"Hey, Mr. Paligulia," Jolene said, rising from her seat and giving the old man a hug and kiss hello.

"Please, stop it with the Mr. Paligulia. Sonny, please. It's Sonny. Call me Mr. Paligulia when I'm brought downtown for something. Not here. Now, how's everything going with you two?" Debarsi and Hartley looked at each other and smiled. "I was worried that you guys were on the outs. Like I said, haven't seen you in months."

"Just busy working, Sonny," Ronny responded.

The old man turned slowly to Jolene with wide eyes and a hand raised in disbelief. "Can you believe this guy?" he began, talking to the beautiful woman before him as if Debarsi was not present. "Calling me Sonny? It's Mr. Paligulia," he said, bending down and staring at Ronny. Sonny laughed heartily after a few moments and added, "Only beautiful ladies like this one can call me Sonny. Hell, my dear, you can call me anything you want. As long as I see you around here more."

"My apologies," Ronny said between chuckles.

"Now what can I get you two for dessert? Gelato? Cannolis? Or you two going to take desert at home?" he asked, slapping Debarsi's arm and laughing at his sexual insinuation. Ronny rubbed his hand across his face in mock embarrassment and looked to Jolene, who, at the moment, was bringing her drink to her lips, her eyes leveling on her date as the old man looked on.

She smirked at her Ronny and rose from her chair. "You know what, Sonny?" she said as she wrapped her arm around his shoulders, the old man smiling and reaching up to caress her forearm. "I think I'm going to get dessert at the hotel. That okay with you?"

The question was directed to Ronny, yet Mr. Paligulia responded. "*Dio caro!* You young kids. Get! Get out of my restaurant! No," he exclaimed as Debarsi began to reach for his wallet. "This is on the house. Get! I will see you again soon, no?"

Jolene and Ronny said their goodbyes, each hugging and kissing the old man as they moved off down the street towards his Harley and away from their past. "Dessert at the hotel, huh?" Debarsi asked. "You know there isn't an ice cream shop there, right?"

"Oh, I know," she said, sliding onto the back of the bike and smiling.

"Oh, woman," Ronny said as he took his seat in front of her. "You're going to be the death of me." They pulled away in a roar, Mr. Sonny Paligulia waving from the restaurant windows after them.

FIFTEEN

Jolene Hartley decided to not stay the night in Ronny's hotel room mainly for the fact that there would not be a lot of sleeping going on. She had done the unusual earlier in the day by coming in late and leaving early and although she had enjoyed it, she felt a sting in the pit of her stomach that could only be guilt at not focusing on the case more.

She had stayed for several hours, most of which was spent rolling around the sheets in the hotels fancy, plush king-sized bed. She had showered before heading out, leaving the room just after eleven-thirty, Ronny calling from the bed as she exited for her to stay the night. She smiled as she left and promised they would see each other again soon, but she had to work the case for the entirety of the following day.

The ride home was slow as the taxi weaved in and out of late night city-goers. Jolene began to drift away from Ronny and their lovemaking to the conversations she had had with Kimberly Banneau the previous night. *When did your vic get out of the gang life?* she heard in her mind, as clear as if Banneau were seated next to her. *Things happen and make people change. I'd look into his past.*

Banneau's voice in her head grew deeper and began to carry a Mexican accent swirling in the inaudible mumblings. She thought earlier to the interview with Miguel Gomez, her vic's cousin and the son of Maria Gomez, the murdered mother from three months back. *He saw some dude get killed ... he was wigging out. Just killed this guy and walked off.*

The quick, jerky resonance of Miguel's words transformed in her mind as the vocals became deeper and more stretched out, the image of Jerome Grazer forming in Hartley's thoughts. The man she had tackled in a rotting stream came into view through the haze, the interview of how he witnessed the killing of Gomez, of how the killer calmly watched her die, standing out on the edges of her reveries.

She leaned forward and knocked on the window separating her from the driver. "Excuse me" she said. The driver looked up to her in the rearview. "I need you to take me to Area One police headquarters." The driver nodded and adjusted his GPS system, making a sudden left to get in line with his destination.

Too many things were floating through Hartley's mind at the moment, all of which seemed to somehow be connected with Benjamin Ochoa in a cluster that was unclear, yet completely undeniable. Hartley pulled out her phone and punched in the first three letters of her partner's name, hesitating and then hanging up, realizing she needed time to look into these leads without the pressure and tension of Barailles. She knew her partner was a valuable asset when tracking down leads and finding clues, yet with everything they had gone through personally and were now facing within the past few days, Hartley could not take the chance of him bringing the event up and scattering her mental connect-the-dots to hell. She needed to focus.

Hartley knew she would not find much on Benjamin Ochoa in the system besides the few arrests for destruction of property they had pulled up before. Miguel Gomez had made it clear that Ochoa was not the serious gangbanger his cousin was and that the dangerous life was something he had wanted out of soon after joining. Her route to get to know Benjamin Ochoa did not lie in Ochoa's records, but possibly in the records of another murdered man, the low-level politician that Miguel had mentioned while speaking with them. Hartley figured she would have a much easier time finding connections in this murder rather than Ochoa's or Gomez's. Politically charged acts of violence tended to garner more attention than gang activity, regardless of how low-level the politician was. Hartley just hoped her hunch was right and it was not another dead end.

The taxi pulled up to the station just before midnight, letting Hartley exit the cab into the warm Chicago night air, her lungs filling with the moist air. The streetlights illuminated the squad cars parked in front, reflecting off the newly washed vehicles like a row of giant Christmas lights. Uniformed officers stood outside against the brick walls of the station, puffing on their cigarettes and chatting casually about the events of their day. They nodded their greetings to Hartley as she made her way up the steps, each eyeing her as she past, wondering what in the world she was doing at the precinct at that hour.

Hartley made her way to her desk and took her jacket off, setting it on her chair and pulling her hair back. She had grown tired near the beginning of the cab ride, yet the thoughts swirling through her head had jolted her up like no cup of coffee could. She logged into her computer and opened a browser window, searching for political deaths in the city within the last six years. If memory served her right, whatever had happened in Benjamin Ochoa's life had happened nearly five years prior to his death. *Moving into an apartment takes a while,* Banneau had said at their dinner. *I'd see if there was anything going on within the last five or six years.*

Hartley had her timeframe set. If he had witnessed a murder of a politician, maybe he had stuck around to tell the officers what he had seen. *If only I could get that lucky,* she thought to herself.

Her query into political deaths in the city brought up a number of results. There had been two judges within the past six years killed in automobile accidents and a lawyer that had been hit by a drunk driver while walking along the lake and died three days later at the hospital. Add to that a city councilman that had committed suicide after a scandal arose that included sexual favors by a transvestite prostitute. The councilman left behind a wife and three daughters.

Through it all, two results caught Hartley's attention: One was the murder of an alderman; the other the brutal slaying of a female lobbyist in Hyde Park. Hartley opened the latter of the two up and read through Mrs. Burnett's final moments as recorded by the reporter.

> *Mrs. Alice Burnett, 36, fought for her life in Hyde Park last evening, the coroner said, a fight that unfortunately ended in her death early this morning. It happened in the north end of a park near a popular bike path and duck pond, a spot usually inhabited by tourists and bird lovers, yet last night only by the agonizing screams of Burnett, a young and upcoming lobbyist for...*

Hartley stopped reading and looked to her desk in thought, remembering this case. Alice Burnett was found fully clothed with the lower half of her body submerged in the duck pond, her hands placed on her stomach and blood dripping from the back of her head where she had received a fatal blow. The case had stumped detectives for several months until it was discovered that Mr. Burnett, the jealous, manic-depressed husband of Alice, had, in fact, brutally raped and killed his own wife.

This was not the murder she was looking for. Hartley turned her attention to the other listing, a murder of an alderman by the name of Daniel Vincent, a husband and father that, she remembered, had a knack for helping the underdog make enormous leaps against much heftier opponents. She had not followed that case much due to the fact that she had been busy chasing her own murderers, yet knew it had remained unsolved, an outcome which had cast a shadow upon the police force.

Hartley moved to the desk opposite hers and slid the mouse across the surface, waking the computer and searching through the database of cases for Vincent's. She pulled up a number of items associated with the case and chose the link to view the crime scene photos, landing first on the blood-smeared face of the man that had once lived a full, giving life dedicated to the people, yet now stared blankly into the camera lens. She flipped through the digital photos, taking in the crime scene and noting if anything caught her attention, stopping suddenly at the fifth image. Displayed before her was a view of the crime scene, Vincent's body sprawled on the concrete in the background, a group of officers huddled around a civilian dressed in black jeans and a dark red shirt, the typical colors of the Five Ones.

Benjamin Ochoa.

This had to be the event that had transpired five years prior that had spooked her victim. He had witnessed the gruesome murder of Alderman Daniel Vincent and had decided he did not want to end up the same way, a cold lifeless corpse lying on the hard, gritty pavement of a parking garage. Hartley's mind was reeling. Although she had most likely pinpointed the time in which Ochoa had altered his path, this still did nothing for her current case. She still had no solid connection between her current investigation and either the Gomez or Vincent murder other than the coincidental relations between Maria and Benjamin and the witness of the alderman's killing.

She flipped forward in the series of images, all of them focused on Ochoa speaking to officers, the photographer making sure to include the blurred body of Vincent in the background. An ambulance had made its way to the scene and had checked on the couple that had arrived shortly after Vincent had expired. One of the photos showed Ochoa resting on the bumper of the opened ambulance, looking to the ground as the officer turned to speak to the detective on hand. From the left of Ochoa, a dark-haired man with a stubble-filled face was caught talking to Benjamin, pulling on his shirt to get the gang-banger's attention. A series of these images etched a verbal exchange between the two, yet nothing more.

Hartley checked into the files regarding the mysterious stubble-faced man, yet found nothing. *Probably some nut in the crowd wanting to know what had happened,* Hartley thought to herself. She leaned back again and glanced at the wall clock. 2:45 a.m., it read. She yawned and closed her eyes, stretching her neck and rubbing her shoulders, wondering if she should catch a cab home for a few hours of sleep or crash in the break room like she had so many times before. *Break room,* she decided, not wanting to lose any of the mental notes she had in the works on an exhaustive ride back to Lakeview.

Hartley turned her attention once again to the monitor, pressing the button to continue through the crime scene photos. She fell into a trance as she worked her way into the night Daniel Vincent was murdered, envisioning how the killer had made his way into the garage and hid, not noticing the gang-banger down the way hiding in the shadows and watching his every move. She heard the footsteps of the alderman approaching, his shoes echoing as they fell in the parking garage of her mind. She saw Vincent approach and sprang from the shadows with weapon in hand.

Hartley stopped her mental film from spinning. "How were you killed?" she asked aloud, realizing in her haste to find Ochoa she had passed by crucial information that may or may not help her determine if there were any more connections. She skipped through the digital photographs and fell on an image that made her gasp. Hartley leaned back in her chair and gripped the armrests, her knuckles going white as she stared at the monitor.

Daniel Vincent lay on the pavement, his head towards the right on the photograph, his feet to the left. His shirt was soaked through with blood, yet Hartley could make out two distinguishable puncture wounds, one on each side of his chest, and the life-ending slit to his throat. Hartley sighed and scratched her head, returning her gaze to the monitor and image. "It's the same killer," she said aloud, thinking to the Maria Gomez case and the murderer's M.O. that now seemed to have spread to two slayings.

Hartley smiled, deciding that her hunch had indeed been correct. There was something bigger going on with her investigation than the killing of a random ex-gangbanger. She had realized that Benjamin Ochoa may show up in her search for political deaths, yet the method in which Maria Gomez and Daniel Vincent were murdered were identical, as well as the description of calmness the killer displayed while in the brutal act. Questions formed in Hartley's mind, inquiries that were now trying to connect the two murders and her current investigation together, conjuring ways to form some chain of events that ended in three dead bodies over the course of five years.

She looked to the wall clock again and yawned. It was now 3:15 a.m. She would indeed stay put tonight, possibly catching a few hours shut-eye in the break room before starting up again in the morning. Then again, she had pulled all-nighters before. Maybe a cup of coffee would get her moving again. She stood and moved to the kitchen, filling the coffee pot with water and emptying a packet of grounds into the filter, thinking to herself that tonight was her penance for missing nearly half of the previous day.

SIXTEEN

Barailles exited his taxi in front of the precinct just after seven o'clock in the morning carrying a coffee in a ceramic mug and a bagel wrapped in a paper towel. He had rushed out of his apartment earlier knowing well that Hartley, having missed some of the previous day, would feel the need to buckle down and make a huge dent in their investigation.

As he walked up the exterior steps a group of uniforms exited the building, one of them pointing towards Barailles and nodding his head in greeting. "Good luck in there, detective," he said as he passed and patted him on the shoulder.

Barailles stalled and turned with his arms wide. "Good luck? What for?" he asked the man.

The group of officers chuckled. "That partner of yours has been in there since midnight, I've heard."

"Hartley? Hartley's been in there since midnight?"

"Midnight," the officer repeated. He smiled at the quizzical look that had spread across the detective's face. "I could be wrong, but that's just what the other guys told me. Said she came in and hasn't left. Said she's on her third pot of coffee."

"Did you see her?" Barailles asked.

"Yeah," the officer responded. "Looks great." Barailles dropped his arms and looked at the officer sternly. The officer caught the detective's drift. "Yeah, sorry. She's got files spread out all over your desks."

"Files for what?"

The officer laughed loudly. "Yeah, I'm not going near that. No clue." He waited to see if Barailles had any other questions then replied, "Well, like I said, good luck to you." He descended the stairs and entered a squad car, raising his hand up and waving as he pulled away.

Barailles turned back towards the precinct entrance, though he remained glued to his current spot, pondering what his partner had found in the early hours of the morning, what breakthrough had occurred in her mind and where it had led her.

And last but not least, why she had not called him to come in to help.

* * * * *

Hartley stood next to her desk, staring at a chalkboard filled with facts and questions, eraser markers and fresh chalk lines. New images of crime scenes with their unfortunate victims were taped near the top. Hartley sat on the edge of her desk, her eyes scanning the items on the murder board, her hands shaking ever so slightly from the amount of caffeine coursing through her system.

Barailles walked up behind her, setting his bagel and mug on a cleared corner of her desk. "I'd offer you coffee," Barailles said, "but I've heard you're good on that."

Hartley did not remove her eyes from the board. "Yeah? Did that shithead Milton tell you that?" she answered calmly.

160

"Yeah," Barailles responded. "Told me you've been here all night. Is that right?"

"Milton," she said, ignoring the question. "You know that jackass tried to grab my ass the other week in the gym?" Barailles remained silent as he glanced at the board. After a time Hartley acknowledged her partner's inquiry. "Yes, I left—I had some ideas last night and came in."

"Why didn't you give me a call? You know I would've come in and helped you."

"I needed to make sure my hunch was good. Then I just got sucked in."

"Still could've called. I could've picked up—"

Barailles stopped short as Hartley turned towards him and glared. "Do you want to know what I've found?" she asked. He forced a smile and raised his hand, giving her his attention. She moved her focus back to the board and began to play out their investigation as she saw it. "Okay," she began, pointing to a picture of Benjamin Ochoa in the upper left of the chalkboard. "Ochoa is our focus. Miguel said he got his cousin out of the gang about four years ago because Ochoa had gone through a change. The night I went out to dinner with Banneau, she said that some of the cases that deal with kidnappings involve a family member that goes through some sort of change. Like an altercation in the past that eventually leads up to the abduction. Following?"

"No," Barailles admitted. "But keep going. I'm sure it'll click soon enough."

"Well, on my way home, I kept thinking about Miguel Gomez talking about Benjamin witnessing the murder of a politician and about how it freaked him out because of the coldness of the killer just standing over the guy and watching him die. Then I thought to Jerome Grazer and how he had said the same thing. The killer just stood in front of Maria and watched her go, calmly leaving right after."

"Jo, a lot of people get satisfaction out of killing. They like the rush."

"Right," she agreed, pointing at Barailles. "The rush. People get used to taking a life and it gives them pleasure. But this guy, these killers in these two cases, there is no satisfaction. There is no rush. Both of the witnesses told about the killer being completely calm. Almost made them sound like the acts were routine, part of everyday life. Like brushing your teeth."

Barailles crossed his arms across his chest and leaned back onto a desk. "Business as usual. Right, I get it."

"So," Hartley continued, "I looked into political murders within the last six years and brought up this." She pointed to a printout of the Daniel Vincent murder scene, a non-descript image that showed the entirety of the chaos within the parking garage. "Alderman Daniel Vincent."

"Yeah," Barailles said standing and walking towards the chalkboard. "I remember that. Guy was killed coming out of a restaurant couple years back."

"Five," Hartley corrected. "Five years back. Right around the time that our vic decided to get out of the gang life." She retrieved another printout from her desk and handed it to Barailles. The image was of the officers standing around the man in the red shirt. "Recognize anyone?"

"Holy shit!" Barailles said with a smile. "That's Ochoa. So this is it, huh? This is the murder he witnessed."

"Right. And I'm assuming that this is the murder that scared him straight."

"Great," he replied, setting the image back on her desk.

"That's not the best part," she commented. "See, this entire case, nothing makes a whole lot of sense. We have the murder of Vincent five years ago, witnessed by our vic, leading him into a righteous tailspin that sends him running from his Five One brothers. Four years and nine months later, our vic's aunt is brutally murdered, which, after years of comfort in his new-found life, once again turns him into a nervous wreck. Not knowing the identity of either the Vincent or Gomez killer, why do you think this would make Ochoa a ball of crazy?" She paused, letting the question sink into her partner's thoughts.

"I don't know," he answered. "Seems to me that, sure, the Vincent murder would make him agitated. But the murder of Gomez, other than the pain of losing your aunt, shouldn't make him flip out. If anything, Miguel should be the one flip-ping out."

"Unless the details given to him of the murder scene of his aunt and remembering what he had witnessed the night of Daniel Vincent's killing were similar enough to make Ochoa think that the killer had come back." Hartley pulled the two images of Maria Gomez and Daniel Vincent from the pile on her desk and held them aloft before Barailles. He stared at them intently, noticing, as had Hartley, the identical method the killer had used.

"It's the same guy," Barailles stated, looking over the pictures to Hartley who nodded her head.

"Same killer," Hartley said aloud.

"Unbelievable." They looked to the board again. "So how does this fit in with our current case?"

Hartley paused before answering. "I don't know," she said, staring at the board and playing with her fingernails. She could feel Barailles's gaze moving from the chalkboard to her, knew that eventually this conversation would head to their current dilemma on the pair having no solid leads.

"Well," Barailles said, realizing that Hartley was, for the moment, stumped. "There's got to be something else we can go off of. Maybe our answer to this investigation lies in one of these cold cases. Have we gone through everything in the case files?"

"No," Hartley answered. "There are still more pictures in the database. I just couldn't look at them anymore." She sat down in her chair and leaned back, pulling her hair out of the ponytail and letting it fall past her shoulders as she looked towards the ceiling. "There's also a box or two on your desk for both the Gomez and Vincent murders." Barailles moved to his desk and opened a box containing items related to the Vincent investigation. "Oh," Hartley said, sitting straight up and shuffling through the printed images. "Almost forgot. There are a couple pictures of this guy talking to Ochoa after the police showed up." She stood and walked to Barailles's desk, handing over the images. "I doubt it's anything, but I ran it through facial recognition and got nothing." She moved back towards the chalkboard and resumed her viewing, rocking back and forth on the balls of her feet.

"Don't recognize him," Barailles said as he set the images down next to the opened box. He reached inside and removed a packet of files and a bag, revealing a set of photographs hidden beneath. Barailles pulled them out and held them up to his face. "Jo," he said. Hartley remained fixated on the board. "Jo," Barailles repeated.

"Barailles," she responded with a scowl, "don't call me Jo while we're—"

"Hartley, did you see this picture in the database?" he interrupted, turning the image around and revealing a photograph of a drawing done by the sketch artist of the Daniel Vincent case.

Hartley walked closer and grabbed the image, studying it. "Like I said, I didn't get through all of them." The sketch she gazed upon now was that of a young Caucasian male, mid-to-upper twenties with short hair. The drawing was descriptive, yet the completed material could match any one of the thousands of young, white males roaming throughout the Chicago streets. The item that set it apart, however, was an inset in the lower right corner showing the back of the suspect's head, revealing a tattoo of a thin black circle on his neck just above his shoulders. *Not unique enough,* Hartley thought to herself, understanding that the case was, to this day, still unsolved, the killer remaining at large somewhere in the world. She looked up to her partner who was gazing at her. "'A white guy with a tattoo on his neck,'" Hartley said. "Jerome Grazer told us that the guy who killed Maria Gomez was a white guy with a tattoo—this guy."

They stood facing each other, glancing from the chalkboard to the boxes of files, Hartley yawning and running her hands across her forehead. "What now?" Barailles asked, breaking the silence.

"I don't know," Hartley answered. "I need to get out of here for a little bit. I'm going to run across the street to the diner. Just—I'll be back in a little while."

She turned and made her way towards the stairs, Barailles watching after her as he fought the temptation to follow. He looked down towards the box of files and back to the stairs where his partner had just descended. The box of files would have to wait, he decided, draining his cup of coffee and moving in the direction of the steps. Files were important, he knew, but nothing beat the mind of Detective Jolene Hartley on an all-night caffeine-induced brainstorming session.

SEVENTEEN

Hartley sat near the front of the diner so she could lose herself in the bustling city street outside. She watched as pedestrians moved in and out of her view, some lost at the edge of her vision, others disappearing around building corners or stopped city buses. She felt drained yet satisfied at discovering what she had during her midnight rummage session. Her frustration still lay in the fact that her current investigation had somewhat stalled. She had new information regarding the two other murders, yet nothing of significance to her current case.

"Hey, Detective," shouted a burly man from the back of the diner.

"Hey, Louie," Hartley shouted back.

"You want your usual? Coffee and a muffin?"

Hartley shook her head. "Maybe some eggs over easy and a couple pieces of bacon."

"You got it. Late night?"

"You have no idea," Hartley said as she sipped from her glass of water. She turned her head away from Louie and back towards the street just in time to see Barailles cutting through traffic. She stared at him for a moment and then brought the water glass to her lips as if to douse the flames before they started.

Her partner entered the diner and moved immediately to his right, waving to the waitress behind the counter and to Louie in the back. "Coffee, please." The waitress nodded and grabbed a carafe and a mug, following in her customer's footsteps towards the table. "May I?" he asked as he approached Hartley's table.

She nodded her head and glanced outside. "What's up?" she asked.

"You look exhausted," he replied, deflecting the question.

She looked back to him. "Thanks," she said sarcastically.

"I just mean you—"

Hartley raised her hand in submission. "I get it. Don't dig yourself a bigger hole, Barailles."

Barailles smiled and took a sip from his coffee cup. He focused back on her and remained silent for a moment. Hartley could feel his gaze fall upon her yet she remained fixated on the outside world. "Where do we go from here then?" he asked after a few moments. She turned her attention to him again, not sure if he was talking about the case or bringing up their mistake from the other night. "With the case," he replied quickly, catching that his inquiry worked on several levels, one of which he knew his partner wanted to avoid at all costs.

Hartley shrugged. "I don't know. I'm losing steam right now. What do you think?"

"I think maybe we look into the Gomez and Vincent cases a little more, see if we pick anything else up from them."

"Okay," she agreed. "I went through them both earlier and the way I'm seeing it is we have the same killer for both murders, a kid who is connected to both, but no way of connecting anything from those two to his. Maybe it's just me being completely wiped out, but I'm having trouble figuring out where to go."

"Well, I'll run through them again. Maybe there's something that I'll find that maybe you missed. Not saying that you did, but working an all-nighter, sometimes you can skip over some things." Hartley nodded. Barailles sipped his coffee as the waitress brought out a plate of eggs and bacon for each of the detectives. "Thanks, Lou," he yelled over the counter, receiving a wave in response.

They ate their breakfast in silence, Barailles looking up every so often to glance at his partner, a stunning vision even with no sleep under her belt. Small, dark bags had begun to form underneath her still alert eyes and her hair had taken on a carefree, hippie-ish look, no doubt from the constant up and down of her ponytail combined with her fingers combing through every now and again.

"So," he said, breaking the silence after they had finished their meal, "have you seen him?"

Hartley looked up and answered, "Seen whom?"

Barailles remained silent for a moment before responding. "Debarsi." She stared back at him, not responding. *How does he know about Debarsi being in town?* she asked herself. "He called the other day after you left." Hartley glanced out the window again as Barailles pushed the subject. "Have you seen him yet?"

Hartley thought for a moment, trying to determine why she felt as if she were on the wrong side of the interrogation table. Debarsi and her had no bearing on Barailles and her relationship. It was also none of his business. Yet she felt heated at the question, as if she were under the microscope and he was judging their partnership based solely on this one inquiry.

"Yes," she answered finally, nodding her head and sitting straight in her seat, her gaze settling on his face. She forced herself to shake the nervousness that was forming, to stay clear of the proverbial eggshells she knew she did not need to walk on. She needed to remain the strong willed woman she had always been.

Barailles held her gaze. "Is he back for good?"

"No," she responded.

"What's he doing back? I mean—Did he come back for—" He left his statement hanging.

Hartley, seeing where the line of questioning was heading, let her irritation come forth. Her face became rigid, making her already attractive features that much more pronounced. "Come back for what, Tony?" He leaned back in his seat and glared at her. "For me? No. What's with the third degree from you?"

"Jo, I'm just looking out for you—"

"No, Tony, you're not. You're looking out for you. You want to know things that don't concern you in the least."

"How doesn't it concern me when I'm faced with my partner getting blindsided by her prick ex-boyfriend and losing her edge on the—"

"Fuck you," Hartley said, creating a silence that had never occurred between the two before. Barailles stared at her, unable to process what had just come out of her mouth. Hartley calmed slightly, yet the fire still burned. "Look, I don't have time for this. I'm exhausted." She pulled a wad of money from her pocket and tossed it on the table, standing and walking towards the door.

She stopped and turned back towards the table, Barailles still seated, his back facing her. "Tony, don't ever say I'm losing my edge again. You know, you never even got to know him.

But I don't care. I don't care that you think he's a prick. I don't care that you think he was wrong for me. But what I do care about is your feelings for me clouding what you should be doing. We're on the job now. We have a case that needs to be blown wide open and I need my partner to stop worrying about what I'm doing before and after work and just worry about me on the job. Can you handle that? Can you put whatever is going on here behind you and focus? Because if not, this isn't going to work." She stared at her partner who sat still, glancing from the window to his plate. "I'm heading home, Barailles," she continued. "I need some rest. Call me if you find anything. I'm sorry."

Hartley turned and left, leaving her partner to stew over the harsh words she had left hanging in the air between them.

EIGHTEEN

Jolene approached her apartment door and yawned, sliding the key into the hole and turning the knob while she conjured up an image of herself asleep on the couch, the cool breeze blowing through the open windows and across her face as she lay motionless under the blanket. She opened the door and let out a loud scream as Debarsi moved out of the kitchen and into view.

"Jesus Christ!" she yelled, her hand to her mouth as she calmed herself. "Ronny, what the hell are you doing here? You scared the shit out of me!"

"You scared the shit out of *me!*" Ronny rebutted. "What are you doing back so early? I thought you had to stay on the case all day."

Jolene moved to the couch and removed her jacket, revealing the same clothes she had been wearing for the previous twelve hours. "I went in after I left your hotel last night. Had a couple things I needed to look at, which turned into a couple more things. Just kept—What are you doing here?"

Ronny smiled as he reached for a plate on the counter, holding it out to her. "Breakfast. The hotel doesn't have a stove in the room to make breakfast."

171

"You do know that most places serve breakfast though, right?"

"Yeah," he responded, placing the plate on the kitchen table, "but the eggs are always scrambled and the bacon is just disgusting. Nothing like doing it yourself." He pulled out a chair and raised a hand for Jolene to have a seat.

She smirked and sat in the assigned location. "I just ate," she replied, "but I'll take that cup of orange juice if you don't mind."

"Absolutely," he responded as he pushed her chair in and handed her the glass of juice, taking a seat next to her as she slid the plate of food in front of him.

"Ronny," Jolene said.

"Yeah?"

"Next time you scare me like that, I'm shooting you in the leg."

"That's fair," he responded as they laughed.

He finished his breakfast as Jolene downed the last of the orange juice, the gears in her mind slowing to a stop after being pushed to the extreme for the last half day. She set the glass on the table and looked wearily to Ronny. They stared at each other for several moments, Debarsi grinning and Jolene trying to retain her smirk, the exhaustion starting to creep into her body. "How did it go last night? Did Anthony come in too?" Jolene's smirk faded. "Everything okay?" he asked.

"Yeah," she answered as she stood and let her hair down. She walked towards the couch and retrieved her jacket, moving to the closet and hanging it up. "Ronny," she said, turning.

"Yeah?" he answered.

She remained silent for a moment before continuing. "Who are you here for? Are you here for your mother? Or is it for me?"

His smile faded almost to nothing, yet his gaze remained fixed on the lovely woman before him. "A lot of both," he responded. "What's going on?"

"I need to know what we're doing here? I care for you just as much as I did when you left, and I'm guessing it's the same for you—"

"It is," he interrupted, wanting her to know that he still felt just as strongly for her.

"Is this something that is going to go someplace again? Or is it just what it is?"

"What do you think it is?"

"You showing up out of the blue and us having a great time. Like you never left. But you will leave." He nodded his head. "You will leave," she repeated. "So is this just us sleeping together until you're gone, or are you going to want to make us work again?"

Ronny stood and moved away from the table, stopping in front of Jolene and running his hand through her hair, brushing a strand back behind her ear. "I don't know. I miss you. I'm still in love with you. I just don't know how we can make it work, you know? The job—it just takes too much. And with the distance …" He paused. "I better leave—"

"No," she interrupted. "I don't want you to go. I didn't bring this up as an ultimatum. I just want to know what I should be expecting."

"I don't know. I know what I want, but I know that the odds of that working—"

"I know," she interrupted again. "Never mind. Forget about me bringing it up," she said, forcing a smile and wrapping her arms around his neck, pulling him in for a kiss.

"Where'd all this come from?" he asked as she moved her mouth off his. "I mean, I know where, but—" He stopped, letting his question hang in the air.

Hartley looked into his eyes, remembering the partner she left sitting alone in the diner across from the precinct. "Nowhere. Just my mind racing from no sleep and a lot of coffee. "

"Well, maybe a hot bath would help you."

"Maybe," she replied. "Is this a bath for two?"

"I don't think I should after the conversation—"

"Let me rephrase," she interjected. "This is a bath for two. I need someone to talk with so I don't fall asleep in there."

* * * * *

"Barailles said that?" Debarsi chuckled as he slapped the water, sending bubbles flying into the air. Jolene laughed loudly as she moved the suds around with her arms, nodding her head to him. They were both submerged up to their shoulders, the warm water easing their bodies from the workout they had the previous night, calming Jolene's frame as she sat with her right leg extended along the rim of the tub. Ronny ran his fingers down her shin and to her toes, the feeling sending tingles down Jolene's leg and into her stomach. "I can't believe he said that."

Hartley shrugged. "I can," she replied.

"That you were losing your edge? Or that I'm a prick?"

She giggled. "More that you're a prick."

He splashed water at her. "You know I'm not trying to be a—"

"I know, Ronny. I know. You're not a prick. He just looks out for me."

"A little too much it seems."

"He's a good man," she said, laying her head back and closing her eyes. She sat like that for several minutes, Debarsi swirling the water with his free hand, glancing up at her from time to time, taking in her beautiful, damp neck and her sensual facial features like he would never see them again. Her wet, brown hair fell behind her ears and just past her shoulders, beads of water dripping from the ends onto her upper chest and disappearing into the suds.

"So how's the case going? Any headway on the overpass killing?" Debarsi asked.

"Some," she responded. "Although it looks like I'm getting more leads with the other two murders."

"Don't you love that? Finding nothing on your investigation, but turning up a whole mess with another?"

"Tell me about it," Jolene agreed, taking in a deep breath before submerging into the water, staying under for a few moments, letting the warmth work its way over her eyes. She reemerged and ran her hands over her face and into her hair as she wiped back the stream of water that ran over her brow. "We figured out that Maria Gomez—my victim's aunt—was killed by the same guy that murdered Alderman Daniel Vincent five years back. Killed them the same way: Stab wounds to both lungs and cut their throats. Pretty gruesome."

"Man," Ronny exclaimed. "That's tough. But nothing else on your guy's killing?"

"Nothing solid. I think whatever happened five years ago spooked our guy into going straight. Then again when his aunt was killed. But his murder wasn't the same style as the others, so I'm not sure how it fits."

"Anything on who the killer of the aunt and alderman is?"

"No names. Got a sketch from the Vincent files, but really, it won't go anywhere. Guy looks like every other shorthaired, mid-twenties guy in Chicago: Good looking, tattoo. Probably would blend in wherever he goes."

"You know, I've been thinking of getting a tattoo?" Ronny said with a smile, trying to hold back his laughter.

"Oh yeah?" Jolene replied.

"Yeah. Maybe one across my forehead. Oh! Maybe I could get a tattoo of a moustache, seeing I can't grow a complete one anyway."

Jolene laughed loudly, splashing water towards him. "Definitely the moustache. May want to draw it on with a pen first, just to see if you'd like it. Test it out."

"Absolutely."

"Be better than the guy in the sketch, anyway."

"Oh yeah? What does he have? Tribal around his arm? *Mom*?"

"No, nothing that good. It's a circle. Not completely colored in, but just the outside, on the back of his neck. Like a giant bulls eye or something."

Ronny's smile vanished and his eyebrows furrowed as he looked at Hartley. "A circle on his neck?" he asked.

Jolene's laughter subsided, leaving her with a quizzical smile. "Yeah, um, at the base of his neck," she replied, touching her skin where the tattoo was located. He looked to the water and back to her before suddenly standing and exiting the tub. "Ronny?" she asked, leaning forward into the bubbles. "What's going on?" Debarsi wrapped a towel around his waist and retrieved his cell phone from his pants laying on the floor, punching in a series of numbers and holding it to his ear. "Ron," Hartley said again, standing and grabbing her towel.

"Hey," he said into the phone, "it's Debarsi. Give me Loften. It's important."

"Ron!" Hartley exclaimed, finally grabbing his attention. "What do you have?"

He moved the phone away from his mouth and looked directly at her. "There was a botched bank robbery about four or five months ago. Two of the suspects were killed and another wounded by a member of their own team. The shooter got away."

"So?" Hartley said.

"He had blond hair and a circle tattoo on the back of his neck," Debarsi explained.

Hartley's face grew taut. "How did you find this out?"

"The wounded suspect pulled through and spilled the beans on the guy. We have a sketch."

NINETEEN

They moved to the bedroom where Hartley dressed and Debarsi threw on his pants before Agent Carm Loften in Philadelphia answered. Debarsi set the phone to speaker so Hartley could join in the conversation.

"Hey, Ronny," Loften answered. "How's it going? How's your mom doing?"

"She's good, Carm," he responded. "Look, something came up here and I need your help."

"Sure, buddy. What's up?"

"Remember the detective I told you about here? Detective Jolene Hartley?"

"Of course."

"I'm here with her now—"

"Hi, Agent Loften," Hartley interrupted.

"Good morning," Loften responded. "What sort of trouble is Debarsi getting you into?"

"This time it seems he's actually helping," Hartley said with a smile to he ex.

"Well that's a first. What can I do for you guys?"

"Hartley's on a case over here that I think has a connection to our bank robbery gone bad from months ago," Debarsi explained.

"Oh yeah? What have you got?"

"I'm working a homicide," Hartley stated, moving closer to the phone and taking the lead. "Kid was killed, shot through the head. Looking into his past we found two other murders: His aunt and a politician in the city named Daniel Vincent."

"Okay," Loften replied. "I'm following."

"My victim witnessed the Vincent murder and we spoke with a guy who had seen the killer of the aunt's murder. Both had mention of the killer being a white male with blonde hair and a tattoo of a circle on the back of his neck. We have a sketch from the alderman's murder."

The line was quite for a minute. "Loften?" Debarsi asked. "You still there?"

"Yeah, yeah, I'm here. Just looking this up. This sounds like our guy, huh Debarsi?"

"Certainly does. Although if he's here, it's more of Hartley's guy."

"Okay, I found it. The sketch I have is of a young white male. Long hair. Circle tattoo. You got a fax?"

Debarsi looked to Hartley as she shook her head. "Not at the moment, Carm. But we can head to the precinct and text you there."

"Sounds good," Loften replied. "I'll keep an eye out for you guys."

"Talk soon," Debarsi said as he hung up, Hartley already having pulled on her shoes and making her way to the stairs. Debarsi followed close behind. "Grab me my helmet there, would you?" he asked as Hartley retrieved her leather jacket. "We'll take the bike over." She nodded and handed it to him, grabbing her keys and sliding into her jacket as they exited the apartment. The exhaustion that had set in hours before was completely gone, fueled instead by yet another connection, this time to Philadelphia.

They had quite a ways to walk, as Debarsi had been unable to squeeze his large motorcycle into any spot on the street, instead checking it into a parking garage nearly a half-mile away. It gave them time to talk.

"Tell me about the robbery," Hartley said, moving in line with Debarsi's longer strides.

"Philadelphia Bank & Trust, four months ago," Debarsi began. "Four guys come in wearing false rubberized faces. You know, like makeup for the movies." Hartley nodded her head. "They secure the exits and get the guards tied up. Hostages are put into supply closets. They get into the vault and ransack it. But not everything is taken. They leave a majority of the cash, only enough for them to carry, which, it turns out, was quite a bit to go off and disappear for a while. One of the tellers inside is able to reach the button and cops show up on the scene a minute later."

"Any requests or anything?" Hartley asked.

"Nothing. Seems like they were just in it for the money."

"So what went wrong for them?"

"Besides us showing up? Nothing. We had no contact in there with the guys. All of a sudden there's some shots heard and the hostages coming running through the front door. We went in and found two of the guys dead and the other barely clinging on. Nothing else. No sign of the fourth guy. Must have gotten out when the chaos started and the hostages ran."

"How long from when the shots were fired until you got inside?"

"Maybe twenty seconds. We rushed in after the hostages came out. Figured something had to go seriously wrong if there was that much mayhem."

"You said you found out about the tattooed guy from the surviving perp?"

"Yeah. Paramedics got there shortly after the shooting and took the guy straight to the hospital where they got him stabilized. He was in critical condition for the first week, but came through. First thing he said when he came to was about how he wanted the guy dead. He was all for ratting him out."

"Just like that, huh?"

Debarsi raised his hands. "Just like that. Crazy. We didn't even offer him a deal, though I don't think he would have cared. He was just pissed off enough to talk."

"So what did he tell you guys about him?" Hartley asked as they stopped at an intersection and waited for the crosswalk.

"Said he was a tough guy. Very strict on how everything was to happen. Military-like. Things weren't going his way, the other guys would hear about it. The guys didn't much like him, but knew he was all business. One of the guys that was killed, he had told our survivor about how the killer had mentioned a murder he had committed here years ago."

"Why mention something like that?"

"I don't know. Bragging rights, maybe." The intersection light changed and they crossed, moving down the street towards the parking garage.

"The way our witnesses talked about this guy, bragging rights don't seem to be high on his priority list."

"Well, maybe he needed to prove himself to get into doing this job. Who knows? The important part is that he told him about the killing and how the victim was a 'man of importance.' He had been paid to kill this man over the building of a casino. Apparently the victim had been putting a halt to the plans to push the casino idea through the city council. A lump of money fell in his lap and he took it."

"Debarsi," Hartley said forcefully. "When I was looking into the Vincent files, I ran across several newspaper articles that dealt with the Silver Ray Casino. Vincent had been against the casino for years. It would have displaced thousands of people in his neighborhoods. Weeks after his death the city approved the plans."

"Did it ever go up?"

"Yeah. The casino is up and running as of two years ago. And just like Vincent said, the neighborhoods surrounding it have taken a nosedive. Drugs, prostitution. You name it."

"Well, I'd say this definitely sounds like our guy," Debarsi said as they turned into the garage. He reached into his pocket and pulled a ticket out, inserting it into the machine and paying with cash. The ticket dispensed itself again and Debarsi grabbed it, turning to Hartley and concluding, "I just hope this sketch matches the one you have from the Vincent murder."

"Me too," Hartley agreed.

* * * * *

Debarsi pulled his bike up to the sidewalk near the front of the precinct just before noon, dismounting and grabbing the helmet from Hartley who turned and walked towards the steps. "Text Loften," she said as they moved into the building. Debarsi reached for his phone and typed in the fax number of the precinct, sending the information to Agent Carm Loften in Philadelphia.

"Fax is being sent now," he said as they stepped onto Hartley's floor. "Cross your fingers."

From the other side of the room Barailles walked towards them, obviously heading out of the building. He slowed as he saw them, eyeing up Debarsi with a furrowed brow and glancing at Hartley as she moved towards him. "Can whatever you're about to do wait for a little bit?" she asked, stopping in front of him with Debarsi, the latter glancing around the room.

Barailles's gaze flipped from his partner to Debarsi and back before he leaned in and said, "I thought maybe we could talk about earlier. Maybe clear the air."

Hartley's features went rigid, her eyes peering into Barailles's soul. "No," she said bluntly, instantly ending whatever plea or explanation about to fall from her partner's lips. "We can't. What we can do is save that for another time and focus on what we've found. Now, can whatever you're doing wait for a while?"

"Fine, Jo," he said with a shrug. "We going to have a group today?" he asked looking to Debarsi, who glanced at him with a smirk.

"Good to see you too, Tony," he responded.

"Debarsi has some information from Philadelphia that may benefit our case. So yes, we are going to have a group today." She turned her attention to Debarsi and pointed at a chair leaning against the wall. "Grab that and bring it over. You'll need a seat. Barailles, there should be a fax coming from an Agent Loften in Philadelphia. Go grab that and come back."

The men turned and did as directed, Debarsi retrieving the chair and placing it next to her desk, taking a seat and setting his helmet on his lap. "Holy shit!" came an exclamation from the copy room where Barailles had reached the fax. "Hartley, check this out." He exited the room holding up a fax of the sketch of the suspect from the Philadelphia bank robbery. Hartley smiled to herself as her partner taped the sketch on the chalkboard next to the suspect drawing from the Vincent murder. Besides the length of the hair, both pictures resembled each one another. They had a match.

"How'd you find this?" Barailles asked. Hartley proceeded to explain what had transpired in her talk with Debarsi and of the conversation with Carm Loften. "Seems like the dumbest thing this guy could've done," Barailles commented after hearing their suspect had broken his silence regarding the Vincent murder.

"Sometimes these guys just slip," Debarsi responded.

"He just seemed so in control with these murders though. Hardly seems he would break ranks and spill something so crucial." Barailles turned to Hartley who was standing in front of the board, studying the images and writings that covered its surface. "What are you thinking, Jo?" he asked.

Her gaze remained fixed. "I don't know. We keep finding items that help out his aunt's murder and the Vincent investigation—"

"And now the Philadelphia Bank & Trust investigation," Debarsi interrupted.

Hartley glanced over her shoulder and then back to the board. "And now that one too, but nothing seems to fully connect these to Ochoa's. I'm just trying to figure out if our case is related or not." She paused for a moment. "Barailles, have uniforms question people in the Six One neighborhood. I want to see if anyone saw Benjamin prior to his murder and if they witnessed any odd activity anywhere on their turf." Barailles retreated to his desk and picked up his phone. Hartley moved her fingers to her mouth, biting her nails and squinting her eyes as she surveyed the board.

"I know that stance," Debarsi said from behind her. She removed her fingers from her mouth and turned. "Yeah, you have something already in your head. You know you can't make it up for yourself though, right?"

"It's not such a stretch," she responded.

"Give it to me."

"Okay—" She stopped as Barailles approached.

"Made the call. Uniforms are asking around now. Should get something back in a little while." Hartley nodded her head. "What do you have?" he asked, glancing from her to Debarsi.

"Why does everyone think I've come up with something?"

"It's your tell. You'd be a terrible poker player," Debarsi said as she threw her arms in the air. He turned towards her partner. "She's got something that may tie all of this together."

"But I can't prove it," she said. "It's just a feeling."

"Let's hear it," Barailles said.

She remained quiet for a moment then said, "What if Ochoa's killer is the same guy as all the others? What if he knew that Ochoa had witnessed him kill Vincent?" She turned her attention back to the board, pointing to Ochoa's picture. "Talking with Miguel, he said that Benjamin got scared from witnessing something in his past. This something coincided with him leaving the gang and receding into a life where he was somewhat of a hermit. We've pinpointed that event to the murder of Daniel Vincent." She moved her finger from Ochoa's picture to the alderman's. "From the records of the night of Vincent's murder, the couple that found the alderman lying on the ground was startled by Ochoa moving towards them, which leads me to believe that Benjamin was hidden very well in the trees." She paused again, mumbling inaudibly to herself.

"But if that was their only meeting," Barailles began, "how would the killer know who Ochoa was? Or know what he looked like?"

185

"I don't know. Hold on." She moved her eyes across the board, trying to find something that had sparked her interest earlier. She found it on another photograph of the Vincent crime scene, this one a shot with the alderman lying in the forefront of the image, his black Mercedes-Benz in the upper right. "That's how," Hartley said excitedly, pointing to the car. "The gang tag. All the gangs of the area have certain tags. And like every artist, every individual who uses that paint leaves his or her own mark on it. Let's assume that the killer didn't see Ochoa, but saw the tag. One could easily figure out what gang that tag belongs to with a little research."

"And with a little more research," Debarsi added, "one could easily find the artist."

"Right. So our killer remembers the gang tag, skips town for a while or lays low until things blow over." Hartley moved to the image of Maria Gomez. "Rudy and Selena Ochoa, our vic's parents, stated that Benjamin started acting strangely around the time when our suspect reappeared to kill Maria Gomez, his aunt."

"But why would he—the killer, I mean—go through the trouble of killing his aunt? What does that prove? Even if he were sending a message, wouldn't it make sense to go after your victim's parents or something?"

"Unless he wasn't trying to send a message to Ochoa," Barailles chimed in. "Maybe he went there to kill Benjamin, not the aunt."

"At the wrong house?"

"He didn't know it was the wrong house," Hartley said, turning towards her partner. "Let's say he got back in town and started researching into the gang tags. He finds one that looks similar and hangs out in the neighborhood. A white guy in a predominantly Mexican area would stand out, so he wouldn't be able to keep a long watch over places."

"And since Ochoa is out of the game, in his brief canvas of the area, he finds the next best thing."

"Miguel Gomez," Hartley finished, smiling and nodding, her eyes lighting up at their speculative scenario.

"I'm assuming this Gomez is related to the murdered aunt?" Debarsi asked.

"Yeah," Barailles answered. "The son." His phone rang and he answered, moving away from the other detectives.

"Which," Hartley added as she rummaged through photographs across her desk, choosing one of Miguel Gomez the night of his mother's murder, "is an almost exact replica of our victim." She held the image up to the board in line with Ochoa.

"Holy crap!" Debarsi exclaimed as he shifted in his seat. "Those two aren't brothers?"

"Nope," Hartley replied. "Freaky, huh?"

"Absolutely. If I had a cousin who was identical to me I'd be asking my parent's some serious questions."

"Exactly," Hartley agreed. "So, he finds out where this look-alike lives and goes to kill him, however, Maria Gomez shows up and—well, we know what happens."

"So you think that the killer stuck around and finished him off on the bridge?"

"Sure," Hartley replied. "Assuming he didn't know where Ochoa lived but knew his routine of getting on the bus, it would be the most likely place to get him."

Debarsi nodded his head and looked over the board. "Okay," he said, "that's not too far fetched at all. Good work."

"Thank you," Hartley responded with a smiled.

"Now where do we go from here? We've connected all murders, have two sketches, but no names."

"You keep saying *we.* Are you somehow including yourself in this investigation?"

"Well, considering I'm an FBI agent with an open investigation into the Philadelphia Bank & Trust robbery, and now you've seemed to connect my guy to more than the two murders in the bank, I think I'm entitled to." He laughed as he looked into Hartley's eyes.

She nodded and smiled back. "Okay," she replied, "but this is my investigation. No pulling your FBI jurisdiction shit on me."

"Wouldn't think of it. I'll just help out where I can. Besides, I doubt I'd get authorization to be working outside of Philly anyways. Apparently they think I have bigger fish to fry than the Bank & Trust case."

Barailles returned over Debarsi's shoulder just then, scratching his head. "Officers got nothing new with asking around. The Five Ones either saw nothing or said nothing."

"Figured as much," Hartley said again, turning towards the board once more. "Which leaves us with a lot of useless information and back at square one." She put her hands on her hips and frowned. "We're missing something."

TWENTY

They ordered Chinese and ate in silence at their desks, Debarsi sharing the little room Hartley had on hers and trying hard not to spill orange chicken on the files. Hartley remained focused on the board. They were indeed missing something, though she could not figure out what it was. Her investigation into Benjamin Ochoa's past revealed nothing other than a few arrests. Same with Maria Gomez. Neither one had any serious enemies other than the global dislike for being involved directly or indirectly with the Five Ones.

Alderman Daniel Vincent, however, was another story altogether. Politicians, big or small, seemed to attract enemies, though most remained unseen and unheard from, taking shots through the mysterious shroud of the internet. "Maybe whatever it is we are looking for includes Vincent's political movements at the time of his murder," she said suddenly. "Did we look into what was going on?"

Barailles nodded. "This morning after you left. I checked into his actions from a year before his murder. There were a couple incidents, but nothing stood out. The one thing that was constant was that casino. He fought that for a while."

Hartley thought for a moment. "Who was he fighting? The city?"

"No. Harold Johnston," Barailles answered.

"Congressman Harold Johnston?" Hartley asked.

"Well, at that time he wasn't a congressman. He was an alderman with connections."

"Don't they all have connections?" Debarsi chimed in.

"Yeah, but not like Johnston," Hartley replied. "He was always sort of the creepy politician. You know, say one thing and do another. Allegedly, a couple mistresses on the side. Somehow nothing was ever pinned to him and he made a successful run to Congress."

"Politicians," Debarsi said, shaking his head.

"It's going to be hard to find anything dirty that would connect Congressman Johnston to the Vincent murder. These guys are dirty, but not that dirty. Usually. Maybe we can take a look into both these guys and see if anything pops up."

"On it," Barailles said, throwing his paper container in the trash and rubbing his hands together in an attempt to cleanse them without soap and water. He logged onto his computer and began searching for articles related to Harold Johnston and the Vincent murder.

"What do you need me to do?" Debarsi asked.

Hartley looked to him and smiled. "How about you go make me a cup of coffee."

Debarsi's jaw dropped as he stood. "Wow," he said, "you detectives really don't like the FBI, do you?"

"Not in the least," she responded with a laugh, kicking him in the rear gently as he passed. She turned to her computer and woke it with the move of her mouse. "Barailles, who are you looking up?"

"I'll take Vincent," he answered.

"Okay. I got Johnston. Check into his people, too. Politicians have a whole mess of people under their wings. Volunteers and such."

"Right."

* * * * *

The Silver Ray Casino & Convention Center had been a decade long struggle to accomplish, mainly for the fact that petition after petition had been signed by the people of the neighborhood where the casino was to be built. Harold Johnston, a brass, in-your-face alderman, had backed the plans to break ground and led a movement through the city council to approve the construction, which, in turn, would also support the eviction and relocation of thousands of residents. Yet the structure would bring in revenue to the city and, more importantly, line his pockets even more than they were.

As Hartley and Barailles researched their chosen politician for the case, each came across the same articles and commentary, each read about the birth, rise and fall of the numerous city council petitions to build the immense structure. Over and over again, more than half a dozen times within a ten-year span the idea was raised, and each time it was thwarted at the last moment, not making it wholly through the committee.

Then, five years ago, there was success. The defender of the neighborhoods where the casino and convention center were to be built was brutally murdered with no trace of who the assailant was. There was no evidence, save for the eyewitness account from a thug gangbanger who had seen the killing while in the midst of spraying the murdered man's car with a gang symbol. The project, without the voice of a fallen hero, was approved and building began months later in areas uninhabited by neighborhood residents. Relocations became the norm as the site grew and eventually the whole of the neighborhood had been moved to various sections of the city, separating families and displacing neighbors that had grown accustomed to one another.

Harold Johnston, Hartley read, showed little emotion to the murder of Daniel Vincent, relaying through the media his "heartfelt condolences to Alderman Vincent's family." He was seen photographed minutes later with union leaders who were set to get the job contract to break ground, all smiling from ear to ear at their great fortune.

"Jo!" Barailles yelled from his desk, rousing her as well as several other detectives in the near vicinity. Debarsi moved to the break room doorway to listen. "You are not going to believe this."

"What do you have?" she asked, looking over her monitor.

Barailles raised his eyes to her, unsure how to proceed in his explanation. Hartley stood slowly and began towards his desk. "I checked into Vincent's political workers. There's a ton over the twelve years he was in office. But you won't believe the name I found on the list." He pointed to the screen as Hartley rounded the corner and took a stance just over his shoulder. On the monitor, above his extended finger, listed in a volunteer employment form was a name she had heard before, yet spelled entirely different: J GRAISER.

"What the hell? That has to be a coincidence, right?" she asked to no one in particular, Debarsi now moving from the break room to see what the fuss was about.

"I'm assuming it is. But that's still weird," Barailles responded.

Debarsi approached from behind Barailles's chair and glanced to the monitor. "Tony," he said, "how well do you know that woman right there?" He pointed across the room at a middle-aged woman sitting at her desk twenty feet away.

"Barb? Are you kidding?"

"No, seriously. You know her well?"

"What does this have to do—"

"Just answer the question."

"Pretty well!" Barailles exclaimed. "I've worked with her for years. Why?"

Debarsi reached down and turned Barailles's desk nameplate towards the detective. "Barb, you say it is, right?" He grabbed a pen and paper and walked to the woman's desk, bending down and speaking quietly with her.

"What is he doing?" Barailles asked Hartley.

"I have no idea," she responded with a grin.

After several moments Debarsi walked back over, pen and paper in hand. "Barbara over there told me the same thing you did. You've worked with each other for years. Talk at holiday parties."

"What's the point?" Barailles asked impatiently.

Debarsi reached back down and flipped his nameplate up, setting the piece of paper down in front of it. "The point is that after years of working together and saying hello over drinks at the Christmas party, Barbara does not know how to spell your name." The writing on the piece of paper was done in a flowing, bubbly script, yet was completely legible, spelling what phonetically sounded like his last name, yet not using the correct letters. "*B-A-R-A-Y-E-S*," Debarsi spelled out loud. Hartley smiled as she looked back to the computer screen and gazed once more upon the Vincent volunteer. J GRAISER. "The way this case is going," Debarsi continued, "I'd say we take a look into J. Graiser."

* * * * *

"Damn!" Hartley yelled as she stared at her computer screen. "Everywhere I look it's nothing but murders."

Barailles popped his head up from his computer where he was in the process of locating a photograph of their newest subject. "Another one?"

"No," she replied, glancing up. "Sorry. Nothing that has to do with our case."

Debarsi came from the kitchen with a cup of coffee and sat in his seat near Hartley's desk. "What's all the yelling about?"

She turned her monitor towards him. "James Graiser. Thirty-year-old male with a permanent address right here in the city. He's connected by more than a volunteer position to Daniel Vincent."

"Tell me about it," Debarsi prodded.

"Says here that when James was twenty, his parents were murdered at their vacation home. His father was stabbed multiple times before being tossed into the lake and his mother was viciously beaten and raped. She died from her wounds later."

"And where was young James at during this time?"

"Report said he was backpacking in Europe."

"Vacation homes and European getaways? Who are these people you're dealing with these days?" Debarsi asked as he smiled and leaned in.

"I know, right? Well, seems the Graiser family comes from plenty of old wealth, all of which James here inherited after his parents passing."

"Seems like a nice motive to kill them to me," Barailles added from his desk, his eyes still locked on his monitor.

"You would think so," Hartley agreed, "but of the money he inherited, little to none has been used. He's popped up across the nation to collect paychecks, probably doing odd jobs to keep busy."

"Why would you work if you had that much money?" Debarsi questioned. "I'd be sitting my ass on a beach someplace drinking *mojitos*."

"No you wouldn't," Barailles said. "You'd get bored."

"How do you know?"

"My cousin opened a software company when she was in college. Made pretty good money. Finally a large corporation made her an offer that allowed her to never work again. Want to know what she was doing three months later? Greeting people at a local home goods store."

"That makes no sense," Debarsi said.

"Sure it does," Hartley replied. "It makes perfect sense. Barailles's cousin got cabin fever from sitting around and doing nothing. The job allowed her to interact with people. Jobs would be different if you didn't base your livelihood on them. If you had enough money to freely leave a job without any consequences."

Debarsi shrugged. "What does it say there?" he asked, pointing. "I see our dead alderman's name."

"Right. So James's parents and Vincent were longtime friends. When his parents were killed, Vincent allowed James to live rent-free in one of his apartment buildings until he was able to get the hang of living on his own. After awhile there seemed to be some monthly payments going into the apartment, but other than that, not much of his inheritance was being used."

"Bingo!" shouted Barailles.

"What did you find?" Hartley asked.

Barailles rose from his desk and walked briskly into the copy room, retrieving a printout of a newspaper article with a picture. "I couldn't find any images for the people working for Daniel Vincent, but I searched for the murder of James Graiser's parents and came up with this." He turned the picture towards them. "I think this may be our item to break the case wide open," he added with a smile.

Hartley's mouth dropped open as she moved closer. The picture showed a young male in his late teens or early twenties walking down the sidewalk surrounded by older, business-like individuals. "I don't get it," Debarsi stated. "How does this guy blow the case wide open?"

Hartley reached to her desk and began tossing around papers, searching for a single item that would explain it all, finally finding it and slamming it on her desk in front of Debarsi. "That's why," she said defiantly. Debarsi looked down at the picture as Barailles walked forward and set his photograph next to Hartley's. "James Graiser," she said, pointing at the photos. "He was there the night of Vincent's murder." Debarsi looked to the murder scene photo, showing Benjamin Ochoa talking with a dark-haired white male, the same individual captured walking next to the older gentlemen in the image Barailles had pulled.

He looked up to Hartley with a smile. "J. Graiser," he said. "How much you want to bet this is who Ochoa wrote down on that piece of paper?"

"We'll find out soon," Hartley said, reaching for her coat. "Let's go get him," she said to Barailles. "You going to be okay here?" she asked Debarsi as the three of them stood, the detectives on the case assembling their necessary items.

"Yeah," he replied. "I'm actually going to take a ride to my mother's again today. Check and see how she's doing. I'll head back here afterwards and see if I can find out anything else on our tattooed suspect."

Hartley smiled and squinted at him. "This is my case," she reminded, "but feel free to use my computer. Let me know what you find."

TWENTY-ONE

James Graiser made his way up his apartment building's stairwell, biting into a half-eaten apple while balancing a brown grocery bag and a stack of mail with his non-feeding hand. He had been back in the states for nearly a month although remained away from the city up till now, traveling from place to place in an effort to extend his time away for just a little while longer. His vacation had been nice, spending it mostly laid out on a beach in Jamaica and helping a friend in Ocho Rios before shuffling aimlessly around New Orleans and the Gulf Coast.

However, it had been time to come back, to return to his home base and recharge his battery before the itch to move would once again light a fire under his feet. It was how it went with him, ever since his good friend Alderman Daniel Vincent was murdered. With the passing of his parents, James Graiser had latched on to Vincent as a child might a favorite stuffed animal, keeping him close at hand for times of need. When he was found dead in the parking garage five years ago Graiser had made his outings more extreme, from weeklong getaways in a multitude of cities, to months-long excursions to numerous continents. He liked to disappear and reveled in the fact that he knew he was off the map, that no one in the world knew what he was doing or where he had gone. It was freedom in its purest form.

He came back, eventually, to his home base in Chicago, plugging into his former life for a short while and checking into any responsibilities that needed tending to. This was one of those times.

He opened a door that led into a dim hallway and continued to the end, stopping in front of his apartment and staring at the door, sighing as he slipped his key into the lock. The door opened to a musty smelling room, stale air wafting into the hallway, escaping into a freedom all its own. He moved inside, flipping on a light and throwing his apple core into a receptacle just below the switch, kicking the door closed behind him with his heel as he set the groceries down on the small dining table.

He lifted the mail to the light, rotating the envelopes to read them. There was nothing of interest in the stack of letters, mainly credit card companies sending their pre-approval letters and coupons to the newest convenience store just around the corner.

He shook his head and glanced up, focusing past the bills to the refrigerator door where the dust-covered silver handle disappeared into the darkness of the kitchen. A shimmer from the grip of the appliance caught his attention, however, light reflecting off it as if dust that had settled in his absence had somehow been wiped away. He set the envelopes on the table and moved forward to the refrigerator, running his finger down the handle and over the cleared spot. *That's strange,* he thought to himself as he glanced up, noticing finally a misplaced chair pushed away from the table, resting against the wall near the corner of the dining area.

It was then that the man in black, hiding in the shadows of the dingy, dusty apartment, made himself known, stepping into the dim light and extending his hand, a large, shimmering knife wielded in one hand, his cold, dark eyes peering from beneath his wool facemask at James.

James stood motionless, staring at the man who had just appeared in the corner. "What do you want?" James asked finally, his voice shaking. "I have money if that's what you're looking for."

The intruder smiled eerily, the silence in the room palpable as the two men stood facing one another, James realizing that money was not the prize this prowler was after. The man suddenly sprung from his place, darting from behind the couch and into the living area, his eyes locking on his prey as James quickly reached to the counter, grasping a long, metal spatula used for his outdoor grill. As the man neared, James stepped sideways, swinging the spatula with all his might, the jagged, serrated edge of the utensil ripping into the man's mask and cheek and striking bone, a groan escaping his mouth as his head jerked back.

The exchange, however, left James off balance and vulnerable. The intruder barreled into him, the knife sinking into his left side, a searing pain shooting up from the wound. James let out a screech as he gasped for breath, dropping the spatula and grasping the man's right wrist in an effort to prevent the blade from entering further into his midsection.

The man, dizzy from the blow across his right cheek, turned his head back to James, his face contorted in a sneer as he tried to focus on his prey. The intruder stumbled away from James momentarily as Graiser raised his right arm high above his left shoulder and brought it forcefully down, connecting with the man's eye socket and sending him sprawling into the kitchen table and over a chair.

James glanced down to the blade that now protruded from his stomach and pulled, feeling the knife tear his flesh yet again as it exited his body and dropped to the floor, blood immediately beginning to ooze from the wound.

From under the table the intruder began to rise, his hand raised to his face and pressing against his eye socket that throbbed with each beat of his heart. James turned and sprinted down the hall and into a bedroom, slamming the door shut and locking it before moving to the window where the fire escape zigzagged up the building exterior.

The intruder regained his feet and retrieved the knife, wiping the blood from his brow where James had struck him. He turned and ran full-speed down the hall, lowering his shoulder just before reaching the door. From the other side, wood splintered and drywall cracked as the man flew through the opening and landed in the middle of the room, popping up and glancing around before noticing the open window.

He hurried to it and glanced down. Two stories below, the fire escape hung precariously from the brick wall, a structure that could be treacherous if a strong wind were to blow. From above he heard a *clang*, turning just in time to see James step from the platform onto the roof. He smiled to himself. It would be easy to catch James on the roof, especially with the stab wound slowing him down.

* * * * *

Hartley and Barailles pulled up to the apartment complex of James Graiser and exited the car just in time to see a panic-stricken man crawl through his window and begin his ascent to the roof, clutching his side as he weaved up the metal grated stairs.

"Barailles—" Hartley said, pointing to the man on the fire escape.

"What's going on here?" Barailles asked to no one in particular as he watched the event unfold before his eyes. The man turned and looked down, his wavy brown hair flopping in the breeze. "Hartley, that's Graiser."

Hartley raised her forearm to the sun and squinted her eyes. "James Graiser!" she yelled, causing the man to glance her way as he stepped onto the roof. James could see the glimmer of sunshine reflect off the woman's silver star and the bulge of a firearm on her hip. He did not understand what was happening at the moment, why a man had been in his apartment waiting, it seemed, to put an end to his life, nor did he comprehend why officers of the law would show up knowing his name.

James looked from the officers in the street to his window again, catching a glimpse of the intruder's hand reaching out to grab onto the brick wall, pulling himself halfway onto the fire escape. "Help me!" he shouted to the officers.

The detectives watched as the masked man emerged from the window, carrying what appeared to be a large knife stained with blood. The figure halted and glanced to the street, eyeing Hartley and her partner before turning and beginning his hike up the grated stairs.

"Let's go," Hartley said forcefully, sprinting across the lanes and onto the sidewalk, Barailles following close behind.

They burst through the front entrance and into an area resembling a hotel lobby fit with a recreation room, reception desk and a security office. The individuals jumped as Hartley and Barailles entered. "Hey!" the guard yelled as they entered the area. "Hold on a second!"

Hartley slowed as they approached, moving her jacket to the side to make her star visible. "Police," she said, glancing around. "I need to get to the roof."

"The roof?" the guard repeated, his arms out wide. "Hold on. You're—"

"Listen to me. I'm a detective. I need to know the easiest and quickest way to get onto the roof." The guard glanced from one detective to the other, remaining silent as he assessed the situation that had presented itself before him. Hartley, growing impatient, slammed her hand against the desk, sending the receptionists jumping through the air. "Now!" she yelled.

The guard nodded his head. "Okay," he replied, realizing the woman in front of him meant business. "Take the freight elevator up to twelve. When the doors open, take a right and then another right. There's a stairway that leads up to the roof. Code to unlock the exit door is 5-8-7-5." Hartley nodded and moved towards the elevators. "What's going on? Do you need my assistance?"

Hartley shook her head. "Stay where you are. Call 9-1-1 for backup." They climbed aboard the freight elevator and hit the button for the twelfth floor, riding it quickly up and entering into an empty workroom. They turned into the hall and hastily made another right, moving past a vending machine and reaching a closed door with the words *NO ACCESS* written in red. Barailles punched the code into a keypad located to the right of the handle, producing a *click* as the lock retracted and allowed them to proceed.

Hartley armed herself as Barailles pushed the door open into an alcove, the ceiling above them breaking away to blue sky as they exited. Hartley rounded the corner and advanced slowly up the steps that led to the roof, her firearm extended in front of her as she peered out across the vast building.

To her right she caught movement, glancing just in time to see the man in the mask disappear behind one of the enormous air conditioning units. She hustled onto the roof and into the open, her eyes wide as she took in her surroundings. Barailles moved after her, sweeping around to her right to cover more ground and lessen the chance their perp would flank them.

He looked to his partner for direction as Hartley stopped, her head cocked to the side, ears open as she attempted to hear over the drone of the air conditioners. The building's roof was enormous and lined with numerous obstacles and hiding places, making the detective's movements slow and riddled with caution, allowing their suspect that much more time to work out a plan of action.

The detectives moved together on opposite sides of the units, Hartley getting glimpses of her partner between the enormous machines as he inched ahead, covering more ground than she. It was only a matter of time before they would meet at the end of the air conditioners, trapping their assailant between them.

Hartley cautiously leaned in between two of the units, noticing an indentation just large enough to be used for a hiding place. She led with her service piece as she jumped in front of the alcove, finding nothing but an ancient, crumbling bird nest jammed into the corner supported by a metal rod.

To her dismay, the sudden sound of fighting from Barailles's direction rose up in the air, the groaning and grunting of two men locked in battle clearly audible to Hartley's ears as she made her way from between the units and around the structures. Hartley rounded the units hurriedly, racing to the end just in time to see Barailles ram the man into one of the machines, the knife in the assailant's hand flying through the air and landing near the building's edge. Though the blow would have dropped most men to their knees, the attacker, however, reacted quickly, wrapping his arm around Barailles's neck and reaching with his other to the gun that was held firmly in the detective's hand.

"Freeze! Police!" Hartley yelled, raising her weapon to the struggling men as Barailles faltered, sliding on the rocks that lined the base of the units. The man looked to her, holding fast to the gun in her partner's grip. Barailles had been forced to move one of his hands to the attacker's forearm in an effort to lessen the noose that was slowly cutting off his airway. "Freeze!" Hartley yelled again.

The attacker, recognizing he had achieved the upper hand with Barailles, raised the gun with the detective still attached and took aim at Hartley, pulling the trigger twice, sending her diving headfirst to her right between two of the units, narrowly missing a metal pipe that protruded from the machine. She landed with a thud on the rocks, her wind escaping her for a moment. When she finally composed herself, she was shocked to see James Graiser staring at her from under a unit, his eyes wide as sweat beaded on his forehead, his hand pressed firmly upon a wound that still seeped blood. She reached down and grabbed her silver star, holding it to the frightened man who nodded his understanding. Hartley rose quickly and peered around the corner, diving back again as another shot was released from the attacker's direction.

Barailles, his life slowly escaping him in the man's vice-like grip, quickly reached into his pocket, searching for the last weapon he had on him: Car keys. Grasping them tightly with the shafts pointing down, Barailles plunged the keys into the man's arm, releasing a guttural growl as the limb loosened, the detective falling to his knees and gasping for air. He turned slightly just in time to see a fist connect with his cheekbone, the wound immediately erupting with heat as he fell to the rooftop, his grip on the firearm going limp as stars filled his eyes.

Sirens blared from the street in front of the apartment complex as police pulled up to the curb. The assailant ripped the gun from Barailles and began towards the edge of the building, realizing that a well-timed leap could clear the small gap between the rooftop and the structure adjacent to the apartment complex, the buildings in this part of the city situated relatively close, if not sharing a wall.

The man ran at full speed and leapt through the air, arms swinging to keep balance as he soared to the building a story below, hitting the roof and rolling across his back, landing on his stomach with the firearm still held firmly in his grasp.

Hartley ran to her partner, her eyes glancing from the man moving across the neighboring building to Barailles as he rolled onto his side and pushed himself to a sitting position. "Are you all right? Barailles?"

"Yeah. Yeah, I'm fine," Barailles answered. "He's got my gun."

A uniformed officer appeared on the rooftop then, weapon in hand as he crossed to the two detectives. "You two all right?" he asked as he approached.

"Go down that way," Hartley answered, pointing to where she had seen James. "There's a man down there. Stab wound to the abdomen. Call in an ambulance." She turned her attention back to her partner who stood, looking more confident on his feet. "Barailles?" she questioned, glancing towards the man jumping to the next building.

"Go," he answered, bending to retrieve the keys the man had removed from his arm. "I'll make my way to the street. There's a shotgun in the trunk. Go!"

Hartley patted him on the shoulder before turning and sprinting after their suspect. She hit the edge at full speed and leapt into the air, soaring over the gap and landing on the building below. She somersaulted and gracefully bounced to her feet, continuing her pursuit without missing a step.

The man had proceeded to the next building and was running in the direction of a looming brick wall of the adjoining structure, obviously searching for a window or door to to hastily make an exit. "Police! Stop!" Hartley yelled, watching as the man stopped on a dime and aimed her partner's gun at her once more, firing a single shot. She slid to the ground like a ballplayer into a base, her foot banging into a concrete partition and stopping her progress. She fell to her right and aimed her weapon at the man, cursing as he moved behind an object and out of view.

Hartley rose and began her pursuit once more, wiping sweat and hair from her face as she tried to calm her breathing and nerves. The urge to track her suspect at a quicker pace pulled Hartley forward, yet her experience on the hunt forced her to be wary. Speed could sometimes be your enemy in situations like this. She had seen too many officers take a bullet thinking they could outrun and outmaneuver their suspect.

The crash of a window ahead on the next rooftop moved her along, affording her the general vicinity in which her suspect resided as well as the space to work more freely. Ahead she could see that the man had indeed found the exit he had been searching for: A hallway window of a hotel eleven stories above ground.

Hartley cleared the second gap and veered away from the window, yet her eyes remained fixed on it. She moved to the front of the building and peered over the side to the street below, watching as Barailles stepped away from the trunk of the cruiser towards the building she had just jumped from. "Hey!" she yelled. "Tony!" He looked up and scanned the rooftops, locating his partner as she pointed to the hotel adjacent to her. He nodded his understanding and crossed the street as another marked squad car pulled up, the officers exiting and stopping before the detective.

Hartley turned her attention back towards the window, raising her gun to the opening as she made her way to it, expecting any second for the masked man to appear with his weapon raised. It did not occur, fortunately, and Hartley proceeded through, eyes sharp and scanning her surroundings. Several patrons of the hotel had congregated in the hall after hearing the crash and now stared wide-eyed at the woman making her way from the broken windowpane. "Police," Hartley said. "Anyone see a man come in here?"

"Down the stairwell," someone yelled. Hartley moved to the stairway door and opened it quickly, her firearm at the ready. From below she heard frantic footsteps descending, running at full speed down the concrete steps towards the ground. Hartley took off after him, clearing three, sometimes four stairs at a time, her weapon still gripped in her right hand as she flew after her suspect.

Barailles and two officers appeared in the hotel lobby, guns drawn as they moved across the highly polished marble floor to the check-in desk. The concierge stepped back as the officers approached. "Chicago PD," Barailles said, flashing his badge. "There's a suspect that just entered the building from the adjoining roof. Get all of the patrons out of the lobby area right now and into secure rooms." He turned towards the officers. "I need one of you with me and the other to stay put down here. Keep everyone out of the lobby."

Barailles and the officer moved to the stairwell, opening the door quickly and raising their weapons. They stood still, listening as footfalls descended quickly above them, Barailles nodding to the officer to begin the careful hike skyward, staying near the walls for a better vantage point.

They made their way to a platform two floors up and stood their ground, guns aimed high as the sounds of shoes slapping onto concrete grew more pronounced. When the sounds were descending the level next to them Barailles shouted out, "Police! Stop where you are!" From their right, on the level directly facing them, Hartley slid into view, falling onto the ground as she tried to stop herself from launching down the steps.

Barailles lowered his weapon and stared at her. "Hartley?"

"Shit!" she responded. "Did you see him?"

"No. Must be on one of the floors."

Hartley stood and leaned into the wall, catching her breath. "We need to get down to street level," she said between gasps.

"Anderson is down there," the officer chimed in. "He's got the lobby covered."

* * * * *

Officer Joshua Anderson walked the lobby, thumbs hooked into his belt as he ran his eyes across the interior of the building. The place was nice, with aged tapestries hanging from the walls directly next to new-wave paintings that no doubt made their hip creators plenty of money. The walls were a crisp off-white, framed by the caramel color of the highly stained wooden border. A chandelier of crystal hung from the direct middle of the lobby ceiling, spanning at least twelve feet across and lined with soft, white orbs of light.

The officer leveled his head just in time to see a masked man approach from his left, extending a pistol to his face and pressing it into his mouth, the hard barrel grinding against his teeth. The man continued forward, pushing the officer towards the revolving doors, the uniform's hands sticking out in surrender. From behind the counter the receptionist noticed the occurrence and yelled out. "Stop!"

The assailant turned momentarily to the counter, just enough time for the officer to reach up towards the gun pressed between his teeth. He managed to remove the firearm, however, the man turned to the side and stuck the officer with the butt of the pistol, sending him sliding along the beautiful marble floors in an unconscious heap.

The clang of the stairway door sent the man flying out of the building as the detectives and uniforms entered the lobby. "Stay with him!" Hartley yelled to the officer, pointing to his partner that lay motionless on the floor.

The detectives raced through the door and followed into traffic, releasing a series of screeching tires and blaring horns as they weaved in and out of the passing cars. Ahead Hartley could see the man running in the direction of an alley, knocking into people as he proceeded down the sidewalk to the left and disappeared.

Hartley and Barailles followed, entering the alleyway with their weapons high, realizing that they had, unfortunately, walked into an open area with little to no immediate areas to take cover. They were instantly aware of the masked man positioned to their right about twenty yards ahead, strategically placed in the threshold of a warehouse door with the gun raised and aimed at them.

Hartley dove to the ground as the shots rang out, sliding through a puddle of what looked and smelled like used fryer grease, slamming into the brick wall behind a dumpster.

Barailles was not so lucky.

As the shots exited the pistol, Barailles was positioned where he could not escape, a spot that yielded no easy dive behind a dumpster through a river of oozing grease and garbage. He turned just in time to feel a bullet enter into his right shoulder, followed closely by another just below in his arm. The impacts spun Barailles back towards the shooter as another bullet pierced his thigh. Barailles let out a cry as he collapsed to the ground.

"Tony!" Hartley yelled, panic and anger filling her being. She turned into the alleyway again, gun raised as she fired several shots towards the doorway, realizing as she did that the man was no longer there, leaving in his wake an opened entranceway into a darkened abyss.

Hartley ran to her partner and knelt beside him. "Tony!" she exclaimed again, her eyes toggling between the doorway and her stricken partner.

He rolled in agony, yet gathered enough composure to answer her. "Shit, that hurts!" he said.

Hartley reached down and grabbed his radio, pressing down the button and bringing it to her mouth. "Officer down! Repeat, officer down! Need assistance across from the Berkshire Hotel North next to DioGiovanni's Restaurant!" She lowered the radio and looked to the street as an officer with gun drawn hastily made his way to them. "Stay here and keep an eye at that door," she said as he approached.

She moved into the threshold with her gun raised, stopping near the door to allow her eyes to adjust to the darkness. Inside, the room opened to a space roughly half the size of a football field with machinery sitting idle in the dusty gloom, light barely penetrating the tinted windows lining the walls near the ceiling. Hartley stepped in, immediately glancing down to the floor where she saw fresh footprints in the dust and grime.

She followed the trail leading straight between several of the enormous machines towards an open door on the opposite side of the warehouse. Light streaked from the adjoining room as Hartley made out the fresh footprints in front of the doorway. She moved swiftly towards them.

From her right, out of the darkness between two mechanical structures, a hollow metal rod swung at her, striking Hartley in the midsection and sending the detective collapsing to the ground gasping for breath, her gun dropping from her hand and sliding across the floor. She pressed her face to the cool, dusty concrete, her arms wrapped around her waist as she tried to gather air, eyes focusing on the firearm out of reach to her left.

She was suddenly lifted to her knees as the man firmly grasped onto her dark locks. The cold metal of a gun pressed to her cheekbone, running down the side of her face and resting directly under her jaw. She bit down hard, tears forming in her eyes as she realized that her life might be cut short, her breath coming easier now as her heart pumped furiously.

The man squatted, his chest brushing against her back as he placed his mouth near the detective's ear. "You're persistent," he said. Hartley remained quiet, a tear streaking down her dust-covered face like a tiny, filthy avalanche. "Why are you following me?" Hartley clenched her jaw, keeping her mouth shut. The man jerked his hand back, pulling Hartley's head towards him with a snap, a movement that caused a moan to fly from the detective's lips. "Why are you following me?" he repeated.

"You shot at me," Hartley responded hoarsely, her breath returning to her ever so slightly.

"I shot at you after you showed up on the roof. Why were you there?"

"None of your business," Hartley said, forcing her emotions behind her police façade.

The man violently yanked Hartley's hair towards the ground, spinning her head and shoulders to him as she landed face up on the concrete. He extended her arms above her head, pain shooting throughout her midsection as he grabbed her wrists with his free hand, resting the gun on her cheek. She looked to the man's masked face, taking in the dark, calm eyes as well as the gash from the metal spatula.

He bent lower and gazed upon her, taking in her beauty through the dim lights. He released her hands yet kept the gun aimed at her head. "You know, I expected your partner to put up more of a fight. But I see you're the one I should be worried about." From outside in the alley the sound of voices erupted as a unit of officers gathered to mount a search for their missing comrade. The attacker calmly moved the barrel of the gun to the opposite side of her face, raising his finger from the trigger and running it across her forehead and down her cheek, grazing her jaw line and making his way down her neck. "You're a beautiful woman, Detective. I'd hate to have to do something to you to get my answers. It's not my style." His finger stopped near her throat. "Why were you there?"

"Look," she pleaded, tears streaming from the corners of her eyes, creating valleys through the dust caked to her. "I'm a homicide detective. I don't know you. I don't give a fuck about you. I work homicides. I had something that led me to the hotel, not you—"

"You're lying!" the man growled, setting the barrel of the gun under her chin.

"Please," Hartley said, clenching her eyes shut. "Please, no."

"How do you know James Graiser? Why were you there?"

"I wasn't there for you," she said between sobs. "Please, I'm a homicide detective. I am looking into a murder from a couple days ago. Not you. Not you. Please."

The man remained quiet for a minute then continued, the amusement lacing his words. "Are you investigating the kid on the overpass, Detective?" Hartley opened her eyes and stared up in disbelief through her tears, wondering if she had dreamed what had just been said. "Yeah, you are," he continued. "Then you've found your guy." He pressed the gun harder into her chin, forcing her neck to arch.

"Please," she squeaked out, her eyes closing again as she awaited her fate. The man glanced up as the voices began to filter through the warehouse, bouncing and arching over the machinery as they grew closer.

Her assailant turned back towards Hartley and smiled, bending closer and whispering in her ear, "If I wanted you dead, you'd be just that. Killing cops isn't my thing. But next time you get in my way …" He paused momentarily for effect before adding, "Goodnight, Detective." He leaned up and, raising the gun high, brought it crashing down onto her head just over her right temple. He stood and moved through the door, losing the mask and pulling a hat from this back pocket as he exited onto the street, loosing himself in the city as the police made their way into the room.

As Hartley faded to darkness, the man's voice echoed in her head. *You've found your guy. You've found your guy. You've found your guy.* The phrase was repeated over and over, the words swirling in the recesses of her mind, fading into the darkness that now consumed her as she tried to focus on the flashlights working their way towards her.

TWENTY-TWO

Hazy lights intertwined with a blood-soaked black mask. The mumblings of voices clashed with the crispness of a man seeming to say her name aloud, yet inaudibly. Her head felt extremely heavy, her mind confused, the sensations of cold and warm, dry and wet, all combining and mystifying her senses and leaving her in disarray.

She slowly opened her eyes and pushed herself to her knees, her arms stretched out to the floor beneath her, her head tilted up in the direction of the lights flashing intermittently in her direction, bouncing from her face to the concrete and back again, like a cruel, tempting strobe light. She felt a warm liquid pass over her lips, drenching the tip of her tongue as she tried unsuccessfully to force saliva forward to spit.

She pushed up from the floor, placing one foot underneath her, instantly losing balance and crashing to the dust, rolling on her side again, an arm extended towards the oncoming lights. "Help—me," she whispered, lying still and falling back into the limbo she had just escaped from.

* * * * *

She sat outdoors on a bench that was in desperate need of a paint job, a drab green chipping away to red that had not seen daylight in a dozen years. She looked around at her surroundings trying to gauge her location. Jolene reached up to her head, feeling the temple where her attacker had pistol-whipped her, amazed that the pressure she put on it now brought no pain whatsoever. She lowered her hand, staring at her fingers stained red with blood from the wound. The dust caked to her face was gone, though residue still clung to her clothes. Her hair was down, flowing to her shoulders as she looked to her left.

A ways down, she could see a bus turning onto the street that lay before her, moving slowly in the calm, early morning sun. To her right sprawled a dingy neighborhood, empty save for a few men walking the alleyways. She glanced down at the bench, realizing she had somehow transported herself to a sitting position on its backrest, her feet planted firmly on the seat. Leaning back she felt the intertwined meshing of a metal chainlink fence brush up her back. Her eyes opened suddenly. Jolene stared into the blue sky above, running her fingertips along the bench's chipped wooden surface before stepping off to her right and turning. She stared through the metal fencing, her eyes peering to the Dan Ryan Expressway below. Cars and trucks were absent from the concrete, yet, near the shoulder, she could make out the backhoe.

Jolene strained her eyes, raising her arm to block out the sun as she stared down to the machine, making out a man in a black mask aiming what appeared to be a long-range military rifle at her. He raised his head and smiled, the voice echoing through her mind as if he were next to her. "Goodnight, Detective." With that he pulled the trigger, sending a bullet speeding through the air towards her, passing through the chain link fence and impacting under her right eye, burrowing into her brain and exiting her skull as it propelled her backwards into the street.

She lay motionless, staring down the pavement at the headlights of the approaching bus speeding towards her, oblivious she was in the way.

Goodnight, Detective, she heard as the headlight reached her body, the glow filling her sight and encompassing her soul. *Goodnight, Detective.*

* * * * *

Hartley jolted upright, grabbing onto anything she could. She teetered on the cement, reaching for her firearm as she looked around. "Detective," a man from her left said. "You're okay now. We're here." She looked up at him, realizing it was the officer that had accompanied Barailles—

"Barailles," Hartley said aloud.

"En route to the hospital, Detective," the officer responded.

"The man—" she said, letting the phrase hang in the air as she reached up to her forehead, shocked to find another hand holding a piece of gauze to her temple. She turned to her right and realized the warehouse was filled with police and paramedics, all of whom now stood either glancing at the detective sitting on the ground or investigating the area around her.

"Did you hear me, ma'am?" the officer asked from her left. She turned towards him again. "What? No. I—"

"The man that assaulted you is gone." Hartley gazed to the door where her attacker had fled. On the ground, yards away, she saw the metal rod that had been used to subdue her and, underneath the corner of a machine, her firearm. She pointed towards it and the officer turned his head. "That one yours?"

"Get me up," she said to the paramedic holding the gauze. He helped her to her feet as Hartley reached for her gun, clicking the safety on before placing it in her holster.

The officer escorted Hartley out of the building and into the alley, sitting her on a rickety crate near the back of an ambulance, a throng of people gathering and staring at the wounded officer holding a blood-soaked bandage to her brow.

"How are you feeling, Detective?" came a voice to her right. She looked up to see an older man wearing blue latex gloves approaching. "I'm Eric. I need to look at you real quick," he said as he lifted her chin skyward, removing the gauze from her forehead. "You have a large cut here that will require stitches. I'm going to patch you up real fast and we can get to the hospital. Is there anything else that is hurting you?"

Hartley grimaced as he dabbed her wound with an antibacterial pad, the sting reaching down into her cheek and spreading across her head. She pointed to where the metal rod had connected. "I—" she began, freezing as an intense twinge traveled up her side.

"Okay," Eric said, glancing down. "I'll take a look at that." He placed a fresh bandage across her forehead and held it in place with several pieces of white medical tape, looking between the crowd and his patient. "Hey, why don't we move you to the back of the ambulance? No need to have an examination in front of a hundred strangers, right?"

She smiled as he helped her to the ambulance, resting the detective against the back end of the vehicle, the doors opened wide to block any onlookers. "Okay, I need to lift your shirt a little bit." Hartley looked at him and nodded, raising her arms up, her face contorting as the pain shot up her side again. "You definitely have some bruising going on here," he said as he placed his fingers on her skin, pressing gently against the discolored area. After a moment he removed his hand and lowered her shirt. "We'll need an x-ray when we get to the hospital. I don't think you have any broken ribs but we better be sure."

"My partner," Hartley said, her breathing slightly labored. "Is he—?"

The medical technician looked at her. "He's stable. Another ambulance is on the way to the hospital with him. He'll need surgery to remove one of the bullets. It was lodged in his upper chest," the man explained, pointing to where his shoulder and torso met. "He should be fine."

"What about the guy on the roof? Had a stab wound—"

"Taken to the same hospital," he interrupted. "Don't know if he's going to need surgery or not." Hartley reached up to the bandage and groaned. "Listen," the man replied, "why don't we get you in here and laying down. I can give you something for the pain. We'll head to the hospital where your partner is and get you fixed up."

Hartley nodded her agreement as he approached her, grabbing her arm and helping her into the back of the ambulance. She laid down on the gurney and closed her eyes, reflecting on the total misfortune that had befallen her and Barailles, the paramedic closing the doors and moving around to the front, seating himself behind the steering wheel as he rolled down the window. "Frankie," he shouted. "I'm taking the female detective to get stitched up. You catch a ride with—" he paused as someone outside yelled back. "Okay," he said, putting the vehicle into drive and flipping the siren on. He turned back to Hartley. "We'll be there in a couple minutes, Detective. Just try and relax."

* * * * *

"Well, those ribs of yours aren't broken," said a doctor as he lowered the x-ray and turned to Hartley who was seated on the exam table. "Just bruised. And let me see that stitch work." He walked over and stood in front of her, reaching up to remove the bandage and taking a long, hard look at the stitches that had been put in. "That looks nice," he said, pressing the bandage gently back into place. "It'll heal good. Probably not even a scar."

"Thanks, Doctor," Hartley said. "Detective Anthony Barailles, do you know where he's at?"

"Yes," the doctor responded. "He's in surgery right now. Should be a while. He's stable, but they need to get that bullet out."

Hartley nodded. "Another man came in, too. James Graiser?"

"Yes, Mr. Graiser. He also required surgery. The blade wound sliced into some of his intestines. He'll be out later today. In the meantime, why don't we get you checked into a room so we can monitor—"

"Thank you, but no," Hartley said, sliding gingerly from the exam table. "I need to get back to the station."

"Detective," the doctor pleaded, "I highly recommend you stay for a while. You took quite a shot to the head. I need to make sure you don't have a concussion."

"I need to check in on some things," Hartley responded. "Call me when either Detective Barailles or Mr. Graiser is out of surgery."

Hartley exited the room and made her way to the front of the emergency waiting area, halting by the doors as she glanced around. "Hey, Officer," she yelled to a uniform standing near the reception desk. He glanced her way as she flashed her badge and began towards her. "Are you heading back to the station any time soon?"

"Just about to leave right now, Detective. You need a lift?" he asked.

"Please, if you don't mind."

"Not at all. Let's go." He turned to the receptionist and waved. "See you later, Tracey. Have a good one."

They exited the hospital and made their way to a marked squad car in the adjoining lot, Hartley's expression tightening as she slid into the passenger seat. "You mind me asking what happened?" the officer asked as they pulled away from the building, moving into traffic as he weaved his way in the direction of the precinct.

Hartley remained quiet, staring out the passenger window as she bit down on her thumbnail. She glanced forward, shaking her head ever so softly, the officer nodding his understanding as her eyes filled with tears. "Maybe just some music then," he said as he flipped on the radio, the sound of smooth, calming jazz escaping from the speakers. Hartley turned back towards the window, leaning her head against the headrest as the city streaked by to her right.

TWENTY-THREE

The officer dropped Hartley at the front of the station, offering his assistance to help her up the steps with the least amount of pain possible. Hartley declined, thanking the uniform as she shut the door, biting her lip and grabbing onto a street sign when the movement almost caused her to collapse in agony. The doctor had told her the ribs were not broken, yet the pain spreading through her midsection just under her breasts made her question that assessment.

She made it up the steps, resting against the outer wall as she withdrew her phone and dialed the person she needed most to assist her once in the building. "Jo," Kim Banneau answered. "Oh my God, are you all right? I heard what happened. How is Barailles doing?"

"He's in surgery now. I'm okay," she answered, turning away from a group of officers glancing her way as they descended the precinct steps.

"You don't sound okay. Where are you?"

"I need you to come outside—"

"You're here?" she asked, a hint of surprise in her voice. "Jo, babe, you need to get to the hospital—"

"Kim, please," Hartley interrupted. "I'm fine. I just need your help."

"Sure. Sure, Jo. Anything. I'll be right down."

"Kim," Hartley said hurriedly.

"Yeah?"

"Bring an elastic bandage."

* * * * *

Banneau helped Hartley through the doorway of the women's locker room located on the far end of the workout area, eyeing several rookies dressing for their evening on patrol. "Go on, you guys," she said, walking towards them with her arms wide as if she were corralling cattle, Hartley leaning against the lockers a dozen feet away with her back to them. "Give us some privacy."

The rookies moved to the exit, peeking over their shoulders as Banneau followed, making sure they indeed left the premises. "Is that Detective Hartley?" one of the women asked as they walked through the doorway. "Is she okay?"

"Fine," Banneau answered. "Rough day on a case." The women left the area and Banneau turned back towards her friend, walking briskly and stopping at her side, eyeing the bandage across the right side of her forehead that was tinged red with blood. Hartley stared ahead at the lockers, her eyes glassy as she tried to once again contain her emotions. Banneau recognized the inner battle raging inside Hartley and took the initiative. "Okay," she began, reaching down and ripping open the elastic bandage. "What do I need to do with this?"

Hartley cleared her throat and answered, "Help me take off my shirt." Banneau reached down and grasped onto her top, sliding it up her back as Hartley began to pull her arm from one sleeve. When she had completed the task, Banneau gingerly spun Hartley towards her, pulling her other arm free and lifting the shirt up.

"Jesus, Jo!" Banneau exclaimed as Hartley's bruising came into view. "What exactly happened?"

"He hit me with a metal pipe," Hartley answered.

"We really need to get you to the hospital—"

"I was already there."

"Well, you should have stayed," Banneau answered as she looked into Hartley's eyes. Tears formed quickly and began to stream down her face, falling off her chin and plummeting to the ground. Banneau moved to her and ever so gently wrapped her arms around her friend, Hartley's arms folding to her own body as she buried her face into Banneau's shoulder.

"He had Barailles's gun pressed to my head," she said between sobs, Banneau running her hand over Hartley's hair as she let her friend release her pent-up emotions. "I thought that was it."

"It wasn't," Banneau answered firmly. "You're still here. And you're going to continue to be here and you're going to get whoever did this to you."

Hartley lifted her head and looked Banneau in the eyes. "Kim, it was him."

Banneau's face contorted at the statement. "Him who?" she asked, her eyes going wide as she began to comprehend. "The guy from your case? The killer?"

Hartley nodded her head. "Yeah," she answered. "He told me I had found the right guy."

"Did you get a good look at him?"

Hartley shook her head. "Had a mask on."

Banneau nodded, her gazing remaining fixed on Hartley. "How did all this happen?" Hartley reached her hands up to wipe the tears from her cheeks, the action sending a new, fiery jolt of pain into her torso, a searing sting that doubled her over, causing her to lean into the lockers. Banneau reached out and steadied her. "You know what, babe?" she said, shifting her friend from the lockers to a standing position. "Why don't we get you fixed up before we talk some more?" Hartley nodded, unable to form words.

Banneau unwrapped the bandage and looked back to Hartley whose eyes were firmly locked on hers, arms together in front of her as if she were trying to hide her injury. "I need you to raise your arms," Banneau said. "It's going to hurt, but I'll be quick." Hartley nodded as she stepped away from the lockers. Banneau approached and opened two doors at shoulder level, creating a spot where Hartley could grab onto and rest her arms as Banneau wrapped the elastic bandage around her torso. "Ready?" Banneau asked.

Hartley took a deep breath and nodded. "Okay," she said, lifting her arms straight in front of her. Her eyes immediately became glassy and tears ran freely once again down her cheeks. She let escape a high-pitched groan before clenching her teeth and staring fixedly at the locker before her. The pain was excruciating, yet she was determined to not let it get the best of her.

Once in position, Banneau began to wrap the elastic bandage around Hartley's ribcage, creating a tubular restraint that resembled a woman's girdle, the pressure of the loops around her body releasing some of the pain from her muscles and allowing her breathing to come easier.

Banneau assisted her with putting on her shirt, taking position against the lockers once they finished, Hartley breathing deeply as she wiped away the tears for what felt like the hundredth time today, a pain creeping into her ribcage once more though not as intense as before.

"Thank you," Hartley said as she looked up to Banneau, smiling.

Banneau grinned back. "I've got something for you," she answered, walking across the room to her own locker and retrieving from her purse a pillbox. She walked back to Hartley and handed her the metal container. "I've had these since my ankle surgery months ago."

"What are they?" Hartley asked, opening the container and glancing down at large, white pills.

"Painkillers," Banneau responded quickly as Hartley cocked her head to the side. "With the amount of pain you're in now, that bandage will only help so much."

"I can't take these," Hartley responded. "I need to be able to think."

"Babe, you won't be able to think with the hurt that's going to come."

"I don't want them."

Banneau looked to her friend and smirked. "Fine," she said, stepping forward and onto the bench that separated the two. She held out her hand at waist level and looked to Hartley. "If you don't want them, hand them to me." Hartley looked to her friend's hand, lifting the container towards Banneau and falling back into the lockers as a jolting pain shot through her battered body, the pillbox clattering to the floor in a noisy clang from just above her waist.

Banneau stepped down from the bench and retrieved the container from the floor, opening it up and setting a pill in Hartley's palm. "See," she said. "What happens if you have to raise a gun? You won't be able to. Take it." Hartley looked down at the pill and nodded, raising her hand to her mouth as she popped the white tablet onto her tongue. Banneau walked to her locker once more and grabbed a bottle of water, bringing it to her friend and unscrewing the cap. Hartley swallowed the pill and handed the water back to Banneau. "I know you want to head upstairs, but you need to go home and rest."

Hartley shook her head. "I can't. I need to look into this case—"

"No," Banneau interrupted. Hartley looked to her questioningly as Banneau turned. "Look," she began, "you're Super Woman. Everyone knows it. Every rookie cop wants to be the next Jolene Hartley. But you need to rest. You need to go home and get better. And I can't be doing my job if I'm wondering if you are getting killed out there because you can't protect yourself. Now, if you are my friend and you respect my opinion, then do what I say. Go home."

Hartley remained focused on her friend, knowing in her heart that Banneau was right and she needed to tend to her wounds. She nodded her head and began walking again, Banneau stepping in line next to her as she pulled out her cell phone. "Hey, Ronny," Banneau said into the mouthpiece, Hartley looking up to her quickly as she spoke. "Meet me out front. Hartley needs a ride home. You guys can take my car. Okay. See you out there."

She hung up and slid the phone into her front pocket, glancing sideways at her friend and smirking. "What, you think I didn't notice that your boy was in town?"

"Well, I—" Hartley stumbled on her words.

"You know, this is the type of gossip that us chicks love. Maybe next time a sexy FBI agent comes into your life for night after night of intense, passionate sex, you can fill me in?" Hartley smiled, reaching out to her friend and squeezing her arm, loving the fact that Kimberly Banneau knew exactly how to brighten her spirits in an otherwise dismal, gray day.

TWENTY-FOUR

Jolene's nearly empty stomache was not exactly the best basis for pain medication, yet she knew there was not much she could do. She needed the relief that the drug gave her. It took less than ten minutes for her head to begin swimming in a groggy, slow motion haze and her extremities to start tingling as if they were commencing their exodus from the rest of her body. Kim Banneau sat with her friend outside the precinct on the bus stop bench, waiting for Ronny to bring the car around. She kept an eye on her wobbly friend, unable to determine at times if she had fallen asleep or just had her eyes closed in concentration.

Jolene was not used to the heavily sedated feeling that now encompassed her. Her only experience with medication of this caliber had been from her youth when she had had her wisdom teeth removed, a feeling, she recalled, that remained unpleasant for several days.

The ride home was uneventful, the conversation between her and Debarsi limited. She peered out the passenger window, her eyes unsuccessful at focusing on anything passing by the car. Debarsi made sure to ask how she was doing from time to time, genuinely worried about her state as he had learned from a fellow detective of the events of the day, of how Jolene Hartley, the woman he cared so much about, had been assaulted and left with bruised ribs and a gash from the butt of a pistol.

Jolene did not speak of the event in the car ride to her apartment, nor did Ronny ask. His goal was to just be there for her.

* * * * *

Jolene awoke hours later in her bed clothed in a sweatshirt and a pair of gray, cotton sweatpants. She leaned up, feeling woozy, yet fully aware of the events that had transpired up to the car ride home, losing all remembrances of entering her apartment and changing into her clothes.

She moved slowly from under the covers, cringing slightly as a dull pain crept into her abdomen. The alarm clock read 2:16 a.m. as she stood and made her way into the dark hallway. Below, the kitchen glowed in the light of the television, a sign that Ronny was still there keeping vigil over her in her time of need. Jolene made her way down the steps and entered the kitchen, pausing at the counter to take note of the pad of yellow paper with Ronny's pen scribbled on the surface. *6:20 p.m. – Graiser and Det. B out of surgery. Tony will be kept at least for several days. Graiser to be released tomorrow morning.*

Jolene glanced towards the couch. There would be no way she would convince Ronny to escort her to the hospital, not at that hour and in her current condition. She weighed her options, debating on her urge to go and meet with her partner and James Graiser or to return to the warmth of her fluffy bed. She scanned the kitchen and caught a glimpse of the metal container Kim had given her early in the day, making her decision as she reached out and grabbed it. She headed back up the steps and into the bedroom, searching a pile of clothes for a relatively clean pair of jeans and a sweatshirt. Jolene turned to her dresser and retrieved some bills for the cab ride to the hospital before placing her finger on the scanner of the lockbox and pulling out her firearm. She snapped her silver star to her hip and holstered the gun, leaving the comfort of the bedroom with a flick of the lightswitch.

* * * * *

Hartley entered the hospital doors and walked to the reception desk, flashing her badge to the young woman behind the computer monitor. "Good morning," the woman said cheerily. "Working late, or getting up early?" She was a young girl, no more than twenty years old, with fair skin and straight, shiny red hair. Her smile was a breath of fresh air and Hartley understood completely why she had been placed at the desk. Had she been in the hotel business, there was no doubt in the detective's mind that this young lady would be a superb concierge.

"Who knows," Hartley responded. "I'm looking for Detective Anthony Barailles's room."

The woman put her fingers to the keyboard and searched. "Yes, Detective Barailles. He's in room three-oh-one. Elevators—" Hartley pointed to her right. "Yep," the woman said. "Up to three and make a left." Hartley waved her thanks and moved into a hallway, weaving her way through the hospital wing until she reached the elevators. She waited as the lifts descended, her head beginning to pound and her breathing causing some pain in her mid section. She reached into her pocket and retrieved the painkillers, removing one and setting it on her tongue. She turned and crossed the hall to a water fountain, taking a long sip and downing the liquid and pill.

Hartley rode the elevator to the third floor and made the left into the hallway, flashing her badge at several of the nurses stationed across from room three-oh-one as she turned the handle and entered.

Tears immediately welled in her eyes as she made her way to the bed where her wounded partner lay, his arm in a sling across his chest, an oxygen tube dangling under his nose. Hartley sat on the bed near his good arm and grabbed his hand, weeping quietly with her head down. She could not help but feel responsible for the position Barailles was in, hooked up to wires and oxygen without the use of his right arm. She knew he was a veteran officer with years of field experience under his belt, yet she was also the one assigned to watch his back, to assist him in every situation to avoid being in this exact spot.

"Hey," a deep, grumbling voice said, waking her from her thoughts. She looked up to see him staring at her.

"Hey," she answered, sliding closer and pulling his hand into both of hers, tears making her eyes glassy. "How are you feeling?"

"Been better. Can't feel much, they've got me so numb."

"Well, that's good." She smiled and raised a hand to wipe away the tears.

"How are you? They told me what happened."

Hartley shrugged. "I'll survive," she answered.

"Your bandage is bleeding a little bit," he replied, glancing to her forehead.

She reached up and touched the fabric, rubbing a small amount of blood between her fingers as she lowered her hand. "Yeah. He, uh—He got me good. With your gun, too."

"I'm sorry, Jo," he said. "I'm sorry I wasn't there—"

"Don't be. You had your own things to worry about."

"Yeah. Like not dying." They both laughed lightly, Hartley looking from him to the door and back. "They said that Graiser made it too. Have you seen him yet?"

Hartley shook her head. "I was going to go see him after you."

Barailles smiled. "Well, at least I'm first on your list right now," he said.

Hartley lowered her eyes and squeezed his hand, realizing had it not been for the painkiller kicking in she would have become flustered at the comment. Instead, she looked back to him and smiled. "Tony, the guy who shot you is Ochoa's killer." Barailles cocked his head slightly and continued to gaze at her. "He told me straight out. He had your gun pressed to my chin and wanted to know why we were there for him. I told him we weren't there for him and that we were investigating a murder that happened days ago that had something to do with James Graiser. He knew who I was talking about. He knew I was referring to Ochoa. Told me that I had found my guy." She paused and stared into Barailles's eyes. "We almost had him."

"What was he doing at Graiser's?"

Hartley shrugged, wincing as the movement sent a sting down her sides. "I don't know. But the only way Graiser is connected to Ochoa is through the Daniel Vincent murder. There's definitely something there, and my guess is that the man who shot you and killed Ochoa is the same man that killed Gomez and Vincent."

"What proof do we have?"

"None. Yet. I'm hoping this Graiser can help with that."

The door to the room opened then and a woman stepped into the threshold. Hartley turned and set her eyes on Cynthia Barailles, the short, attractive wife of her partner, a woman who, despite knowing what being a homicide detective included, despised the job and the relationship between her husband and Jolene.

Hartley forced a smile and turned towards Barailles. "I'll leave you two alone," she said, squeezing his hand as she stood. "I'll talk to you later today. Fill you in on what I find out from Graiser."

"Okay," he said as she moved from the bed towards the exit, nodding her head in greetings to Cynthia as she passed through the door and closed it.

She stepped to the nurse's station and waited, leaning her body against the counter and ever so gently pressing against her ribs. There was definitely a sensation of pain, yet the medication had taken the sting away and a sense of comfort from the pressure invaded her body. "May I help you?" a nurse asked as she approached.

Hartley slowly raised her head up and looked at the woman, a stout, round lady in her mid-fifties with disheveled, curly hair and bowed legs. "Yes, sorry. I'm looking for a James Graiser. He came in earlier this afternoon right around the time Detective Barailles came in." She pointed behind her towards her partner's room, her arm unsteadily waving in the air as if she were conducting an orchestra.

"James Graiser," the nurse repeated as she flipped through a chart. "He's up on five. Five-sixteen. Just head up the stairs here and once you're on the fifth floor, turn right."

"Thank you," Hartley said, moving off towards the stairs. She made her way to the fifth floor and walked up to a nurse crossing from room to room. "Excuse me," she said, the nurse turning to her with a smile. "James Graiser? What room is he in?"

"Graiser. Graiser," she repeated as she walked back to the nurse's station and reached for a chart. "Cute kid," she said with a smile and a coy look to Hartley. "Had several of these younger gals actually doing some work when they had to visit his room." Hartley nodded her head, unsure of what to say. "James Graiser. He's gone," she said matter-of-factly, lowering the chart and turning away from Hartley to take a seat behind the computer screen.

Hartley looked at her in disbelief, not sure she had actually heard the nurse's word correctly or her sedated mind had conjured them out of thin air. "I'm sorry," Hartley said. "Where is he again?"

"Gone," the nurse replied, her attention still on the monitor. "Checked out a couple hours after he woke up from surgery. Says here it was against the surgeon's advice. But yeah, he's gone."

Hartley lowered her head, glancing at the countertop. "Who was on duty when he was here? What nurse?"

"I was," came the reply from behind her. Hartley turned as an attractive blonde approached from down the hall, squeezing past the detective and into the station, taking a seat next to the other woman. "I'm assuming you're talking about that Graiser guy?"

"Yeah," Hartley responded. "Why did he leave?"

The nurse shrugged. "No idea. He came to and hung around for a little while, then once he got his bearings he took off."

"Did he say where he was going to?"

"Nope," she said as she tapped the other nurse's shoulder. "Kind of pissed. He was a pretty good-looking guy. Thought he'd say bye, at least." The nurses laughed together, quieting after a moment as the detective continued to stare at them with a grave expression. "I told the same stuff to the other officer that came up here looking for him. You guys don't really talk much do you?"

"There's a lot of us—" Hartley paused, her eyebrows furrowing as she walked closer to the blonde nurse. "Did you happen to get a name from the officer?"

The girl shook her head. "Usually we don't ask since we can just see the name tag, but this officer was in plain clothes. Must have been involved in a scuffle or something."

"Wait," Hartley said, raising a finger. "He was injured?"

"Yeah," the nurse answered.

"Are you talking about the detective down on three? Anthony Barailles?"

"I don't know. I haven't been on three all day. Did this guy—"

"Detective Barailles."

"Right. Did he have a gash across his cheek? Like he had been sliced with a knife?"

Hartley felt her arms and legs tingle as her adrenaline began to pump, the jolt starting a battle with the medication she had taken for her pain. "Give me your phone," she said, reaching across the counter.

"What?" the nurse asked, suddenly nervous.

"That wasn't a cop," Hartley explained. "Give me the phone." The nurse handed the receiver to her and placed the base on the counter. "This guy. What did he look like?"

"I don't know," the nurse said, arms raised as she tried to recall earlier in the day. "Blond hair. Long. Pulled back in a ponytail. I remember thinking to myself that I'd never seen a cop with long hair before."

Hartley began to dial in a number. "And he had a cut on his right cheek?"

"Correct."

"Anything else? Anything that stood out?"

"Besides the gash on his cheek—" The nurse thought for a moment, shaking her head as she continued. "He had some sort of tattoo on his neck. I didn't get a good look at it because his hair was covering it."

Hartley looked up at the nurse, focusing on her eyes as she fought off the fogginess from the medication. "Why would you notice a half covered tattoo?"

The nurse shrugged, turning her head and lifting her own ponytail high, revealing a tattoo of a black star just below her hairline. "When you get a tattoo you just kind of start noticing other people's." She dropped her hair and turned back to the detective. "Just something I saw when he turned his head. Just couldn't make it out."

Hartley nodded. "How do I get an outside line?"

"Dial nine and star," replied the other nurse.

"Thank you," Hartley responded, dialing the series of numbers followed by the line to the precinct. "Captain," Hartley said as her boss answered. She remained silent as the man on the other line talked. "I'm okay. I'm at the hospital. Listen, the guy we went to talk to today, James Graiser ... He's gone. He's not here any—" Her eyebrows came together again. "What? He's there? How ... Nevermind. I'm on my way." Hartley hung up the phone and pushed it back towards the nurses. "If you see the guy with the blonde hair again, call the cops."

The nurse nodded her head as Hartley turned into the hallway. "Excuse me," the blonde nurse said, stopping Hartley in her tracks. "Let me clean that dressing before you go. It'll take two seconds." Hartley began to decline but the nurse was already in motion, grabbing fresh gauze and spraying some antiseptic onto the surface. She peeled back the old bandage and replaced it with the clean one, securing it with some medical tape. She smiled at Hartley as she finished. "Next time you're in here, stop by and we'll make sure that's clean."

Hartley nodded her head and thanked her, moving towards the elevators, realizing that over the past day her case had broken wide open, pulling with it two cold murders that had haunted detectives for the past five years.

TWENTY-FIVE

As Hartley ascended the stairs into the precinct, she could not help but feel as though she was entering her home. Her life, especially in the last several days, seemed to revolve around this building, meshing with the bricks and mortar and concrete of the façade, intertwining with the linoleum flooring and wooden skeleton of the interior. Her own apartment felt foreign to her, an alien country that she seemed to visit on occasion yet never settled in.

She did not mind the feeling, however, as she had faced it many times before, getting sucked into an investigation that kept her away for more days than even her current case had. Yet she had never been faced with such animosity in a case, such terrible dread that resulted in so much violence. Her partner, having wrestled their suspect on the roof of an apartment complex, was later shot several times and now rested fitfully in a hospital bed following surgery to remove one of the bullets. Hartley herself had been involved in physical altercations in other cases, yet none had resulted in her being spread out on a dusty floor, gasping for breath and praying for her life as her suspect held a loaded pistol to her chin.

She shook the thoughts from her head, focusing on the task at hand: James Graiser. She walked to her floor and immediately saw James sitting in the break room, head resting back on the couch as the warm light shined throughout the office. To the left, her superior, Captain Henry Nolan, sat in his office behind his large, oak desk, donned in his street clothes as he aimlessly rifled through a stack of papers. He glanced up as Hartley entered the room, forcing a smile as he threw the papers back on the desk. "Hartley," he said as she stopped before him. "Have a seat."

"No thank you, sir," she responded. "What is he doing here?"

"Came to see you," the captain responded. "Hasn't said much. A uniform saw him hanging around outside a few hours ago and brought him in here when he mentioned your name. I got called in when they couldn't reach you." Nolan paused for a moment, raising his finger towards Hartley's head. "You okay? You need me to put someone else on this case?"

"No, Captain," Hartley replied. "I'm okay. Just a little banged up. I'm fine."

"Good, because the only other person I could have spared is Barailles, and I don't think he'll be back on a case for a while."

"No, I suppose not," Hartley agreed, the realization that she would be working alone from here out slowly sinking in. "How long have you been here, sir?"

The captain glanced to his watch. "About an hour," he said, smiling and shaking his head. "Damn rookie cop woke me up out of a great sleep. Bethany almost had a heart attack at the phone ringing. I'm sure I'll hear about it later on."

"I'm sorry, sir," Hartley replied with a grin. "I was resting at home and—"

The captain raised his palm to her. "You deserve a week straight off, the way you work. You don't need to try and explain."

"Thank you, sir."

He glanced past Hartley into the break room where James Graiser was standing, having finally noticed the female detective in Nolan's office. The captain directed his head towards Graiser, saying to Hartley, "You may want to see what's going on with him. Why you're killer was tracking him down in the first place. I doubt this is coincidence."

Hartley nodded and turned, eyeing the man across the precinct. "Right," she said. "Thank you, sir."

"Yep. Keep me posted," he answered, rising from his chair. "I'm going to go hit the gym. Haven't been up this early in years," he said as he walked past Hartley and out the door.

Hartley turned out of the office, flipping off the light and making her way in the direction of the break room and James Graiser, his eyes fixed on her as she weaved through the desks towards him. She was incredibly beautiful, he thought to himself, even with the labored walking and a bandage taped onto her head, a purple discoloration creeping from underneath the gauze.

Hartley looked over James as well, an attractive man with a certain shyness about him that most likely drove the girls crazy. He had messy, dark hair topping a chiseled, yet slim face covered in yesterday's stubble that had morphed into a neatly trimmed beard.

As she neared James she raised her hand in greeting, stopping as her desk phone began to ring. She smirked and raised a finger to Graiser before turning back to her desk. "Hartley," she answered.

"Jo," Debarsi said from the other end. "Just making sure you're okay."

"Hey," she replied. "Yeah, I'm fine. Sorry. I didn't want to wake you."

"That's all right. When did you leave?"

"Um, just after two, I think. I left my cell on the counter. I saw your note and wanted to see how Barailles was doing."

"How is he?"

"Hanging in there."

"Good," he said through a yawn.

"Why don't you go back to sleep? I'm here with James Graiser."

"Oh, I'll let you go then. Give me a call later."

"Okay. Talk to you later." Hartley hung up the phone and walked back towards James. "James, I'm Detective Jolene Hartley. How are you doing?" she asked as she pointed to his midsection where he had been stabbed.

James's hand reached up to touch his waist as he nodded his head. "I'm okay. A little sore, but okay."

"Good," she replied.

"How, uh—How are you?" He pointed to her ribcage. "I heard you were brought to the hospital as well. The nurses told me what happened."

Hartley smiled and waved her hand in the air. "Just a few bumps and bruises. Part of the job. Do you mind if we talk for a little bit? I have some questions for you."

"Sure. Absolutely," he answered as he turned into the break room, extending his hand to the couch to offer the detective a seat. "Would you like me to make you a cup of coffee or anything?" he asked.

Hartley smiled wider as she passed, quickly removing the grin as she turned towards him. "No. No thanks," she replied. "Please have a seat." Hartley took a spot on the end of one couch, leaning delicately into the arm and bracing herself on her elbow. She was surprised when James moved into position next to her, taking his place at the other end of the sofa, curling his right leg under his left and shifting his weight as he sunk into the cushions.

"How's the other detective doing? Is he your partner?"

Hartley nodded her head. "Detective Barailles. He's making it. He was shot in the alleyway across from the hotel. Got out of surgery early in the evening."

"That's good. I'm not really sure what all of this is about, but I'm glad you two showed up when you did."

"Well, I hate to tell you, but us showing up like that was purely coincidental. We came to talk. We didn't know all that was going to happen."

"Then you were coming for me? How come?"

Hartley shifted her weight into a more upright position, cringing as she did so. She folded her hands and looked to the man gazing innocently at her. "James, I'm a homicide detective. I'm investigating a murder that happened a few days ago."

"Oh," he replied, confusion etching across his face. "A murder? Sorry, but you think this has something to do with me?"

"Does the name Benjamin Ochoa ring a bell?"

James thought for a moment, his brow scrunching down around his eyes as he perused the recesses of his mind, finally coming upon the memory of five years ago near a parking garage. "Ochoa? I remember him. He was at Daniel's murder. He saw it."

Hartley nodded her head. "Right."

"Is Ochoa ... Was he the one murdered?" Hartley nodded again as James sat back into the couch. "That's awful."

"How well did you know Benjamin?"

"Not at all. The only time I talked to him was the night Daniel was killed."

"Nothing after that?"

"Nope."

Hartley paused for a moment. "Do you know of any reason why that man was in your apartment today?"

James shook his head. "I have no clue. I was hoping maybe you would have an idea."

Hartley looked to her hands and shifted in her seat. "We're not sure either," she responded, looking back up at his face, his soft, innocent eyes connecting with hers. "The day Ochoa was murdered we found a piece of paper in his pocket with your name on it."

"Me?" he asked incredulously.

"It was was spelled incorrectly and there was only an initial for the first, but yes."

"How do you know it was me then?" he asked.

Hartley smiled. "It's a long, complicated story. Looking into all of this, though, we found a connection between Ochoa and two other murders, one of them happening to be Daniel Vincent's. We believe that the man who killed Vincent also killed Ochoa's aunt almost five years later, then murdered Ochoa himself three months after that."

James stared at her, a puzzled, yet optimistic look crossing his face. "Do you know who he is?"

Hartley stared intently at James. "We don't have a name, but I think whoever is responsible for those was in your apartment today." James leaned back into the sofa, sighing heavily as he did. "James," Hartley continued, "all of these separate pieces I've looked into, no matter how absurdly distant they seem from each other, seem to be coming together."

"Am I one of the pieces?"

Hartley nodded. "But I don't know why this man was there today. We looked into the three cases I mentioned and in the Vincent case we came across your name as a listed volunteer for the campaign teams."

"Among other things," James replied.

"What other things?"

"Benefit dinners, fundraising. I helped him feed the homeless at the shelters once or twice a week."

"What was your job with Vincent other than that sort of thing? What did you do while he was campaigning for re-elections?"

"I was part of the team that would look after the funds allocated to the campaign. I worked with the treasurer of his party. We were to keep track of every last dime and where it came from and all that. Just so we had a paper trail and could show proof if anything were to ever come up against Daniel."

"Did things come up a lot like that?"

"Financial issues? No. I mean, here and there we'd be accused of something, but having the papers and files made it simple to prove the falsity of the accusation. Those politicians at that time were pretty big on digging up dirt on each other."

"Did anyone from Vincent's team ever find any on other parties?" Hartley asked.

"Sure," James answered, nodding his head emphatically. "Harold Johnston."

"Congressman Johnston? The guy responsible for the Silver Ray Casino?"

"Very same. Although he wasn't a Congressman at the time, and the Ray hadn't been approved by the city council."

He paused for a moment. "Don't you remember the Johnston scandal?" Hartley shook her head. "Years before his murder, Daniel began looking into funds allocated into the Johnston campaign. Harold Johnston came from wealth. He really didn't need any funds from the communities, but he took it anyway. No harm in that. But what we found was that someone in his office was laundering money they had acquired working back alley drug schemes. There was a whole outfit formed to handle and collect money from the neighborhoods. Gangs and prostitution and whatnot. Pretty messy business."

"Were the authorities involved?"

"Authorities as in police?" Hartley nodded. "Not at first. We did our own investigation, not wanting to undermine a political power in the area if the evidence turned out to be false."

"Was it?"

"No. We found proof, and a paper trail that led back to Robert Thames, Harold Johnston's treasurer. We took it to the authorities after that and news broke of the story. Johnston immediately fired him and Thames was indicted on a number of charges. I think he's serving a twelve year sentence."

"What happened with Johnston at the time?"

"Nothing, which was a big mistake."

"Why do you say that?"

"He had to be in on it," James stated blatantly. "There's no way that someone as controlling and well funded as Harold Johnston allows laundering and a whole mess of illegal activity to go on under his nose unless he was mixed up in it too."

"Any charges ever brought against Johnston?"

James shook his head. "From my understanding, there wasn't even a muscle moved to look into it. There was just so much damning evidence against Robert Thames that once they arrested him, there was no need to look any further." James sighed and looked around the room. "Anyway, things like that happened all the time. Not to that magnitude, but they happened."

Hartley sat back and thought for a moment, watching James as he yawned deeply next to her. "James," she began, "you said you spoke with Ochoa once, correct?"

"Right," he responded.

"We have a picture of the scene that evening and in one of them you were shown speaking with Ochoa. Five years later, after one brief encounter, your name was pulled from our victim's pocket. Can you tell me why you think Benjamin, after all that time, would be walking around with your name in his pocket?"

James thought for a moment. The event had been brief five years ago, yet he knew without a doubt the reason why Benjamin had been carrying around a piece of paper with his name written on it. "I do," he said flatly, staring towards the couch cushions, feeling the woman's beautiful eyes peering at him, worrying that when the words finally fell from his lips the detective sitting near him would turn cold. "Do you know my past, Detective?"

Hartley nodded. "I do. Some of it."

"Then you know my parents left me money?"

"Yes," she replied.

He took a deep breath. "What I said to him that night I said out of anger and pain. I was blinded by the hurt and the rage that had welled up inside of me."

"Why did he have your name in his pocket, James?"

James looked into her eyes and spoke. "I told him that if he ever found out who the killer was, or ever saw him again, I'd give him more money than he could ever dream about." He looked down to his hands again, his voice breaking as he thought about the night.

"What for?"

He remained silent, then responded, "To have someone kill the man who killed my friend."

"You were putting a price on the man's head?" Hartley asked, James remaining silent as he stared to the couch cushions. Hartley continued to gaze at him, surprised that his words had not gotten a reaction of disgust from her. She had heard the revenge talk before and each time she had been disappointed in the person seeking it, knowing that they had taken several steps down their ladder of humanity. Now, as she stared at the emotional, soft-spoken man seated next to her, Hartley smiled to herself. What was it about this man? He was a person of interest in her current investigation, a man connected to three murders, directly or indirectly, and she somehow found herself on his side even after the omission of revenge.

She shook her head and looked towards the opposite couch. "I was young and stupid," James said after a moment, pulling her attention back towards him, their eyes meeting again. "I left soon after that and began traveling more and more. Staying away for longer periods of time. I actually had just gotten back that moment when that guy attacked me."

A silence hung in the air as Hartley looked up to the wall clock. 4:53 a.m. She looked back to him. "James," she began. "Why don't you stay here tonight? I'll go grab a blanket and pillow. You can sleep on the couch."

"Are you sure that will be all right?" he asked as she rose slowly.

"Yeah, it'll be fine. I'll close the doors. The officers won't bother you."

"Are you heading home?"

Hartley turned and smiled, unable to hold it back. "Well, by the time I got there I'd have to turn right back around. So, no. I'll be out by my desk if you need anything." She left the room momentarily and returned with a pillow and blanket, handing them to James as he smiled and thanked her. She nodded her head and smiled back, leaving the room and closing the door behind her.

"I need some sleep," she said to herself as she reached her desk, embarrassed at how giddy she felt from having talked to James Graiser, like a schoolgirl kissing her crush for the first time. She leaned into her desk and stretched out her arm, resting her head on it and drifting to sleep within minutes, her surroundings fading as she slipped into a soothing darkness.

TWENTY-SIX

Jolene awoke to brilliant light pouring in through the precinct windows, illuminating the activity of officers darting around the pit. She squinted her eyes and began to rise from the desk but was forced to a quick halt as a shooting pain coursed the entirety of her right side. Her stomach muscles tensed and forced her forward with a pain that she had forgotten about during her sleep. "Shit!" she said aloud as the sting finally subsided, her breathing returning and eyes opening.

"Here, take a couple of these," came the voice of Captain Nolan as he walked up to her and set a bottle of Aspirin next to her head before moving quietly back into the seclusion of his office. Hartley lifted her forehead from the desk surface and watched him shut the door. She eyed the bottle of Aspirin and leaned back in the chair slowly, meticulously moving and pausing every couple of inches until she was reclined. The wall clock read 9:26 a.m. as she rubbed the sleep from her eyes and fingered the gauze pad clinging to her forehead by en ever-dwindling amount of adhesive.

Jolene stood and pealed the bandage from her skin, leaving behind a grayish-red glob of tape that she scraped off with the tip of a nail, wincing as her finger grazed the stitches.

251

When the pain subsided she moved slowly to the water fountain near the break room, catching a glimpse of James standing between a couch and the coffee table, his shirt bottom between his teeth as he attempted to wrap fresh bandages around his waist, tying his clothing into the bindings as he proceeded.

Jolene laughed and turned into the restroom, making her way to the sink where she pulled the extra-strength painkillers from her pocket and set one on her tongue. She filled her hands with water and swallowed the pill, closing her eyes and tilting her head towards the ceiling as the cool liquid ran down her throat.

After splashing some water on her face and fixing her disheveled appearance, Jolene made her way from the restroom and entered the break room, halting in the threshold as she watched James unsuccessfully wrap himself into a shoddy cocoon. His shirt was tucked into the dressings near his back and somehow he had succeeded in reversing the bandages, working his way in the opposite direction. Hartley bit her nail to keep from laughing, an action Graiser noticed out of the corner of his eye as he dropped the end of the bandage and turned. He glanced up and immediately let out a chuckle, his cheeks flushing red. "You know, you would think this would be a lot easier," he said, his arms out wide as he tried to shake the missing bandage end into view.

Jolene shook her head and moved into the room. "I don't know how it's that hard for you," she said. "Keep your arms up and turn around." Jolene reached up to untie the knot he had created near the small of his back. She straightened the bandage and pressed it firmly to his skin with her palm. "Give me your hand," she said, stretching the dressing to him. "Wrap that around the other side and hand it to me." James did as directed, continuing the motion until they had succeeded in covering his midsection with the bandage. "You know that the gauze and tape over the stitches would have done just fine? The elastic bandage probably won't do much for you except roll up and pinch."

James smiled as he turned back to her. "Maybe it was just a ploy to get you to rub my back," he said, taking a seat on the couch.

Jolene remained standing and rested her hands on her hips, staring intently at him. "Maybe next time I'll let you sleep in a cell," she responded, pulling a chuckle from James as she held his gaze.

A knock from the doorway broke the tension in the room as Captain Nolan carried in two mugs of steaming coffee. "Here," he said, setting the cups on the coffee table.

Hartley glanced at her boss quizzically. "Uh, Sir?" she started.

He continued towards the door, raising a hand as he went. "You're welcome," he said as he left. Jolene glanced to the cup of coffee and breathed deeply, the aroma of the beans seeming to be the exact thing she needed at that particular moment. James tilted his head up to her and raised his arm towards the couch, offering the detective a seat. She shrugged and took the spot indicated, reaching out to grab her mug of coffee from the outstretched hand of James. They each took a long sip from their respective vessel, Jolene letting the warmth of the liquid swish around her mouth before swallowing. James quickly frowned at the flavor.

"What?" she chided. "Were you expecting freshly roasted beans?"

"I seriously don't know how you drink this day after day," he said, staring into his mug and setting it on the table.

"You get used to it," Jolene replied.

"I guess," he responded. He remained fixed on the coffee for a few moments as Jolene took several more sips, bathing in the warmth and comfort of the drink. "My parents used to take a trip to Jamaica every year for a couple months," he continued. "Sometimes I'd go with, other times I'd stick around the area. They had the best coffee there. We'd always have a freshly roasted pound or so in the villa they rented. It was the best to wake up and have a cup of that, looking out to the ocean. Just the smell of that stuff was enough." He smiled as he spoke, Jolene watching how intense he was when reminiscing about the past.

"What happened to your parents, James?" Hartley asked, realizing the words had been spoken aloud.

James looked up to her and his smile faded slightly. "Is this part of the investigation into Benjamin Ochoa's murder?"

Hartley gazed into his eyes, shaking her head and shrugging at the same time. "No," she responded. "At least I don't think so. But the way this case is going, who knows?"

James sighed. "They had left for a three week trip to our vacation home, to relax and my father had some sort of business deal he was looking into. From what I understand, a couple nights before they were scheduled to head home, someone came to the house. They caught my father off guard while down by the boathouse and stabbed him to death. Threw him in the lake to try and get rid of any evidence." He paused for a moment, staring down to the coffee table. He reached for his mug and held it between his palms to extract the warmth. "My mother," he said. "She was in the house getting dinner ready. They came from behind and beat her and raped her. She survived for a couple hours, but had internal bleeding and died on the way to the hospital."

Hartley remained silent for a moment, watching James relive the event once more. "I'm sorry," she said finally.

"It was a long time ago, Detective," he replied.

"Call me Jo," Hartley responded, smiling to him as he glanced up and looked upon her face.

"Jo," he repeated. They stared at one another for a moment, unable to turn away. Hartley knew she was walking on thin ice. Becoming dangerously close to a person of interest in an open investigation could spell disaster for her role on the case, let alone lead her into a vulnerable position. She knew the emotions inside her now—the tingle in the pit of her stomach and the pounding of her chest—was as much the need and yearning for a connection as it had been that fateful night with Barailles.

Yet she could do nothing about it. She would continue to do her job the only way she knew how, with full determination and focus, yet there was no reason that she could not skirt the edge of temptation while doing it.

"James," she said, "how about breakfast?"

James smiled at her. "Are you asking me on an early morning date, Detective? Because I have to say, I don't think I've ever been on an early morning date. I've been on a date and I've had breakfast but—"

"No," Jolene interrupted sternly. "No, this is not a date. If you keep it up I'll just go get you a donut from the kitchen. They're right on par with the coffee."

"No, thank you," James responded. "Breakfast without a stale donut sounds much better."

They walked together across the street to the same diner where Jolene had her confrontation with Barailles, a scene in which she wanted to erase from her mind completely, especially now with his extended stay in the hospital. James walked briskly near her, glancing nervously from side to side as he made his way up the curb. "Don't worry," Jolene said, "this is a safe spot. Every cop in the precinct will be in and out of here all morning."

"Sorry," James replied. "Just can't help thinking he's going to jump out of nowhere and try to kill me again."

"Not in here, he won't. He'd have to be the stupidest man alive to try that, and, unfortunately for us, I don't think he is."

They opened the door and walked into a packed house, police officers and random businessmen and women starting their day with a good meal. Jolene motioned for James to grab a booth being cleaned by the diner's staff and they sat, ordering two coffees from a middle-aged, homely waitress behind the counter. "You weren't kidding," James stated. "Cops galore in here."

"Yep," Jolene responded as the waitress set a mug of coffee in front of her. "I told you."

They ordered their meals and ate in silence, each starving and unable to sustain any sort of conversation even if they wanted to. The quiet was nice, Jolene thought to herself. It was calming, soothing, and she enjoyed that she felt comfortable enough to let speech fall to the wayside.

They finished their meals and raised their mugs, each taking long sips before the waitress returned with a carafe, filling them once more to the brim. Jolene could see James in her periphery, a smile creeping onto his face as he looked from his coffee to her. "What?" she said finally, amused at the childlike actions he displayed.

He froze as he looked to her, hands flat on the table and a grin spanning from ear to ear. "Well, I just have to say that was the best breakfast date I've ever—"

"Oh, shut up!" she interjected, rolling her eyes and shifting in her seat. "I told you, this is not a date. This is me buying a person of interest in my investigation breakfast. Nothing more. Consider it a public relations move."

"Oh," he replied, nodding. "Understandable." He laughed as Jolene shook her head and glanced around the room. "Is it so unrealistic?"

Hartley turned back to him. "Is what so unrealistic?"

His cheeks flushed slightly. "A guy like me taking someone like you on a date?"

Jolene grinned as she leaned back in her seat. "Someone *like* me? Or me?"

"You," James replied.

She smiled as she looked to the table. "James," she began. "I can't."

James nodded his understanding as his smile faded. "I understand. Worth a shot, right?"

Jolene looked back to him. "My life is just crazy now. I have this case, my partner in the hospital."

"A boyfriend," James added.

She remained silent, gazing intently at him for several moments. "Someone. Not sure what at the moment."

"Well, whoever he is, he's a very lucky man." She remained fixed on him. "And I guess I am too, now that you're the detective saving my ass. Thank you."

"Any time," Hartley said, though she still felt as if she had let James down. She took a deep breath and leaned forward. "James, maybe at another time it could be more realistic. Just not right now." She paused. "I don't take everyone involved in my cases out to breakfast, you know."

He laughed as he raised his coffee to his lips, taking a long sip as he looked upon the detective's beautiful face.

257

"Hey, how's Detective B doing?" came the voice of Louie from in the kitchen. "I heard he took a couple."

Hartley turned her attention to him. "He's hanging in there, Lou. In fact, I was going to go see him this morning. I'll tell him you said hi." Louie waved his hand in the air and returned to the steaming grill. Hartley looked back to James. "Do you mind hanging out for a while at the station? I need to go see my partner and have a talk with Harold Johnston. I'd like to run through some items regarding the investigation, if you're up for it. Maybe you can help out."

"Sure," James responded. "Don't really want to go home and find that guy sitting at my kitchen table. Not sure how I can help, but I'm game."

"Good. Depending how long I am, maybe I'll pick up lunch. Meatball sandwiches sound good?"

James nodded. "Another public relations event?"

Hartley smiled at him as they rose. "Maybe more like a working investigation luncheon."

"Sounds great. It's a date," James chided. Hartley rolled her eyes at him, throwing money down on the table and leading the way to the door, smiling as she exited with James following close behind.

TWENTY-SEVEN

Hartley left James inside the precinct break room having introduced him to Detective Kim Banneau, telling him if he needed anything at all, Kim was the one to see. Prior to exiting the building, Hartley made a phone call to the hospital and was redirected to Barailles's room.

"Hello?" a woman answered.

"Um, yeah," Hartley began, slightly taken aback by a female's voice. "I'm looking for Detective Anthony Barailles's room. Can you redirect me?"

"This is his room, Jolene," the woman responded, an annoyed tone extending through the phone line to assault Hartley. "He's sleeping," she continued coldly.

"Oh," Hartley replied. "How's he doing, Cynthia?"

"He's fine."

"Good. That's good." Hartley halted, unsure what to say. "I'm glad you're with him."

"You know, I understand what you two have," Cynthia rushed into the mouthpiece, like the words would forever be lost if not said at that exact moment. "I understand that this job requires you two to be each other's guardians." She halted abruptly as her emotions began to take hold. "Damn it, Jo!

He'd follow you through hell and back, do you know that? Do you know what it's like to be in love with a man who worries and thinks constantly about another woman? Do you know how that feels?"

Hartley remained calm, a tinge of pity forming in her body as she nodded her head. "It's what the job requires, Cynthia. I know. We're partners. I'd do the same for him."

"And I would too! I know I shouldn't blame you. It's wrong, but I don't know how not to, you know? This job made him feel for you. You two being at each other's side constantly because of it made him hold you up on a pedestal. I don't want to blame you anymore. I just don't know if I can let it go."

"I know," Hartley replied. She remained silent as she weighed the words that had just come from her partner's estranged wife, words that, without saying as much, were a form of apology from a figuratively bruised and battered woman. "He loves you, Cynthia. Know that. Regardless of the job, he loves you."

"I know," Cynthia said after a brief moment. "I know he does. But it's a love that I have to share with you."

There was silence then as Hartley ran her fingers through her long, dark locks. She understood the turmoil within Cynthia's soul. She had always understood it, yet there was only so much she could do to curb the hatred that was directed towards her. "Let him know I'll check in on him later, okay?"

"Okay," Cynthia responded.

"Tell him I'm going to have a talk with the Congressman. And Cynthia?"

"What?"

"Keep at him. He's a good man."

"I know," Cynthia said as she hung up the phone.

* * * * *

Hartley hopped into an unmarked squad car in the garage and gunned it out of the tunnel, flipping on the siren as she sped her way through a light traffic. Through a couple phone calls to connections she had within other departments, Hartley had found out that Congressman Harold Johnston had a one o'clock lunch meeting with the Second District Judge at Harper's Bistro, followed by the grand opening of the Aberdeen Club later in the afternoon, a members-only guild for the city's wealthiest entrepreneurs and businessmen located in River North right off the waterway. The odds of forcing her way into a men-only club with the likes of congressmen and judges seemed beyond her grasp, so she set her sights on the restaurant.

Harper's Bistro was an antique of a restaurant overlooking the river from the north, a place where mobsters from ages past used to lounge on the outdoor deck, smoking cigars and flaunting their wealth. Not much had changed except the lawyers and politicians had replaced gangsters and their muscle. The differences between the two groups had been jokingly ribbed throughout the papers for decades.

Harold Johnston was a man of great power within the city, having had overseen some of the wealthier neighborhoods for years before turning his sights towards bigger things, namely a seat in Congress. Apart from the new information she had learned from James Graiser and the overall feel of the man being an utter creep in the tabloids, the only other thing Hartley knew of him was he was said to be a womanizer, lusting after females of all ages wherever and whenever he could.

Knowing this, Hartley pulled her squad car to the curb a block down from Harper's Bistro and entered the first clothing store she saw. Inside she purchased and changed into a low-cut, form-fitting black dress that ended just about mid-thigh, her long, tanned legs jutting out of the fabric and screaming for attention as they worked their way into a pair of cheap, yet acceptable, three-inch stiletto heels. She began to pull her hair back yet thought better when she grazed her stitches, sending a sting into her temple.

"I can't believe how good you look!" the woman at the register exclaimed as Hartley walked up. "It's like you're a different woman than when you first came in."

Hartley smiled as she handed the woman some money, shoving her clothes in the bag that was placed on the counter. "Thanks. Big day at work today," she replied back.

The woman looked Hartley over, noticing the gash on her forehead and the skimpy dress she now wore, concluding that her work consisted of the unspeakable. "Well, we all have to make a living, right?" she asked with a better-than-thou tone.

Hartley stalled for a moment, glaring up at the woman behind the counter before reaching into the bag and pulling out her holstered firearm and silver star, setting them on the counter and forcing a grin. "Not that kind of work," she replied.

"No, no!" the woman stated, stammering over her words as her face turned a bright red. "I'm sorry. I, uh—I didn't mean—"

"Yes," Hartley cut in, "yes you did. Now, maybe you can hand me that little black purse just over your left shoulder. I need something to hold these."

The woman turned quickly and retrieved the bag, handing it with shaking limbs to the detective before her. "Maybe you just go ahead and keep that one. It's on me."

"Thanks," Hartley replied as she set her badge and firearm in the bag. "You have yourself a nice day." She turned and began towards the door.

"Miss," the woman yelled, "I'm really sorry. That was awful of me to assume that."

Hartley turned and looked back to her. "Don't worry about it," she replied, catching a glimpse in a mirror. "I do somewhat look like a hooker right now. Must be the clothes." She smoothed the dress down over her thighs and exited the store, tossing the bag containing her old clothes in the squad car and beginning her trek in the direction of Harper's Bistro and the womanizing congressman.

TWENTY-EIGHT

Heads turned. Eyes stared at the vision in black as she entered the door, her dark, silky hair shifting in the breeze from the ceiling fans, her lips parted and her tongue resting against her bottom teeth as if she were about to speak, the corners of her mouth curled slightly in a grin. She knew the attention she was getting. That was why she was there. She had business to attend to, yet with whom was anyone's guess.

She strolled gracefully through a group of men mouthing cigars, flashing sideways glances to a score of them, smiling seductively before approaching the maître d', her hips shifting from right to left, her thighs tensing as she lifted her long, refined leg for another step.

Hartley was aware of what she was doing. She knew she was above average in her physical appearance, knew that men from all walks of life, all ages, felt a yearning in the pit of their stomachs—and lower—when she walked by. However, throughout her life she had known that flaunting her physical beauty in the way she was doing now was not the way she wanted to appeal to the opposite sex. Sure, there had been instances in college where she had used her angelic features to get what she wanted, once in a great while that being a young, sexually-charged man, yet she had always been able to control her needs and desires. One-night stands, for the most part, were not her way. Yet as she moved to the host of Harper's Bistro, she turned her sexual beacon on, sending out vibes throughout the establishment that this was a woman in need.

From the corner of her eye, in a far, secluded nook of the restaurant, Hartley caught a glimpse of the gray-haired congressman sitting with the judge. She stopped in front of the maître d'. "Hi," she said, smiling and batting her eyes at the man.

"Good evening, miss," the man replied back, swallowing hard and losing himself in her eyes. "May I help you?"

"I don't know. I'm new to the city and was looking for a fun, sophisticated place to have a drink." She laughed daintily and leaned forward, glancing from side to side as she placed her tongue on the edge of her front teeth. "Maybe a place with some men."

The maître d' reached up and wiped his brow as he became heated. "We have a lovely bar here, miss," he answered, stepping to his right and swinging his palm out wide. "Our establishment is of highest class and full of lively, fun elite. If you don't mind me saying so, miss, I don't think you'd have any trouble meeting a young gentleman. You've just stopped the hearts of a group of them by just walking in." He nodded his head towards the men with the cigars, Hartley turning ever so slowly to glance over her shoulder and smile enticingly at the group, each one beaming back at her as they looked her over from head to toe.

"Cute," Hartley said, stepping up close to the maître d' and leaning towards his ear. "I'm, um, more interested in an established man. A little older. One that—" she paused as she giggled once more, looking up and catching the man glancing down to her breasts. "One that knows women," she finished.

The man cleared his throat and looked to the floor and back to Hartley. "Yes, miss, well, there will be plenty of, as you said, established men in and out of here all day and into the evening."

"Great," Hartley said with a smile, her eyes still locked on the maître d' as he squirmed under her seductive stare.

"Please, follow me. Let's get you a seat at the bar."

"Yes, let's." Hartley followed the man to the end of the bar, pulling her stool out as she slid into place, Congressman Johnston just beyond the stack of liquor bottles on the opposite side of the restaurant.

"Can I tell the barkeep to get you anything?"

"Please. I'd love a glass of merlot."

"Certainly," he said, stealing one more glance as Hartley purposely crossed her legs in front of him, giving him a front row glimpse of her dress creeping up her right thigh. He moved to the other side of the bar where the bartender was readying his drawer and whispered her order, the man glancing up and raising his finger. Hartley nodded and made herself comfortable.

Her goal, as she sat there in what equated to a tight, long t-shirt stretched into a dress, was to peruse the establishment's customers and make herself known, which, up to this point, she had done miraculously. She knew that her badge in places like this, with people as powerful as Congressman Harold Johnston, could, in all actuality, be a hindrance instead of an object to gain her access. Congressman Johnston, like many of the politicians and judges that frequented Harper's, had extreme pull when it came to the city council, and had in their power the ability to wreck careers if warranted.

Hartley had to play her cards just right with the congressman. She needed to get in his good graces if she were going to gain any insight into his mind's vault of five years ago.

"Excuse me, ma'am?" a voice said to her right. Hartley turned to gaze upon a well-dressed, handsome young man in his mid-twenties from the group she had just passed through, holding a tumbler of what appeared to be gin.

Hartley jolted back into character, her eyes going wide as she looked upon his face. "'Ma'am'?" she said incredulously. "Ma'am makes me sound so old, and I'm guessing I can't be much older than you, sweetie."

"My apologies, miss," the young man replied. "I didn't mean anything by that. You don't look a day over twenty-five."

"That's more like it," Hartley purred. "What's your name?"

"Philip. Philip Humphreys. May I ask yours?"

"Philip, is there a reason all of your friends behind you are glancing this way and giggling?"

Philip turned and glanced at his group of friends, shaking his head slightly to them as they nervously shuffled in their seats. "I'm afraid they think I'm going to make a fool out of myself. Just waiting to give me a hard time when I return."

Hartley smiled and glanced quickly to the congressman's table, noticing Johnston gazing across the room at the commotion Hartley had created amidst the younger males. He stalled as he saw her, stunning in her black dress, her sparkling eyes meeting his as a smirk crossed her face. She held his gaze for a moment and said to the young man, "Philip, your friends are going to have to wait. Why don't you have a seat and join me for a drink."

Philip smiled from ear to ear as his friends stared in disbelief. "It would be my pleasure," he responded, excitedly pulling out his stool and taking a seat close to Hartley, his leg brushing up against hers, a move that, she knew, had been purposely planned out to get her in arms reach. She glanced quickly again to Johnston's table, connecting with the congressman's eyes once more as he spoke with the judge.

This kid just may be more useful than I originally thought, she said to herself, realizing that a touchy-feely, groping young buck tended to bring the larger animals out to defend their territory.

"So tell me your story, Philip," Hartley said, leaning closer to him as she smiled and gazed at the congressman, pulling each of the men into her web of seduction.

* * * * *

It took nearly an hour of conversation mixed with innocent pawing at the beautiful woman at the bar to rile Congressman Harold Johnston from his seat to the opposite side of the bar. The judge moved off to the recesses of the restaurant and had left their table empty, save for a few empty glasses of scotch and a container holding what most likely were extremely expensive cigars.

Johnston stood opposite Hartley, grabbing the bartender as he passed by and placing his order, stealing glances to the dark-haired beauty just feet away. The move did not go unnoticed by Hartley as she laughed and flirted with Philip Humphreys, the young male taking every chance he got to reach out and brush her arm or place his fingers on her thigh. Hartley allowed the actions, although deep down she felt disgusted. Nowhere in her real life would she allow a over-confident, touchy-feely young man run his hands over her body. Yet the fingertips gently grazing her skin had done their job, pulling the congressman out from his table and into the ring, readying him for a bout with a far lesser opponent.

Hartley glanced up to the congressman and held his gaze with lustful eyes, taking a sip from her wine glass just at the exact moment that young Philip reached up to touch her shoulder, a movement that sent Johnston into battle.

He walked slowly around the bar, passing the group of young men still dampening their cigars with their mouths and parked himself directly between the young man and Hartley. Philip slowly turned to glare at the older gentleman as Hartley remained facing the bar eagerly waiting for the inevitable.

"Can I help you?" Philip said with brave tone.

Johnston ignored the pipsqueak. "Miss, I couldn't help but notice you for the past hour. You are a vision."

Hartley turned her head slightly and smiled. "Thank you," she replied.

"Excuse me, sir. I don't mean to be a bother to you, but I'm talking to this woman and—"

"Son, why don't you go have a drink with your buddies? I'll buy you a round. Whatever you want." Johnston's gaze remained fixed on Hartley.

"I don't think you under—"

"Philip, dear," Hartley interrupted. "Why don't we take a break? Have a drink with your friends and I'll see what this gentleman wants." Philip eyed Hartley intently before rising. "Don't worry, sweetie," she continued. "I'll be back." Johnston took a step back to allow the young man an exit from the bar, which he did slowly and angrily, having just lost out on an extremely attractive woman to a man that looked as if he could be her grandfather.

"Would you care to join me for a drink at my table?" Johnston asked. "I've taken the liberty of ordering you another merlot."

Hartley turned towards him slowly, a seductive grin spread across her face, leaning back as she threw her arm across the back of her chair, her breasts jumping into view as she arched her back. "That's a very bold move, ordering a drink for a woman already deep in conversation with another man."

"No need to play hard to get. That infant wouldn't be able to handle a woman of your caliber."

"And you think you could?"

Johnston smiled. "I think I could. I'm definitely going to try."

"And what would your wife think about this?" Hartley asked, placing her finger on the congressman's wedding ring.

The congressman smiled wider. "She doesn't have to know. She'll be home after we're through here, and with a wonderful dinner on the table." Hartley smiled, her fingers sliding across the man's hand and resting back on her stool. "And I'm guessing you are just fine with this."

Hartley glanced to the congressman's table and back. "Very secluded spot you have back there."

"We'd be alone to ... talk," he responded.

"Lead the way," she said, standing.

They worked their way back to the table, Hartley sliding into the rounded booth as Johnston set the glass of merlot in front of her. He sat down directly next to her, setting his arm on the booth backrest around her neck, his other hand reaching out to rest upon Hartley's crossed thigh.

Hartley's heart jumped as the congressman made the move and it took all her will to not reach out and bend his thumb back until it broke. "I saw you trying to get over here for quite some time," the congressman said, sliding his fingers up and down her leg slowly. Hartley forced a smile yet said nothing, taking another sip of her merlot. "You're a beautiful woman," he continued. "What leads you in here today?"

"Oh, I don't know," Hartley said. "Just interested in something."

"Oh, yeah? I'm assuming it couldn't be that young man over there. The one giving me the evil eye for stealing you away."

"No, not him," she responded.

"By the way you kept looking over here, I'm going to guess it's me that you were interested in." Hartley nodded her head. "And why's that?" he asked, his hand sliding up her thigh, fingers inching their way into her dress.

Hartley smiled and looked into his eyes, lifting her purse to the table and leaning towards him. "Well, Mr. Johnston, there's numerous reasons."

His eyes went wide as he grinned at her. "So you know who I am?"

"Yes. I know who you are."

"And am I the reason you came in to this restaurant today?" Hartley nodded her head. He laughed as he looked around the room, working his hand back down her leg to her knee. "Well, darling, why don't we just cut to the chase? There's a room in the back we can go to. I've got pull to get us in there."

Hartley looked around, connecting back with the congressman. "I think we're secluded enough here, don't you think?" She opened her purse as the congressman gazed at her.

He glanced around quickly and grinned. "Sure, sweetheart. I think we are." With that, Congressman Johnston removed his hand from her leg and reached to his pants, unzipping the front and reaching into his underwear, pulling out his member and laying it across his lap, reaching towards Hartley's legs once again, this time with lust in his eyes as he unsuccessfully tried to work his fingers towards her panties. "Why don't you put that sweet mouth around it?" he asked abruptly, setting his hand upon Hartley's head as he tried to pull her to him.

"Why don't you use that foul mouth to tell me what I want to know?" Hartley answered, stunning the congressman as she removed a shiny police badge from her purse and waved it in front of him.

Johnston's eyes scrunched together, his hand halting its progress up her thigh, his exposed parts still at attention below her. "Jesus Christ! You're a cop?"

"Yes, sir, and I'd like to ask you a few questions, if you don't mind."

"Absolutely, I fucking mind!" he said, composing himself and zipping up his trousers.

"Well, maybe you won't mind as much if I arrest you for exposing yourself to an officer in a public area." Johnston remained silent, glancing around the room. "Or you answer my questions and we forget about the whole incident. Your choice."

Johnston glared at her and nodded his head, waving to the bartender for another scotch. "You have balls, sweetheart. You know I could crush you, don't you?"

Hartley nodded. "Most likely. But I'd be taking you down with me. And whom do you think the public will side with? An officer of the law with an impeccable record or a politician with a line of scandals following him around?"

The bartender set the drink upon the table and moved back to his seat at the bar. "Fuck you," Johnston said to Hartley quietly. "Scandals happen every day in politics. If you're clean, then you're clean."

"Maybe some of us just know how to wash the dirt away a little better than others."

Johnston took a long sip from his tumbler before responding. "What is this about, Officer?"

"Detective, sir," Hartley replied.

"Whatever."

"A murder. Three, actually."

"So this has nothing to do with me then," Johnston stated.

"Daniel Vincent," Hartley said flatly. Johnston stalled while bringing the tumbler to his lips. "Remember Daniel Vincent?"

"How can I not? The man was one of my biggest opponents. What about him?"

"Can you tell me your relationship with Vincent around the time of his murder?"

"Are you serious?"

"Sir, answer the question or I swear to God today will chase you around for the rest of your—"

"Okay," he interrupted, holding up his hand in surrender as he set his glass down, clearing his throat. "It's no secret Vincent and I didn't like each other. He was against the Silver Ray Casino being built. That was a plan that would have brought millions to the city at the time."

"And to your pocket as well, I assume?"

Johnston gazed into Hartley's eyes with hatred. "Yes, it would benefit me too. It *has* benefited me. I've made enough money off of that to retire twice."

"Did you realize what that casino was going to do to the neighborhoods adjacent to it? Mainly the ones that Daniel Vincent oversaw?"

Johnston nodded. "Politics is dirty, Detective. There's no clean-cut line. It's all shades of gray. You want something done, people are going to get their toes stepped on. Some will get their feet cut off."

"Beautiful," Hartley exclaimed.

"Things get done to make money and better the city as a whole," he continued louder. "It's a shame that Vincent was murdered, but in the end that casino was good for this city."

Hartley remained fixed on the congressman. "What about Robert Thames?" she asked.

"What about him?"

"He was a member of your team, correct? Ended up getting a dozen years for fraud?"

"What does it have to do with me?"

"Seems odd that a man of your power loses track of what's going on right under his nose, wouldn't you say? A large scale money laundering and fraud scheme, right in your headquarters, and you know nothing?"

Johnston smiled eerily at her. "Thames was found guilty by a jury of his peers, Detective. That's that."

"The paper trails that led to the conviction started in the Vincent party, did you know that?"

"So what?"

"So, sir, sounds like a motive to me: Corruption found by a rival party, plus the same party is the only thing stopping the Silver Ray and your bank account from taking off."

Johnston leaned in towards her. "What are you saying, Detective? I'm hoping that you aren't accusing me of having anything to do with Daniel Vincent's murder. That, my dear," he exclaimed with a raised voice, "just may push me over the edge to take your actions to your superintendent. I suggest you leave. Now!"

"Have you ever heard of Maria Gomez?" Hartley continued unfazed.

"Detective, I'm—"

"What about Benjamin Ochoa?"

"Get out now, or I'm on the fucking phone!"

Hartley held up her palms in surrender, grabbing her purse and standing, placing her badge back in her bag and straightening her dress. She looked back to the congressman, his face contorted in anger. "Thank you for the time, Congressman Johnston." He glared at her as she turned. After several feet, she stopped and turned back to him. "Maria Gomez, by the way, was murdered three months ago. I'm sure you don't know her. But you know what the kicker is? She was killed in the exact same way as Daniel Vincent. And by the same killer. Had a tattoo on the back of his neck." She paused and studied Johnston's face, anger trying to mask a hint of anxiety as it flashed across his brow. Hartley caught the sign and smiled. "We're getting closer to figuring out everyone involved. You should be happy to know your neighborhoods will be safer soon." Hartley reached down and smoothed her dress, rubbing a red mark on her thigh that Johnston had left while trying to reach between her legs. "That should go away, I'm sure. But I bruise like a peach." She glanced up once more, the smile fading as she glared at him, finally turning and walking towards the door, Johnston's eyes watching as the beautiful siren made her way past the group of young men.

Hartley paused near Philip, bending down and kissing him on the cheek. "Thank you for the drink."

"My pleasure," he said, watching as she passed through the door and into the midday sun.

TWENTY-NINE

Hartley's heart was pounding as she entered her squad car. She realized, without a doubt, she had just made the biggest, most aggressive move in her career with, in not so many words, accusing a United States congressman of at least conspiracy to murder, possibly more. She had gambled big time and Johnston's reaction to the man with the circle tattoo had paid off.

Of course, Hartley had no proof of Johnston being involved in her investigation, yet she had a hunch. He had reacted nervously, showing a hint of anxiety about the information she had let him in on, leading her to believe more than ever that the congressman was indeed tied into her case.

She popped one of Banneau's pills for her injuries and took off back to the station, radioing in and leaving a message for Captain Nolan, asking him to meet with her once she got there on an extremely important matter: She needed a tail on the congressman. She needed to know what connection, if any, this man of power had to her case. She needed to know if he had any part in the demise of Alderman Daniel Vincent and, in turn, if he knew who the killer was.

The precinct was buzzing with activity as investigations into this missing person or that murdered individual were looked into with the utmost care. Hartley charged up the steps, noticing officers glancing at her as she passed, forgetting the fact that she still wore her tight black dress that accentuated her toned body. She went to her floor and entered Captain Nolan's office, glancing towards the break room to catch a glimpse of James. "He's not in there," the captain said from behind his desk. "And I'm guessing you're looking for the club three blocks down on the right."

Hartley turned quizzically towards the captain, then, as her face flushed red, looked down to her outfit. "Oh, shit!" she whispered, clasping her hands under her chin to hide the low-cut shirt.

The captain looked over his glasses at her as a father to a daughter and waved his hand. "I'm sure you'll explain momentarily."

"Um, yes, sir. I will." She glanced back to the break room. "Do you know where he went to, sir?" she asked.

"Last I saw, he was playing bridge with some of the holding guards," the captain said with a laugh.

"Excuse me, sir?"

"Yeah," he said, removing his glasses. "That kid is quite the charismatic young man. Everyone's taken to him around here." He laughed and shook his head. "You know, Mac came by a while back. Would you believe Mac offered to buy that kid breakfast? Haven't seen him offer to buy anything in years!" Hartley smiled. "Anyway, I got the message. What do you want to see me about? Find anything new? Need a copy of my teenage daughter's nineties dance hits?"

Hartley nodded her head, her smile fading as she thought quickly how to ask for her request into getting the congressman a tail. She looked sternly up to him and came out with it. "Sir, I have reason to believe that Congressman Johnston is involved in this case somehow." She stopped cold, waiting for the captain's reaction.

"How?" he asked after a moment.

"Sir, I'm not sure," Hartley said quietly. "But I would like to request you put a tail on him. Someone—"

"No," he said matter-of-factly.

"Sir, please—"

"Do you know what you are asking of me?" Captain Nolan interrupted.

"Yes, sir, but—"

"Jesus, Hartley! Putting a tail on a congressman? I need something better than 'I'm not sure.'"

Hartley glanced around the office. "This," she said, unclenching her fists and swinging her arms to the side. "This got me into Harper's Bistro today. Congressman Johnston was there."

"What did you do, Jo?"

"Captain, just listen. I didn't do anything to jeopardize this precinct. He didn't even know who I was, except that I was a detective—"

"Don't you think a man of that magnitude would be able to track you down?"

Hartley looked at him intently, her eyes reflecting confidence. "He won't," she stated. "Not after what he tried to get away with today at Harper's."

Captain Nolan looked at her silently, weighing his options. "Do I want to know?"

"No, Captain," Hartley answered. "But I got him to talk to me."

"About what?"

"Daniel Vincent and what was happening between the two at the time of his murder. He showed his hand when I mentioned our killer with the tattoo. He knows something, and whatever it is it goes back to Vincent's murder." Captain Nolan remained silent, staring up to Hartley as he thought. "Sir, please, just put surveillance on him. Just for a day or two. I got him riled up, and now's the time he'll act if he has something to hide."

Captain Nolan looked to his desk and shook his head as he thought. "I can't do it, Jo."

"Sir, please—"

"He can have our badges like that!" he said, snapping his fingers. "I like my job, Jo, and I'd rather not go fishing on this one."

"Sir, it's not fishing. I promise you. I've never led you astray before, have I?" She waited momentarily for the question to sink in. "Please, Captain. This isn't just a gut feeling. I know he's involved. Please."

"Okay," the captain said, nodding his head. "If you think something's going on with him, I'll do it. But, Jo, you better be damn sure you don't do anything foolish. I'd hate to see one of my best detectives go down in flames."

"Yes, sir," Hartley said with a smile. "Thank you, Captain."

She turned and began towards her desk. "Oh, Hartley," Captain Nolan said quickly.

"Sir?" she said, stopping near her desk.

"Debarsi came by here. Told me to tell you he's been requested back to Philly. He's checked out of his hotel and was heading to your place."

"Shit," she said, glancing from her desk to the break room.

"Jo," the captain replied. "Go see him off. Take the rest of the day off. I'll get the tail on the congressman and we'll see what happens. James will be fine. We'll keep him here for another night. I'm sure he'll be okay with that."

"Thanks, Captain," Hartley said. "Call me if we get anything on Johnston." The captain gave her thumbs up as he retrieved his glasses from the desk, Hartley turning and moving out of the precinct and to the street, flagging down a taxi to take home, her thoughts drifting from the congressman to Debarsi and back again, wondering what, if anything, they would find on Johnston, and when she would see Ronny again.

THIRTY

Debarsi sat at the kitchen table with a pen and paper, scribbling a note down for Jolene as she entered her apartment, stopping in the threshold and staring at him. Their eyes met and Ronny smiled, looking Hartley up and down as she stood motionless in her small black dress. "Did you rent me a dancer for my birthday?" he asked. Jolene flashed him the bird, cocking her head to the side with an evil grin.

She closed the apartment door and moved towards the couch, tossing her purse on the cushions and leaning against the back, arms propping up her body. Ronny tapped the pen on the paper. "I was just writing you a note," he said.

"I heard you got called back," she replied.

He nodded his head. "Phantom Robber is back at it."

"Oh yeah?" she asked, intrigued.

"Hit a Philly bank this morning. And guess what then?"

"What?"

"He vanished." Debarsi smirked as he stood.

"So it's not just a clever name," she said, standing with him.

"Exactly," he responded, moving towards her and placing his hands on her hips as she wrapped her arms around his neck. They hugged then, a tight, comforting embrace that lasted well over a minute. "I don't know when I'll be back," Ronny said finally.

"I know," she replied, leaning away from the hug and gazing up at him.

"This bank heist—I just want to catch him. It's like he—"

Jolene pulled him to her, their mouths meeting, tongues caressing as Ronny wrapped his arms around her slim frame, lifting her up and placing her on top of the couch backrest. "When do you have to leave?" Hartley asked between kisses.

"Need to be on the road by at least six tonight," he responded.

"Well, then we better get to it," she replied, pushing him back and sliding from the couch with her eyes staring up at him. She bent slowly to remove her heels, kicking them towards the door then standing motionless, her legs reflecting the light from the windows, her hair dangling around her face. She reached up and grabbed hold of her dress, pulling it down towards the floor, sliding the fabric over her skin as Debarsi watched in awe. He had seen Jolene naked hundreds of times, yet was still amazed at her incredible beauty. Even with the intense bruising in her midsection, she was flawless.

She let the dress fall around her ankles, stepping out of it as she stood in her underwear staring up at Debarsi. She reached her arms back and unhinged her bra, pulling it down her toned arms and tossing it on the couch, the coolness of the apartment causing goose bumps to rise across her skin. She grabbed onto the straps of her underwear then, toying with them as she stared seductively to Ronny, who had begun to undress as well, though at a quicker pace than his counterpart. She inched her panties down her thighs, running her finger along her legs and stepping from the garment as she stood in front of him, fully nude and comfortable in her own skin, a vision to behold.

Ronny smiled as he walked to her once more, knowing he needed to make the most out of the remaining time he had with her. He laid her down on the floor, kissing her passionately, sinking into to her as the world around him disappeared.

* * * * *

They fell fast asleep on the floor for several hours, intertwined in each other's arms, all their worries and investigations leaving them for a time. Debarsi woke to find himself alone behind the couch, covered with a blanket, his head resting on a throw pillow. He shifted and saw Jolene seated on the couch, facing a blank television screen and biting her nails. "You okay?" he asked, standing and moving around to take a seat next to her, throwing the blanket over her naked body.

"Hi," she responded with a smile. "Yeah. Yeah, I'm fine." She had woke after a hard sleep, slightly disoriented from the pain killer she had taken for her bruised ribcage and full of ideas about the murder suspect in her case and why he had tried to kill James Graiser.

"You sure? Want me to get you anything to drink?" She shook her head and continued to stare into the gray television screen, her eyes glazed over as her mind worked. "What's going on in there?" Ronny asked finally, pointing to her head.

"James Graiser," she responded matter-of-factly.

"Oh," he replied. "He seems like a good guy."

Jolene turned her head towards him. "How—" She let the question hang in the air.

"When I stopped into the station earlier to say goodbye. I ran into Graiser talking to Kim." Hartley nodded her head slowly. "He seems to like you a little," he said, smiling up to Jolene as her face flushed slightly.

"How did you—What was said?"

"Just the way he talked about you to Kim. He didn't know who I was."

Hartley looked into his eyes. "He's just a person of interest in the case, Ronny," she said, not entirely believing the statement herself.

"Jo," Ronny said, reaching out and grabbing her hand, "I understand what we are. I know both of us want more. But I also know where we are in our careers, you here and me in Philly. I know you need to live your life not waiting for me to come around once a year. I do too." He paused as they looked at one another. "I just want you to know that I understand the need to live your life and let people in."

Jolene smiled at him, saddened, yet able to breathe easier at the fact that they knew completely the ground in which they now stood. They cared greatly for each other, that fact was clear. Yet having the clarity between them that dating others was understandable and acceptable was a load off both of their shoulders.

"Now," he said, slightly more upbeat, "you said you were thinking about James."

Hartley returned to the recesses of her mind again, searching her hazy thoughts once more, trying to reel in her ideas. "Right," she began, grasping onto the trail she had been following. "James is part of this investigation, that much is for certain. He has connections with Daniel Vincent and Benjamin Ochoa through Vincent's murder." Debarsi nodded his head. "Yet that's it. He doesn't know Maria Gomez and, according to James, never had any contact with Benjamin after that night five years ago."

"So what are you thinking?"

"I'm thinking that it's not a coincidence that our supposed killer is hanging around Graiser's place waiting for him. There's got to be a reason that he shows up looking for James. And why now?"

Debarsi leaned back and scratched his head. "Let's see what we got," he began. "You said that your vic had a note in his pocket with Graiser's name on it, but spelled differently. Maybe your killer saw the note and searched him out."

"Yeah, but that would mean he would have had to seen the note in the apartment. Mac said the ink was slightly smeared from Ochoa putting it directly in his pocket after writing it. And CSU found the same pad of paper and pen near Ochoa's phone when they conducted a search."

"Maybe he searched him after he shot him?"

"No," Hartley replied quickly. "Video from the bank has him killing Ochoa and leaving. He didn't go anywhere near the body." She thought for a minute, replaying the events from Ochoa's murder until her talk with Congressman Johnston. Jerome Grazer passed through her mind along with the subsequent chase and questioning. The circle tattoo and the murder of Maria Gomez jumped to the forefront, quickly replaced by the image of a hovering man holding a gun to her chin.

Goodnight, Detective.

She snapped her eyes up and looked to Debarsi. "When the killer had the gun to my head, he said the name James Graiser."

"So? From what I heard, didn't you yell James's name out as they were going up the fire escape?"

"Right, but it's the way he said it. 'How do *you* know James Graiser?' Like *he* knew who James was."

Debarsi sat up straight. "Ochoa was killed for having seen the killer's face—"

"But James never saw the sketch. They were never made public by investigators," Hartley interrupted. "Which means only one thing: James may have a name."

Debarsi cocked his head to the side. "Even if he does, it makes no sense why he would be there to kill James. No one knew Graiser was part of this until after the attack happened. It wasn't like James was interviewed and then targeted because of his involvement."

"Right," Hartley added quickly, "but the photo of the crime scene with Ochoa and Graiser was released in an article a little while after the murder as an update piece regarding Vincent's death. Neither of their names was mentioned."

"You said yourself that the killer could have tracked Ochoa down through the tagging. There would be no reason as to how he could have known who James Graiser was."

"Unless he knew who he was before the murder."

The two thought for a moment before Debarsi shrugged and said, "Still, the question stands: Why was James targeted? Would there be any reason to kill him because of this? It's not like Ochoa could have described the killer well enough for James to know exactly who he was. And we know he didn't pass any names to him, because five years later we still don't have one."

The two remained quiet, their brainstorming session coming to a halt. Debarsi looked up to the wall clock. "I've got to head out in a few minutes," he said, stirring Hartley from her daze.

She smiled at him before glancing to the clock herself. She looked back to him and pulled herself to her knees, inching her way towards Ronny, shifting the blanket around her back as she did so. "A few minutes, you say?"

"Yeah," he said, smiling as she straddled him. "About ten."

"Can you give me a ride?" she said, smiling wide and giggling.

"To the station?" he asked. "Or now?"

Jolene bent down to kiss him, pulling away and placing her mouth near his ear, answering in a quiet, seductive tone. "Yes."

THIRTY-ONE

For a time, Jolene lay there quietly, nestling cozily in the embrace of a man that was once again leaving her for an extended period of time. She had convinced Ronny to wait until morning to leave, just as he had convinced her to move to the bedroom. Now, as the early morning sun crested over the horizon, she felt saddened by his inevitable departure, yet more relaxed knowing the two of them had come to an agreement, one that was based solidly on the "if it was meant to be, it will happen" argument that millions put stock in. The two of them were no different.

Each was a highly attractive specimen, yet each had also shied away from advancements from the opposite sex, longing in the back of their minds for one another. Yet things were different now. Things seemed simpler. Things seemed like they had come to a closure.

Each was free to now live life as they saw fit, without that burning question of whether or not the other would be mortified to find out their counterpart was testing the waters of the dating pool once more.

Jolene rose finally from the confines of her cozy, warm bed and moved to the bathroom, showering and readying herself for the day ahead of her. She was surprised when she exited into the hallway and looked over the railing, seeing Debarsi sitting at the kitchen counter sipping coffee, his motorcycle helmet resting next to him. "What time is it?" she called down.

He looked up at her and smiled before glancing to his watch. "Five thirty-six."

"Still want to give me a lift to the precinct?" she asked.

"Absolutely," he responded.

"Okay," she replied. "I'll be right down." She entered her bedroom and threw on a pair of jeans and a white, short-sleeved, button-up blouse, pulling her hair back into a ponytail as she retrieved her badge and firearm.

Downstairs, she drank a mug of coffee in two gulps and snatched up her leather jacket, throwing it on over her shoulders as she turned and faced Ronny. "Ready?" she asked.

"No," he answered with a smile. "But it has to be done."

They exited her apartment and made their way across the street to his bike, sliding their helmets on and mounting the motorcycle as Debarsi made the machine growl to life. They peeled away from the curb, setting their sights on the station, the traffic on the city streets not yet awake at this early hour of the morning.

* * * * *

Ronny dropped Jolene off at the curb in front of the precinct, dismounting the bike and removing his helmet, gazing into her eyes as she smiled up at him. "Thank you," she said, hands on her hips.

"For what?" Debarsi asked.

"For coming back," she replied. "I needed this."

He reached out to her and pulled her in for an embrace. "You're welcome. I did too." They remained together for several moments before Jolene stepped back. "Listen," he continued. "If you ever make it to Philly, look me up. Boyfriend or no, I'd love to see you and catch up."

She nodded her head. "Absolutely." He stepped forward and kissed her then, passionately locking lips before he pulled away and fitted himself with his helmet once again. He mounted the bike and set it to life before smiling and pulling away into traffic, heading back to fight the battle waging with the Philadelphia banks.

Hartley watched him leave then turned and made her way up the precinct steps. In the early morning, the precinct was still full of life with patrol cops making their way in and out of the station as well as investigators checking into certain leads before the day's madness began.

She breathed deeply as she neared the entrance, letting the warmth of the morning air circulate in her system. The day was set to be a brilliant one, packed with little to no clouds and a breeze that was sure to cool down the swelter of the sun.

Hartley entered the precinct and made it to her floor, surprised to see Captain Nolan seated at his desk at such an early hour. She walked up to his office and leaned into the doorframe. "Sir," she began as he looked up to her, "this is two days in a row you're here before nine. Is everything okay?"

He smiled at her. "You're funny, you know that?" he chided back. "Just thought I'd get in here early, that's all. Seems I can get more paperwork done when no one is bugging me."

Hartley smiled. "Sorry, sir." He waved a hand after her as she turned back towards her desk, catching a glimpse of James sitting comfortably on the break room couch with a book opened on his lap. She grinned as she made her way towards him, entering the break room slowly with her thumbs tucked into her back pockets. "Seems everyone is ready to go early here, huh?"

James looked up and smirked. "Yeah," he began. "These couches are only so comfortable. Plus, not much to do all day in a police station but read and take naps."

Hartley looked down at her shoes. "Yeah, sorry I didn't make it back yesterday."

"Oh, don't worry about it. I survived." He paused. "Although, I'd be lying if I said I didn't miss you." He smiled wide as Hartley glanced up to him.

"Shut up," she said, moving to take a seat on the couch next to him. "James, I know you're probably looking to get out of here. I would if I were stuck for two days straight."

"Last night, absolutely. After hours of playing gin and teaching euchre, things tend to get a little stale." They both giggled. "But right now seems to be looking up."

Hartley looked to him with innocent eyes, their connection lasting for a moment before she glanced away, eyeing her investigation board through the break room windows on the opposite side of the floor, half hidden by a coat rack. She looked back to James. "Listen, would you help me out?"

"Sure," he replied.

"I am trying to figure out some things regarding the case." He nodded his head as she continued. "Last night I was thinking about Ochoa and the other murder victims. Bear with me." James nodded. "Vincent is murdered for whatever reason by our killer. Ochoa, who is there at the scene putting a gang tag on Vincent's car, hides and sees the killer's face. Almost five years later, Maria Gomez, Ochoa's aunt, is murdered in the same way Vincent was. Again, there is a witness to the killing. Three months later, Ochoa himself is killed, presumably by the same killer. The question I'm faced with is this: Why did our killer commit these acts? What was the reasoning behind each murder? Vincent, I can't be sure of why the act was committed. Gomez, I believe, was murdered because the killer thought he was entering Ochoa's home."

"Why would he think that?" James asked.

"Because Ochoa and his cousin Miguel looked almost identical. If the killer was trying to locate the witness from the Vincent murder based off of the tag Ochoa put on Vincent's car and a crime scene photo that was published later, it's not unreasonable to think he found what gang the tag belonged to and tracked it down. Eventually Miguel or Benjamin would have shown their faces on the streets."

"So you think the killer followed Miguel to his home?"

"It's possible. Found out where he thought Benjamin lived and went in to kill him, but ran into Miguel's mother instead. There would be no reason to keep her alive. Just another witness. So eventually he finds the right guy and kills him at a bus stop over the Dan Ryan all because Ochoa has seen his face, which tends to be a downfall for someone on the run."

James raised his hand as if he were part of a classroom lecture. "Then why me? If you think the killer of those three murders was the same man in my apartment, why was he after me?"

"I've been thinking about this. Other than knowing Daniel Vincent and speaking to Ochoa at the crime scene that one time, you have no other connection to this investigation at all. Yet our killer was still in your apartment waiting for you." She paused for a moment. "The investigation into Vincent's murder held back some key items from the public, mainly the sketch that was created from Ochoa's description of the killer and names of witnesses, like Benjamin himself and the couple

293

who first got to Vincent. An item that was not left out was that a witness had seen the murder take place."

"Which was why he was killed in the first place, essentially?"

"Correct," Hartley confirmed. "Sketches can prove faulty in a court. But having an eye witness tends to hold more water."

"Okay," he said. "But you still haven't answered my question: Why me?"

Hartley looked at him intensely. "My guess is that you know who the killer is."

James remained quiet for a moment. "You think I know who is killing these people, and who stabbed me, but I'm not telling you?"

"No," Hartley replied with her hand raised. "Not like that. I think the killer went after you because if you were to see him, you would know who he was and could help this investigation."

James thought for a moment before responding. "But why would he come after me now? Like you said, the only time I intersected with this case was five years ago for five minutes. It makes no sense that he would look for me now."

"James, this man has been connected with two other murders in a botched heist. The men he killed were part of his team to rob a Philadelphia bank, but one survived and gave the investigators a lengthy description of him. It's only a matter of time before the investigation goes to the courts, and cases like that tend to garner national attention. The more people who know his description or name, the easier it is for him to be found. Killing off key witnesses just makes it possible for him to disappear that much quicker.

"There's also the fact that directly after Vincent's murder, your pattern of disappearing from the public eye was sporadic, at best. Our killer could have been trying to find you all along, but you being in the city at random times, following no schedule whatsoever could have thrown him off. Who knows?"

"So what you are saying is that you think this man came after me because I can identify him?" He paused as Hartley nodded. "But like you said, there weren't any sketches released to the public. So how would I know who he was? I'm sure this guy kept an eye on the news to gain an upper hand, so he had to have known that there weren't any descriptions out."

Hartley nodded her head. "Right, there were no sketches released. But remember when I said there was a crime scene photo published later as an update?" James nodded. "That photo was the same one that showed you talking to Ochoa that night."

"Great!" he exclaimed. "So you're thinking this guy came to get me—five years later—because of the photo in the paper? But you said there were no names given."

"No, there weren't," she agreed. "I'm guessing he found Ochoa from the image and the gang tag." She paused again, looking into his eyes. "And you ... I'm thinking he saw that photo and knew exactly who you were."

They remained silent for a minute, Hartley thinking over the scenario she had just presented. "Come with me," she stated, rising from the couch and making her way to her desk. "Wait here," she said to James as he braced himself on the top of her desk, scooting a box of files over to make room for his rear. Hartley fetched the investigation board and rolled it towards him, spinning it around and revealing the outline of their work thus far.

James began from the upper left of the board, skimming through the images and ramblings the detectives had pasted to it, trying to make sense of the writings as well as the conversations Hartley had had with him.

Hartley stood to the right side, blocking a quarter of the board as she, too, retraced her steps over the last week. Things had come along since the case began. Leads had appeared out of thin air, others working their way into the light through hard work and determination. She could not help but think of her partner taking a number of bullets in the alleyway, falling down onto the pavement in agony as she pursued the assailant. She reached to her head and fingered her stitches as she recalled the scene in the warehouse, the gun pressed to her chin as she pleaded for her life. She needed—

Hands grasping her waist caused her to flinch and turn her head away from the board. James stood in front of her, his palms resting just above her hips, his eyes cast down towards her shoulder. She froze as he made the movement, unsure of how to react, yet slightly aroused by the sudden contact. "What?" she finally asked as he began to push her away from the board.

"Taylor," he said, releasing Hartley as he stared intently at the sketches from the Vincent murder and Philadelphia bank debacle.

Hartley's eyes bolted to the sketches. "Taylor? Taylor who?"

James slowly looked back up to Hartley, his eyes the epitome of certainty. "Jo," he began, "there's another reason why that man was in my apartment besides that newspaper photo."

"Why?" Hartley asked, taking a step forward and placing her hand on his forearm.

"I'm the one who put his father in prison. He was there to kill me for ruining his life."

"Who is this man, James?" Hartley said, pointing to the sketch.

"Taylor Thames," James answered. "His father is Robert Thames, Congressman Johnston's treasurer."

THIRTY-TWO

"We looked through each of the lists of volunteers and the name Taylor Thames is not on either," Hartley said as she shuffled papers around Barailles's desk, thinking to herself that she needed to call her partner this morning to update him on the progress of the investigation.

"Well, he wouldn't be listed as Taylor Thames," James said as he made his way over from Hartley's desk. He stopped next to her, his chest resting against her arm as they both peered at a sheet of paper with a list of names. "There," he said, pointing at a line. "Nathan Maddux. That's him."

"Did he change his name? I'm confused," Hartley replied, straightening and making eye contact.

"No, just used a different one."

"How does someone working for a politician get away with using a false name?"

"Well, technically, it wasn't a fake." Hartley looked at him quizzically. "It's his middle name and his mother's maiden name. Nathan Maddux."

Hartley shook her head. "How do you...?" She let the statement hang in the air, waiting for a response.

James looked at her with large eyes, his brow raised. "I'm wealthy, Detective."

"Jo."

"Jo. Sorry."

"And what does that mean? 'I'm wealthy.'"

"Money goes far if you need it to. Do you really want to know?"

Hartley thought about it for a minute before waving her hand in the air and turning towards her desk. "No. I don't." She took a seat at her station and glanced up at James with a smile. "There's more to you than you show, you know that?"

James smiled as he sauntered to her, pulling a chair from the wall and placing it directly across from her. "I can tell you all about it on our date," he said with a laugh.

She paused from her typing and stared at him. "Unbelievable," she said, shaking her head and controlling her smile. She began to search for anything related to Robert Thames or his son Taylor, typing in the latter's alias and pulling up everything from the accusation of fraud to Robert's current status in the federal penitentiary, yet wielding nothing regarding any children. "Damn!" she exclaimed after a few minutes. "There's nothing on this guy."

"What do you want to know?" James asked.

Hartley slowly glanced over to him, amused that her new friend was having such a grand time assisting in her investigation. "James, I'm working with a highly efficient police database that tracks criminals all over the country. What do you think you know that it doesn't?"

James smiled. "I tell you and it proves useful, you let me buy you a cup of coffee when all of this—"

"James," Hartley interrupted, "this is an investigation into three murders! I need to know what you have."

"Fine!" he said with his arms raised in surrender. "It was worth a shot." He shifted in his seat. "I'm sorry."

"It's okay. Look, you prove useful to the point of catching this guy, I'll buy you dinner."

"After work. Not as a public relations thing."

"Fine. What do you know, James?"

"Well, you're looking into a database full of files of investigations and past crimes. You won't find Taylor on there."

"Why not?"

"Because he was an enlisted man without a record. He went into the military and became Special Ops."

"You're kidding me?" Hartley said, leaning back in her chair as if she had been dealt another blow across her ribcage.

"That's what I heard. Why?"

"Benjamin Ochoa was killed on an overpass from a shot that originated on the shoulder of the expressway below. Mac had said that whoever made that shot knew how to use a rifle and may be military or ex-military."

"That makes it sound like he is definitely your guy then."

"Yeah, it does," Hartley agreed. "Too bad we can't find any pictures of this guy."

"Oh," James said, walking around and squatting next to her, "I think I can help with that." He opened a web browser and searched for *James Graiser Apex Charity Ball*. "See, Vincent had us looking into the fraud for at least a couple years before we went to the authorities, but that didn't mean we stopped all the fun." He turned to Hartley. "Most of the time different parties would have events for fundraisers or whatnot separately. No need to mingle with the enemy, you know? But this one, the Apex Charity Ball, it was an event run by the local chapter of a national fraternity. They were raising money to put towards campaigns against drug addiction, to infiltrate neighborhoods that were falling on hard times and to teach them that dealing and using wasn't the way to turn. It happened once a year and was the only event that Daniel and Congressman Johnston would attend together. Of course, they would bring some of their party with them."

"And why would searching for yourself help me out in this?" Hartley asked.

He smiled. "Well, one, because I'm strikingly handsome, and two—" He paused as he enlarged an image on the search results page. Across the screen displayed a picture of a younger James surrounded by a smiling, obviously intoxicated crowd of at least a dozen people. James pointed a finger to the edge of the image, drawing Hartley's attention to a blonde-haired young man with a chiseled jaw line. "Taylor Thames."

Hartley leaned into the desk, eyeballing the image on her display as James peeled the sketch off of the board, holding it next to the monitor. The two were a match. Hartley looked to James and smiled wide opening her mouth to say something just as Captain Nolan burst through his door. "Hartley," he said, stopping her before she could start.

"Sir," she answered, standing.

"Surveillance on Johnston sent in a picture taken about an hour ago," he said as he moved towards the two, handing a manila envelope to her. "Seems that our Congressman was seen talking to a white male in the park."

"Please tell me he has a circle tattoo on his neck," she said, smiling as she pulled the photos from the container.

"Even better," the captain replied. "He's got a nice little cut across the right side of his face." The captain tapped James on the shoulder, smiling as he glanced down.

"What's the plan, sir?" Hartley asked.

He looked back to her and chuckled. "It's your case, Detective. You make the call."

She nodded. "I'll put out an APB on Taylor Thames. Can you find out where Congressman Johnston is today?" The captain nodded. "It's about time that asshole tries on a jail cell for a while."

"What about me?" James asked.

"I'm going to have patrol escort you to a safe house like we planned. We'll keep you there until we find Taylor and bring him in, which hopefully won't be too long. Don't want to take the risk of putting you back in your place if he's just waiting for you again."

Everyone nodded their approval and sprang into action, James remaining seated as Hartley called in the APB on their suspect. Captain Nolan picked up his phone and began making inquiries as to the Congressman's whereabouts, though James could not hear what the conversations entailed. He became fascinated as Hartley kicked into gear, morphing from the sweet, humorous, young woman into a high-octane, down-to-business detective on a mission. He sat back and smiled, knowing his life was in the right hands.

THIRTY-THREE

"We got him!" Hartley said enthusiastically, slamming her desk phone down. She stood and pulled her leather jacket from her chair as she stared over James to Captain Nolan exiting his office. "Got a hit on the name Nathan Maddux. He's got a permanent address at an apartment building about ten blocks from here. Just got off the phone with the superintendant of the building that said Maddux came back the other day with a bloody gash across the right side of his face. Claimed it was from a hockey stick from a game at the rec center."

"Circle tattoo on the neck?" Captain Nolan asked.

Hartley smiled. "Like a bull's-eye," she replied.

"Good job," he stated. "Is Taylor still there?"

Hartley shrugged. "He wasn't sure."

James looked over his shoulder at the captain and back to Hartley. "What now?" he asked.

Hartley glanced up to her boss. "Sir?"

"I'm off to pick me up some political scum. You take care of the rest."

Hartley nodded, looking back to James. "For you, it's either here or we find a safe spot for you. Either way you'll have a police escort."

James thought for a moment. "Going on three days and kind of getting stir crazy. I'd rather get out of the station, if I'll have an escort to look after me."

Hartley smiled and nodded. "Understandable. Do you have someplace where we can take you? Someplace that you know is safe, where you haven't been in a while?"

James looked around the room as he thought. "I have a friend I met a few years back while spending some time in Peru. He lives down by Navy Pier. I haven't seen him in at least a year and a half."

"Great. Give him a call." Hartley picked up her desk phone as James moved down the hall to make his connection. "This is Detective Hartley with Homicide," she said into the mouthpiece. "I have a key witness that needs a patrol escort to an undisclosed location near Navy Pier … Yes. Thank you." She hung up the phone and waited as James spoke into his cell, his mouth moving and a smile forming before he turned her way and hung up. "Everything good?" she asked.

"He's there. Said I'm free to stop by."

"Okay. You're going to follow me down to the garage where a unit will take you. The officers will stay with you until I call in. Got it?"

James nodded. "What about you?"

She smiled at him. "Just worry about yourself. I have a job to do."

* * * * *

Hartley watched as two officers escorted James from the precinct, driving up the ramp with their lights off and taking a right onto the city street. James glanced out the rear window and waved to Hartley as they made the turn, disappearing around the corner.

Hartley walked to her unmarked vehicle and popped the trunk, taking off her leather jacket and pulling out a Kevlar vest that she strapped to her frame. She entered the car just as a SWAT van pulled up behind her, the officer in the passenger seat hopping out and walking up to her door. "Hartley?" he asked as she bent to retrieve a small pistol from the glove box.

She sat up and turned. "Hey," she responded.

"You all set?" Hartley nodded. "Where to again?"

"Grand and Peoria. There's an alley around the back of the building that should offer us some secrecy. We'll pull in there and secure the exits."

"Got it," the officer replied. "Half the unit in the front, half in the back."

"I'll be joining yours," Hartley responded, staring up at the man.

He shrugged as he turned back towards the van. "Suit yourself. But you're on my ass like we're dancing."

Hartley smirked as she strapped the smaller pistol to her shin, pulling her pant leg down to cover the piece. "Sounds good. Let's go."

* * * * *

James rode in silence for several blocks before engaging the officers in a brief conversation, one made more out of his nervousness than the need to speak. He peered out the window behind the driver's seat as they crawled through traffic, smiling as the sun brightened up the city and warmed the late morning air. It was beautiful out.

"Hey, don't they have that fair at the pier?" one of the officers asked.

"What fair?" the other chimed in, James turning his head to listen.

"You know, the fair at Navy Pier. Shit, what's the name of it?"

"Man, I don't know! Not like I've had a day off in the last year to go to a fair."

"You just had a day off the other week! What are you talking about you haven't had a day off?"

"It was for a funeral, dumbass!"

"Hey, still a day off."

James laughed as he turned back to the scenery outside of the police cruiser.

* * * * *

They were set. The SWAT unit had secured all of the exits and now waited silently like ghosts for patrols to show up and relieve them of their babysitting duties near alleys and escape doors. There was one main stairwell in the dilapidated apartment complex that spun around the central elevator system rising seven stories above the lobby.

Hartley followed close behind Shane Vills, the SWAT team member she had spoke to in the precinct garage before departing to Grand and Peoria. As they surrounded the door, Hartley held her weapon with both hands and breathed deeply, settling the nerves she had felt while working her way up the steps, composing herself just as a door opposite her opened and a woman with rollers in her hair peered out. Hartley raised her badge. "Police. Please stay in your apartment, ma'am." The woman nodded furiously and shut her door quickly.

Hartley looked back just in time to see a SWAT team member step into the hall and with one, forceful motion, throw his shoulder into the entrance, splintering the frame as he flew into the room. The team followed close behind with weapons raised, filing into the apartment in a single, hectic line and fanning out.

Commotion and yelling followed quickly as the men stormed aggressively about the interior of the apartment, clearing rooms and closets as they made their way. Hartley followed last, gun raised as she entered the home of her suspect. It was a dreary place, with one singular light bulb dangling from the ceiling, exposed to the room like a dancer that had lost her tutu. The mustiness floating throughout the rooms coincided well with the chipped, flaking wall paint and grungy carpeting. Linoleum flooring in the kitchen and hall was scratched and cracked, years upon years of battery with little to no cleansing.

"Detective," Vills said once the apartment was cleared. "You may want to take a look at this." He held up a number of large photographs as Hartley holstered her piece, squinting as she made her way across the room and to a table. A lump formed in her throat the moment she grabbed the images and glanced to the tabletop.

* * * * *

"Bratfest!" yelled the driver of the squad car, laughing hysterically as he made a turn towards the pier. "It's Bratfest at the pier!"

"Dude, it's not Bratfest!" the other officer responded. "I'm sure if it was Bratfest, you'd have taken a day off. Shit! We both would've." They continued their drive, James sitting comfortably behind the driver as he made a phone call to his friend from Peru, filling him in slightly regarding the matters at hand and, more importantly, setting up their meeting and subsequent catch-up session. James had not spoken to his friend in quite a while, yet knew without a doubt he would help James in his current situation.

James hung up the phone and looked to the officers. "Isn't it something like Hamiltonfest, or something like that?"

"Harrisonfest!" the officer in the passenger seat yelled. "That's it! Harrisonfest. Nice one, Jimmy."

James smiled and responded, "To be honest, I'd much rather it be Bratfest. That just sounds delicious!"

"Oh! Absolutely!"

"You're right about that!" They stopped at an intersection, each of them searching the streets, smiling as the day began to liven up with pedestrians walking the pavement as they moved about the city.

A half dozen cars behind the police cruiser, a dusty conversion van sat in line at the intersection light, waiting its turn to proceed towards the pier. The man behind the wheel studied the area, noticing the throngs of people walking the sidewalks towards whatever festival was underway a mile ahead. He knew he was limited in his actions at the moment, yet he did not care. This needed to be done. His mission had to be carried out.

He reached down to the center console and grabbed a pair of aviator sunglasses, resting them on his face, the right lens partially concealing the newly cleaned gash crossing his cheek. He reached down again and retrieved a pistol, setting it in his lap as he looked back up in just enough time to begin crawling forward, following the procession of cars through the intersection. He would have to plan this just right.

* * * * *

The bullets strewn across the tabletop matched those that Hartley and Barailles used for their Glocks. The hard, black case lying near the wall revealed a broken down rifle with loose .22 caliber ammunition. On the floor amidst dust bunnies and dead insects lay a cloth bag, which, once unrolled, revealed several military-issued knives. One of them was missing.

Yet Hartley lost her breath when she finally eyed the photographs Shane Vills handed to her, multiple shots of the precinct with herself and James crossing the street as they headed back from breakfast. The images were taken in succession, showing James and she laughing as they made their way up the station steps and disappeared into the building, an otherwise happy exchange from what looked to be two normal individuals. But nothing was normal about the situation. Nothing was normal about having been stabbed in the abdomen. Nothing was ordinary about having a gun pressed to your chin. And it was certainly not customary to have photographs of a detective and witness in your possession.

Hartley continued to flip through the images, moving from the breakfast shots to photographs of her driving out of the precinct and heading to meet with Congressman Johnston. There were photographs from inside the boutique as she purchased the clothes. There was a set as she walked down the street in the direction of Harper's Bistro.

Hartley dropped the photographs on the table, knocking over bullets as she glanced up to Vills, their eyes locking as she reached her hand out. "James," she said quietly.

"What?" he answered.

"Give me your radio!" she said forcefully. He unhooked the two-way from his shoulder and handed it to the detective. "Secure the area and get a team up here to catalog all this," she said as she backed away towards the door.

"Detective!" he shouted after her, though too late. Hartley raced down the hallway and into the stairwell, clearing multiple steps as she bounded towards the ground floor, bursting through the door and into the lobby.

"Everything all right, Detective?" a uniformed officer asked from the back alley as she hurriedly exited the building.

"You two," Hartley replied as she passed them. "Follow me. I need your help."

"But we were told to stay—"

"I don't give a fuck!" she yelled back. "The guy we're looking for isn't here! I know where he is. Now follow me!" The officers jumped from their spots and entered the patrol car, following Hartley's unmarked vehicle out of the alley with lights flashing and sirens screaming. The cars raced through traffic, horns blaring as Hartley made her presence known.

"Dispatch, come in dispatch," Hartley said as she pressed the radio button.

"Dispatch," came the grainy reply.

"Dispatch, this is Detective Jolene Hartley. I need you to connect me to patrol unit 2046. That's patrol unit two-zero-four-six. It's an emergency."

"Copy that, Detective. Contacting patrol two-zero-four-six."

Hartley waited nervously, eyeing the traffic patterns ahead as she made her way in the direction of the precinct, the marked vehicle behind her swerving in her wake, the officers bouncing in their seats as they tried to keep up. The man they were looking for, Taylor Thames, was a dangerous individual, scouting and studying his victims before he acted, making the vengeful, hideous act of murder into a meticulously planned out affair. Not only was Taylor thorough, he was exacting. If what James said was true, Taylor's military background and subsequent Special Forces involvement made him a force to be reckoned with. He was a trained killer with the knowledge and ability to vanish into thin air. Hartley needed to get to James before Taylor did. "Detective Hartley, this is patrol two-zero-four-six, copy."

* * * * *

The officer in the passenger seat released the button on the radio and waited for the reply, glancing at his partner who was shifted forward in his seat, staring in the side mirror. "What is this joker doing?" the driver asked to no one in particular. Their car was moving along now, having successfully passed through two consecutive city intersections without being caught by a red light. Behind them, however, weaving from the correct side of the road into oncoming traffic, a large van was moving towards them.

"… James on … dio!" came the static-y yell from the other end.

The officer lifted the radio to his lips, stopping before he could say anything as his partner raised his hands in the air in disbelief. "What's going on?" he asked, turning to look out the

311

rear window. James turned also, unable to make anything out behind him.

"This guy behind the wheel of this van has to be drunk," the driver answered. He's flying up the wrong side of the road!"

"Unit 2046, do you copy?" came Hartley's voice through the system again, this time clearly save for the always-present graininess.

"Two-zero-four-six. I read you, Detective. Go ahead."

"Damn it! Listen to me! We did not apprehend the suspect. Repeat: We did not apprehend the suspect!"

"I copy, Detective. What's the plan then?"

The officer released the button and immediately Hartley's voice came through again. "Our suspect has been watching the precinct! He's been waiting for a move! Abort where you are going and get back to—"

It was the last audible thing any of them heard from the radio as the large conversion van cut across traffic and rammed its front right bumper into the driver's side door of the squad car. Glass shattered and flew about the inside of the vehicle as each of the men rocketed towards the point of impact, slamming against doors and bodies before being lifted and thrown in the opposite direction, the squad car ramming into another auto and turning on its side in an inevitable tumble. The car grinded down the nearest vehicle and came to rest on its hood, the police cruiser's left headlight resting heavily on the pavement as James careened once again with the door he had just been looking out of, popping it open and falling to the street below. He landed with a thud, looking up to the cruiser suspended in the air.

Inside, the officer behind the wheel was motionless, head dangling to the street, blood smeared across his face as his partner tried to shimmy his way out of the seatbelt, grabbing the radio. "Unit 2046 requesting immediate assistance! There's been an accident and there's an officer down! Requesting an ambulance to the entrance of Navy Pier … Shit!" The officer was unable to finish his sentence as gunshots rang out, James's watching from his back as people scattered from the sidewalks. "Shit!" the officer yelled again.

James rolled to his side and searched the ground from where he landed, finding a pair of legs half hidden behind the black van's driver side door. James shifted on the pavement to get a better view.

"Taylor," he said to himself, glancing around quickly. He turned to the entrance of Navy Pier, regaining his feet and mixing into the mass of people already scurrying in all directions. Harrisonfest was the exact atmosphere he needed at the moment, one in which he could lose himself among the throng of people until Hartley could get to him. His only hope was that she got there quickly.

THIRTY-FOUR

Hartley listened to the commotion on the other end of the radio before it abruptly cut off, leaving her to wonder what had just happened. Dread filled her body as she threw the two-way on the seat next to her, pressing her foot to the floor and sending the cruiser speeding through an intersection, a move that would have gotten her suspended had higher-ups been watching.

The radio clicked to life with muffled, panicked screams from the other end. Something unexpected was definitely happening and she had a hunch that Taylor Thames was involved. "Unit 2046 requesting immediate assistance! There's been an accident and there's an officer down! Requesting an ambulance to the entrance of Navy Pier ... Shit!" The officer's pleas were cut short by the short, loud pops that meant only one thing: Gunfire. "Shit!" she heard the officer yell one more time before the radio cut out.

Hartley focused ahead, catching a glimpse of the pier roughly a mile and a half away. She needed to get there, and fast. Behind her the marked squad car slammed on its breaks, screeching to a halt as a bus flew through the intersection. The distance between the vehicles grew greater as Hartley pressed on at a furious pace, honking her horn and swerving across the two-lane road, nearly missing oncoming traffic and a group of bikers as she barreled through yet another intersection with barely a glance at the cross traffic.

She caught her breath as she pulled up to the street leading into the pier. People scurried about in confusion and panic. Traffic was at a standstill. It was not until she pulled around a delivery truck and stopped her car that she understood why. In the middle of the chaotic scene sat a smoking, black van, its front facing in the direction of an overturned police squad car with a small fire blazing on its underside, a thick, dark smoke filling the clear, blue sky. Inside the vehicle, an officer struggled to free himself from his safety belt, glancing sporadically to the van and the man who stood within the opened driver's side door.

"Taylor," she said aloud, staring through her windshield just as her suspect turned with weapon raised. She opened her door and dove to the ground as bullets passed through the tempered glass, spider-webbing the surface and sending miniscule shards raining down upon her head as she reached for her service piece.

She remained motionless on the ground for several moments, weighing her options, wondering how James and the officers were coping with their current plight. She crawled to the back of the cruiser, rising up to her knees and breathing deep. She needed to be quick and precise.

Hartley counted in her head to three and jumped up, laying her arms on the trunk of the car and firing two shots towards the van. Taylor, now on the front side of the open door, leaned into the surface of the van to guard against the shots.

It was not enough cover for him.

Hartley's bullets zipped through the warm air, one embedding itself in the interior of the van door as the other rose slightly higher, striking Taylor in the left shoulder and spinning him on his heels. He regained his balance and composure rapidly, leaning through the van's window and sending several more shots in Hartley's direction, shattering the rear window and sending her sprawling once more to the pavement.

Taylor sprinted towards the overturned cruiser, hopping onto the hood of the car that cradled the vehicle and down onto the pavement, swinging the pistol into the opened rear door to fire at James who was no longer in the vicinity. The officers within the vehicle remained strapped to their seats, one unconscious as the other gasped for breath from his injuries. Taylor glanced behind him, searching the sidewalks and crowds for his target, catching a glimpse of a man running full speed down the pier and into the mass of people.

Taylor stepped away from the car, raising his gun once more towards the female detective and letting off a shot. Within moments he was moving into the crowds, following his target towards the pier's end.

* * * * *

Hartley remained on her back as a final shot rang out in the clear sky, ricocheting off the surface of the trunk and embedding itself in the exterior of a nearby building. As she lay there the patrol car that had followed her screeched to a halt and the officers bolted to her side, fearing the female detective had been injured. To their relief, Hartley rose and rounded her vehicle, steadily, yet cautiously making her way to the van with the uniformed officers in tow.

They searched for their suspect in the interior of the steaming vehicle, yanking the doors open forcefully with guns raised. A throaty moan from the overturned squad car set Hartley and the officers into motion, running to the scene and dropping to their knees to assist the trapped individuals. "Are you all right?" Hartley asked.

"Get me … the fuck out … of here," the officer in the passenger seat groaned from between short, labored breaths.

"We got you!" the officer hovering over Hartley's shoulder yelled into the vehicle. He motioned for his partner to go around to the driver, throwing him a pocketknife to saw through the seatbelt in a hurried attempt to free the unconscious man.

"Where'd James go?" Hartley asked, moving aside as the uniform reached in through the shattered window. The injured man let out a sharp yelp as his rescuer pulled at him. "Officer, where's your passenger?" Hartley asked again.

The patrolman next to her grabbed the radio dangling near the injured man. "Dispatch. Come in, dispatch."

"Dispatch. Go ahead."

"We need an ambulance to the entrance of Navy Pier. Shots fired. We have two officers down. One with a gunshot wound. The other is unconscious. I can't tell if he's been hit."

"Copy that. Ambulances en route to you now."

Hartley reached into the window and placed her hand on the injured officer's chest, pulling his eyes to hers. "Where's James?"

The officer breathed deep and stared at her. "On the pier. He got … out when we … rolled. He's … on the pier." Hartley nodded and stood, walking hastily around the front of the car and leaping over the grounded bumper before breaking into a sprint, her shoes clicking rapidly against the pavement and wooden planks as she made her way into the mayhem that was Harrisonfest.

* * * * *

James made his way rapidly through the masses, searching his surroundings for law enforcement as well as places he could hide. He had made it far enough into the festival that the attendees near him had no clue as to the event that had occurred near the entrance. Instead of running for safety and covering their loved ones in fear of a stray bullet, these people carelessly made their way along the lines of boutiques and food stations, enjoying the music emanating from the speakers strategically positioned throughout the pier.

As he neared an enormous building that housed the indoor botanical gardens, the crowd parted and an officer came into view, moving towards a bench with his concentration solely on not dropping his chilidog and soda that balanced precariously on his wrist. "Police!" James yelled as he approached. "Help!"

"What's the problem?" the man asked, setting his meal on the bench as the distressed young man neared him.

"Officer, there's a man back there with a gun," he said rapidly, turning his head and raising a pointed finger in the direction of the festival entrance. "He just rammed into a squad car and the officers are trapped. Some shots were fired. I don't know if anyone was hit. I—"

"Slow down!" the officer said, raising his hands to calm the man before him, noticing that several festivalgoers had heard the ramblings and were looking back nervously. "Where are you coming from?"

James pointed. "That way. There's an accident down there and this guy just started shooting at a police car." James paused and glanced in the direction he had just come, catching a glimpse of Taylor making his way towards him. "There!" James exclaimed. "That's him!"

The officer reached up to his radio. "Dispatch, this is Officer Sheffer."

"Dispatch. Go ahead Officer," came the reply.

"Yeah, I'm at the Navy Pier festival. Has there been any recent calls about an accident near the entrance to the pier?" James nervously looked back the way he had come, noticing as his would-be-killer moved closer and closer, lessening the distance and amount of time either James or the officer had to act.

"Affirmative, Officer," the radio reported. "A patrol unit has been involved in an accident. Ambulance is en route."

The officer watched as James began to move towards the doors of the botanical gardens, his eyes fixed up the pier. "Hey," the officer said. "Wait right there." James continued, hastening his pace as he reached for the tinted glass door and pulled. "Stop!" the officer yelled, taking a step towards the man entering the building.

Suddenly a shot rang out as James dove into the entrance, the glass pane of the door spider webbing as the bullet passed into the gardens and lodged itself into the nearest tree. The officer spun, grabbing his service piece and raising it towards the man. "Police! Drop the—" He dropped in a heap to the ground as Taylor let fly two more shots, each connecting with the officer as the assailant continued his march towards the building.

James looked to the pool of blood forming beneath the uniformed man, his eyes going wide as he rose to his feet, fear and adrenaline pulsing through his veins as he bolted into the gardens and past the escaping inhabitants now searching to take flight from whatever chaos was happening just outside the doors.

* * * * *

Hartley halted in her tracks, retrieving her weapon as festivalgoers near her gasped and stepped clear of her, each one listening to the loud pops coming from just ahead. The shots fired gave her some semblance as to where James and Taylor were located, yet her heart began to pound and her mind reel as she envisioned the reasoning behind the gunfire, as well as who was on the wrong end of them.

She approached the botanical gardens and a large group of individuals huddled around what appeared to be someone lying on the ground. "Police!" she said, her gun half raised. The crowd turned in unison, parting and revealing the unconscious officer. Hartley holstered her weapon and ran to him, kneeling down and pressing her finger to his neck, biting her lip and shaking her head as she did so.

She reached to the officer's hip and removed his radio, wiping the blood away and bringing it to her lips as she pressed the button. "Dispatch, this is Detective Jolene Hartley. Officer down outside the botanical gardens on Navy Pier. I repeat: Officer down. I've got a very weak pulse and need an ambulance immediately."

"Copy that, Detective," came the response. "Officer down near gardens on pier. Ambulance en route."

"Please be advised, dispatch: We have an armed and dangerous man on the festival grounds. I need backup and the pier cleared at once."

"Copy, Detective. Sending over units for backup now. Please wait before pursuing suspect."

Hartley shook her head. "Negative, dispatch. I have a witness to an investigation in here as well that is being targeted by the suspect." She looked up and noticed the shattered door leading into the gardens. "Tell backup to head to the botanical gardens interior. I think the suspect is in there." Hartley stood and dropped the radio, ignoring the directives coming from the speaker. The crowd remained standing around her, glancing to the gardens and back to the fallen officer. "Get yourselves off the pier. Now." The crowd began to move off towards the entrance, glancing over their shoulders as they proceeded.

"I'm a doctor," a man said, stepping forward with his hand raised. "I'll stay with him."

Hartley nodded, turning to another man near her who also remained in place. "You, go to that boat and grab the first aid case." The man sprang into action, sprinting down the pier as Hartley reached for her gun, glancing one last time to the man kneeling beside the injured officer.

She took a deep breath as she moved to the shattered door, knowing that just beyond the tinted, broken glass lay a world of danger and uncertainty. She did not know if James or Taylor were still in the building, nor did she know if her suspect had succeeded in his quest to end Graiser's life. All she knew was that James needed her, and she had to focus on the task at hand: To apprehend—or put an end to—Taylor Thames.

She held her weapon aloft and she passed into the gardens, surveying the landscape, noticing the brilliant beauty of the trees and paths and stones displayed before her all weaving their existence together to form a habitat worthy of any tropical jungle. Yet the splendor was masked today by the fact that the twists and turns and hidden alcoves would prove to be an incredible hindrance to her in hunting her target as well as allowing for an ambush at any given spot on the grounds.

* * * * *

The air was dense, a clinging humidity latching onto everything under the roof of the gardens. Water droplets fell from a row of pipes near the ceiling that dispersed throughout the grounds a fine, warm mist that gave the gardens their tropical feel.

James stood motionless behind a large banyan tree, his fingers toying with the rough bark as he surveyed the area. There had been many close calls in his travels, times when he nearly fell from a thousand foot cliff or got caught in a furious rapid only to be saved by a jagged rock catching onto his backpack. Yet as he stood on the pier surrounded by thousands of different species of plants and birds—many of which he had seen in the wild throughout the world—James could not help but think he was going to die.

He thought of his most recent expedition to Jamaica, to his friend's bungalow near the beach, and to the offer to stay on and help him for a few more months. He laughed at himself now as he leaned against the trunk, wondering why he had decided to decline the offer and head back to the States. Next time he would have to accept, if there was a next time.

The flight of birds from a grouping of trees a dozen yards away sent James scurrying around the trunk of the banyan, his face pressed to the bark as he slowly peeked into the opening. Taylor stepped onto the trail, gun held at waist level as he scanned the area, his eyes searching the foliage, his ears waiting for the slightest noise to offer James's hiding place.

"James!" came a call from the far end of the gardens, stopping Taylor in his tracks. "James, are you in here?" James smiled to himself, knowing now that, for the moment, he had gained a bit of ground on his would-be killer.

Hartley awaited a reply as she moved from the path to the walls comprised of tinted glass, the natural light dimmed from the trees that pushed against the panes. She was at a disadvantage in this room, as she always was when chasing a suspect, not having the ability to move at a quicker pace, always having to assume an attack was looming around every corner.

She made her way into an area of tall grasses, concealing herself as she continued along, her feet falling quietly on the moss and dirt as she stepped over a small stream. The confines of the gardens were hushed as Hartley bounded over a large boulder, coming to rest between a wide trunk and a bush with inch-long thorns sticking out in all directions. "Taylor!" she shouted. "Do you hear me?" She waited. "It's over Taylor. We know everything. I know who you are. There's no running from this. Just turn yourself in."

Hartley dropped to a knee with her gun raised as a rustling from thirty feet away sent a new group of birds into flight. A shot rang out from the area, echoing in the interior of the gardens, the projectile embedding itself in a neighboring trunk. Hartley glanced around, scanning the grounds and launching herself forward to an outcropping of rocks, rolling to a stop as another discharge was heard.

"Taylor Thames," Hartley continued. "Your father is Robert Thames, serving a sentence for fraud that was pinned on him by Congressman Harold Johnston. You volunteered for Johnston while your father worked as his treasurer under the name Nathan Maddux." She paused again, lifting her head and peering over the stones, watching as Taylor's frame hurriedly disappeared into the brush on the far side of the gardens. "You murdered two men in a Philadelphia bank five months ago—"

"Jo!" came a shout from a distance to her right. "Jo, I'm—"

"Shut up, James!" Hartley said as more gunfire exploded. She darted to her right, flying around the grouping of stones and boulders towards the voice that had just called her name, knowing in her mind that Taylor had been waiting for James to slip up and reveal his whereabouts. As she rounded the corner, she suddenly saw the tall, muscular frame of Taylor Thames barreling towards where James was. He swung his firearm towards her and squeezed the trigger, the bullet zipping through the air as Hartley attempted to maneuver out of the way.

The bullet struck her on the left side just under her breast, sending her spiraling to the ground as the air shot from her lung. She slid down an embankment and rolled into a small pool, coming to rest with a groan as she retreated into an alcove just above her. A high-pitched squeak escaped from her lips as she painfully tried to draw breath, rolling onto her back and pulling at her Kevlar vest, tearing into the Velcro and pushing a flattened bullet onto the ground. She doubled over in pain, balancing herself with her weapon as she determined she had now, successfully, managed to break at least one rib.

"Detective?" Taylor said in a singsong voice as he made his way to where she had just been standing. "Are you still alive, Detective?" He laughed loudly, sending shivers throughout her body. "Nothing matters anymore, Detective. I go into each of my missions knowing that I'm going to die. As long as I complete my end of the bargain, I'm okay with that."

"Your mission?" Hartley said, the air returning to her. "Who's assigning these missions to you? Is it Congressman

Johnston?" Taylor laughed loudly. "We know about you two meeting. We have pictures."

"It doesn't matter," came the reply. "Johnston is through."

"Why do you say that?" Hartley asked.

"If you know who I am, then I'm sure your team is searching my place. Johnston left me for dead. I did his dirty work, allowing him to profit, and then he turned his back on me. No. Once you find the records in my place, he's done."

Hartley thought for a moment. "What does your father think about you becoming a cold-blooded murderer, Taylor? I'm sure he's real happy," Hartley continued, pushing herself into a standing position and glancing towards the embankment.

"Fuck you!" Taylor yelled. "What do you know, Detective? Princess daughter growing up in a well-to-do family with Daddy watching your back as the local Barney Fife. You had it easy, sweetheart. You know nothing." Taylor stopped short of the embankment, scanning the grounds before altering his path to the left, making his way slowly towards a grouping of trees and a slope that would flank the detective below.

"I know you killed Daniel Vincent years ago," Hartley answered, leaning heavily against the tree, holding back the urge to scream in pain. "I know you murdered a woman in a house the same way you killed the alderman. I have everything I need to put you behind bars for the rest of your life. But if you throw down that gun right now and let me—"

Laughter erupted from over her left shoulder Her heart began to pound uncontrollably as she realized her assailant had maneuvered himself in a position that allowed her no escape. "Toss the gun to the side, Detective," Taylor said. Hartley did as directed, sending the firearm airborne and landing near the base of a large, red-leafed bush. "Now turn around slowly.

Arms wide." She turned, staring up a second embankment to where Taylor stood, his blond hair pulled back into a ponytail as he smiled an eerie grin at her, her partner's gun aimed at her head.

"It doesn't matter what you know, detective," he said with a smile, his dark eyes peering at her from above. "Daniel Vincent was killed because he needed to be. That's what I was paid to do."

"And who funded that?" Hartley asked with a shaking voice. "Was it Johnston?"

Taylor smirked. "Yes. He needed Vincent out of the way to approve the casino. Having an umbrella over the casino can afford a man a lot of leeway when it comes to drugs and prostitution."

"Why Maria Gomez then? I understand why you killed the kid on the freeway, but why her?"

Taylor shrugged. "Wrong place. Wrong time."

"You mean you messed up?" Hartley asked boldly.

"I mean I don't give a shit anymore," he said forcefully.

"Then why continue?"

"Because I had to. My surviving partner from the bank robbery seemed to be giving up a lot of information. I'm not a detective but I understand how things work. Only a matter of time before you're on to me. And who knows what that shithead Johnston would have done. Most likely fed me to the animals when it benefited him the most."

"You're Special Ops, Taylor. You could have disappeared. Why risk it?"

He smiled. "Because I had a tip that your buddy James was back in town. You see, James knows who I am, and I couldn't take the chance that he'd give you any information about me.

Plus, James was the one who ruined my family, so it works double for me killing him."

"I don't see how it works out for you. You kill me. You kill James. But you're stuck then. This whole pier is going to be swarming with cops. There's no place for you to go but jail."

"No, Detective," he said, shaking his head. "I won't be going to jail. You weren't listening to me before. My mission is to kill James. My information is already known. I don't care what happens to me after he's dead. It's a shame you got in the way, though." He raised his arm higher, aiming at Hartley's forehead. "I gave you and your partner chances. I'm a marksman. You know that, right? I could have put a bullet in your partner's head instead of his shoulder."

"And what about the officer outside?"

"Collateral damage." He smirked at her before continuing. "You didn't have to die today, Detective. But you just keep getting in my way."

Just then James burst through the brush, wielding what appeared to be broken tree limb. The sudden ambush surprised Taylor. He looked to his left just as Graiser swung the impromptu weapon with all his might. The limb connected with Taylor's cheek with such force that it spun him on his heels and sent the firearm flying from his grasp to land in the vegetation below. The momentum of the swing, however, carried James into Thames. They collided in a grotesque thud and tumbled over the edge in a tangle of arms and legs, coming to a halt on a moss-covered mound near a large boulder.

James rolled to his back just in time to see Taylor lunging towards Hartley, a large, glimmering hunting knife tightly gripped in his hand, the same kind, no doubt, that had been used to kill Daniel Vincent. Hartley steadied herself as he approached, her ribs burning intensely as she raised her hands to meet his strike, grasping onto his forearm and spinning her body into his. She pulled his arm into her chest, pinning the blade across the Kevlar vest.

Her positioning, however, left Hartley vulnerable as she clenched onto his captured wrist with both hands. Taylor struck the detective in her wounded ribcage with his free fist, sending nauseating waves of pain throughout her body, forcing her to fight both her assailant and the urge to black out.

Fortunately for Hartley, however, Taylor was suddenly ripped from her back, the knife slicing across her forearm as his body was yanked backwards. She fell to her knees, grasping her arm and coming to rest facing the two men struggling yards away. Before her the men were locked in battle, fighting for the knife, James wrapped around Taylor's back as they moved in unison away. Screams of agony escaped Taylor's mouth as James clawed at his wounded shoulder, digging his fingers into the bloody wound towards the bullet.

In desperation, Taylor cocked his head back powerfully, his skull connecting with James's face, the latter's eyebrow splitting open immediately and dropping him to the earth in a daze. Regaining his composure, Taylor turned and raised the knife, a venomous smile etching across his face as he approached the dazed man lying in the dirt. James peered through the blood flowing over his brow at the man lumbering towards him, searching the ground around him for a weapon of any kind, panicking when his hands found nothing but loose soil. He braced himself for the inevitable assault, praying that whatever was about to occur came quickly.

It did, in the form of ear-piercing concussions and a warm spray of blood raining down upon his lips. James looked up as Taylor slowed, Thames's smile fading as he glanced down to his chest, eyeing the two fresh bullet holes through his body.

The knife dropped from his hand and he reached up, rubbing the blood between his fingers before dropping to his knees and glancing over his shoulder at the female detective, her pants leg raised and a pistol in her hand.

Taylor dropped to the earth, his head coming to rest on a bed of lush green moss as his life began to dim. He had come so close to fulfilling his mission, yet it was not to be. He had absolutely misjudged this woman, belittled her potential viability in the overall scheme of things. He should have killed her in the warehouse. He should have killed her at the entrance to the pier. He cursed himself for not having put a bullet in her head just moments prior.

He was not a cop-killer, yet he realized as the feeling in his body faded, he should have become one. If only to accomplish his mission of killing James Graiser.

Now, as his life passed out of him, he stared at her, watching as her beautiful face stared back, gun aimed in his direction, eyes focused and calming as he passed into black.

EPILOGUE

Detective Jolene Hartley exited the hospital room smoothing out the gauze wrapping her forearm. She laughed to herself as she walked the impeccably clean halls. Never in her young life had she ever received stitches for an injury, let alone twice in one week. Now, as she strolled through the hospital towards the elevators, her pain medication taking effect for her two broken ribs, she could not help but laugh and sigh.

The case of Benjamin Ochoa had reached its conclusion, as well as the murder investigations into Alderman Daniel Vincent and Maria Gomez. The acts, carried out by a meticulous, sadistic killer, were finished. There would be no more dead bodies coming from the hand of Taylor Thames, yet the bigger picture, mainly the investigation into Congressman Harold Johnston, seemed to be in its infantile stage. Hartley knew the case against the congressman would prove difficult, yet she had faith that the content against him thus far could, in all likelihood, demolish his political career from here on out.

Hartley caught the elevator up to the third floor and sauntered slowly through the hall towards Barailles's room, thinking to herself that a much needed vacation was in the near future for her. Within the past week she had racked up a list of injuries—both physically and mentally—that needed a few days, at least, to mend. She had been shot at on numerous occasions, struck with a metal rod across her ribcage, not to mention pistol-whipped into unconsciousness. She was sure she would have been killed on two separate occasions had it not been for the approaching group of officers in the warehouse or the Kevlar vest in the botanical gardens. Add to that Taylor Thames having a conscience about killing an officer of the law. She had required two instances of stitches as well as a scan of her upper torso to determine if she indeed had broken her ribs, which, after taking the bullet to the ribcage, she had finally succeeded in doing. Yes, vacation was definitely in the near future.

Hartley knocked on the door to room 301 before turning the handle and entering, shuffling in with a smile spread across her filthy face. Barailles and Cynthia glanced over, their mouths gaping wide as Hartley walked into view. Her hair was draped around her face, which, although smeared with dirt and grime and little pieces of green moss, was still radiant and carried on it a look of contentment. Her left forearm was wrapped in clean, sanitized white gauze, making the grunginess of her once white blouse stand out that much more as she limped on a sprained ankle to the foot of the bed.

Barailles and his wife sat together on the bed, fingers intertwined "Holy shit!" Cynthia exclaimed, sitting up straight. "Are you all right, Jo?"

Hartley nodded slowly, raising her right palm up and sauntering over to the chair directly opposite the bed, the pain medication for her broken ribs making her woozy. "What happened?" Barailles asked, his face drawn.

Hartley sighed and looked to him with a smile. "It's done," she responded.

"What do you mean?" he replied. "What's done?"

"The case. We got him."

Barailles shifted his weight and nodded. "And Graiser?"

"Alive. Getting looked over right now, but he's safe."

The three of them remained silent for several minutes as Hartley closed her eyes and tried to breathe past the pain in her side. "What happened to you?" Cynthia asked finally. "Do you need anything?"

Hartley popped her eyes open and shook her head. "No, thank you."

"Well, fill me in. What did I miss?" Barailles asked.

"A lot. Taylor Thames. That was our killer's name. From what we figured out, alongside what Taylor himself told us, he was hired five years ago to murder Vincent to get him out of the way so the casino could go up. Just like we thought, he came back into the picture for Ochoa because he saw his face."

"Maria Gomez?"

"Wrong place, wrong time."

Barailles thought for a minute. "What I don't get is Jerome. How the hell does he get brought into this all?"

Hartley shrugged. "Coincidence," she replied with a smile. "The biggest coincidence I've ever seen."

"Tell me about it," Barailles chimed in.

Hartley laughed. "The funny thing is that Jerome was a huge part of the Vincent-Gomez connection, yet didn't know it. It was coincidence that brought us to him, but in actuality, he helped us out immensely."

"Don't tell me you're starting to go soft on gangbangers?" Hartley rolled her eyes as they laughed. "And Graiser?" he asked.

"Seems to have been targeted because he knew who Taylor was. That and he's the one that tracked down the paper trail of fraud that led to the conviction of Robert Thames."

Barailles smiled. "So Taylor is Robert's son?"

Hartley nodded. "Ex-military, just like Mac suggested."

"Do we know who hired him to take out Vincent?"

"No solid evidence just yet, but I'm betting an investigation into Congressman Harold Johnston will be underway sometime soon."

"No way!" he exclaimed, slapping his hand on the bed.

Hartley nodded. "I got Nolan to put a tail on him and he made a really bad move. We have some pictures with him and Taylor talking."

"Going to be kind of hard to shake a documented lunch with a mass murderer," Barailles said, glancing to his wife as she looked from him to the floor. His smile faded.

Hartley caught the exchange and slowly stood from her chair. "I'll leave you two. Get better and I'll see you in the precinct."

"About that," Barailles responded from his bed, stalling momentarily as he rubbed his hand across the sheets. "I don't think I'm coming back, Jo." Hartley stopped in the threshold, turning slowly towards him. "Taking those bullets … It was a wake up call. I have children that I'd like to see grow up. I don't think I can—" He stopped as Hartley raised her hand.

"Good," she replied, nodding her head with a smile across her face. She looked to Cynthia. "Take good care of him," she said as she turned and walked through the doorway, beginning the long trek down the hall at a snail's pace to the elevators.

* * * * *

She took a cab home, calling Captain Nolan and explaining she would be taking a few days off to recover from her injuries, a decision he whole-heartedly agreed with. She slept heavily, turning her phone off and purposely not returning calls when she did wake to move about her apartment, knowing that soon enough her life would be once again filled with chaos and fast-paced action. She would enjoy this time to the fullest, not worrying about the paperwork she would need to fill out regarding the case and subsequent takedown of her suspect, Taylor Thames. She would need to write reports including the information James Graiser had given her. Hell, she would need to actually contact James. She had not seen him since the paramedics arrived at the botanical gardens to take each to the hospital. Most importantly, she would need to follow up with Rudy and Selena Ochoa, Benjamin's parents, as well as reach out to Daniel Vincent's family on the recent events.

She smiled as James entered her mind once again, knowing full well that she would be expected to fulfill their deal. He had helped her with the case, providing extremely useful information that led to Taylor's death. She would have to buy him dinner, take him on what he would inevitably consider a date. And who knows? Maybe she would let it be just that. Her future was wide open.

ON THE LADDER
OF HUMANITY

ACKNOWLEDGMENTS

I am deeply grateful for everyone who took the time to read this manuscript prior to publishing, especially my wife, who had to endure months of outlines, edits and ideas before finally getting a completed draft to enjoy.

A special thanks to: Mom, who, right from the start, thought my name would look good on a book; Dad, for being the first to dive in and give feedback; the women of the Frankfort, Illinois bookclub, for taking the time to read an unpublished manuscript and having me sit in on your Q&A session (absolutely a great time); Aunt Lynn, for the keen eye in pulling the words that would become this manuscript's title; Sean, for your first round of edits and the ability to hold nothing back (much appreciated); Angie Berglund, my editor, for wading through the manuscript multiple times and finding the little things; Sam, whose excitement got me even more excited about writing; Michael A. Black, author and officer, for his early guidance in the realm of publishing. Last but not least, James Riordan, for his insight and direction into everything from editing to feedback to the world of words.

Your help has been immeasurable.

RJP

ABOUT THE AUTHOR

Ryan Jennings Peterson was born and raised in the south suburbs of Chicago. His debut novel, *On the Ladder of Humanity*, the first in the Detective Jolene Hartley series and book one of the Humanity Trilogy, was completed in 2012, followed months later by book two, *On the Edge of Greed*. Ryan currently resides in the suburbs of Chicago with his wife and two daughters.

18530000R10180

Made in the USA
Lexington, KY
10 November 2012